ORBIT 20

WITHDRAWN

ORBIT 20

Edited by Damon Knight

HARPER & ROW, PUBLISHERS
New York, Hagerstown, San Francisco, London

PN
6071
S33
O7
no.20

FIRST EDITION

ISBN: 0-06-012429-6

LIBRARY OF CONGRESS CATALOG CARD NUMBER: 77-11784

Designed by C. Linda Dingler

78 79 80 81 82 10 9 8 7 6 5 4 3 2 1

CONTENTS

ORBIT 20

They Say

Like all fiction, science fiction rests on the four sturdy legs of theme, character, style, and plot. For practical purposes, it includes all stories and novels in which "the strange" is the dominant characteristic. Sf's particular problems result from the author's need to make this element—"the strange"—acceptable to the reader.

In the broadest sense, theme is the story's central concern. In a science fiction story, for example, the theme might be the effects of a system of embalming so improved that the dead could be distinguished from the living only with difficulty. (This was the theme of my story, "The Packerhaus Method," in which the chief character's father was proven dead only by the fact that he could not get his cigar to draw.) Notice that the theme has nothing to do with what *happens* to the characters. Theme is what the story is *about.*

In science fiction, it is imperative that the theme of each story be fresh or treated from a new angle: If the theme is not original or given a fresh treatment, it cannot be "strange." The most common—and the most disastrous—error beginning sf writers make is to assume that editors want more stories on the same themes as the ones they have already published. The writer reads the collected works of Isaac Asimov and Jack Williamson, for example, and tries to write a robot story like theirs. His story cannot be "like theirs" because their stories were fresh and original when they appeared; an imitation cannot be either.

On the other hand, it is still possible to write original robot stories. In "It's Very Clean," I wrote about a girl who posed as a robot because she could not find work as a human being. I like to think that was original. In "Eyebem," I wrote about a robot forest ranger, and in "Going to the Beach," I described an encounter with a robot streetwalker down on her luck.

The trick (and I think it one of the most difficult in writing) is to see things from a new angle. I have found three questions useful in stimulating sf story ideas.

The first is: *What if something new came along?* Think of something some people (not necessarily everyone) would like to have, and imagine that it has been invented. During the Vietnam War, for example, it occurred to me that the Pentagon would probably like to be able to grow soldiers in laboratory flasks. I added an almost inevitable near-future development, the unmanned, computer-controlled battle tank, and came up with a story called "The HORARs of War." . . .

The second idea-generator is: *What if it gets better?* Take some existing art, skill, or what-you-like, and imagine that some brilliant technician is to spend his life improving it. What will it be like when he is finished? What will the social consequences of his improvements be? *What if it gets better?*—the source of my "The Packerhaus Method." A less macabre example is "The Toy Theater," in which I had life-sized marionettes equipped with remote controls.

The third question: *What if those two got together?* Combine two existing customs, practices, sciences, or institutions. In "Beech Hill," I merged the writers' conference (where people who write fiction assemble) with the class of the poseur, the person whose life is his fiction. What I got was an annual gathering of those who pretend to be what they are not—a "secret agent," an "international adventuress," a "wild animal trainer," "the richest man in the world," and so on. My "secret agent" was really a short-order cook, and he wrote the rest of the story.

—"The Special Problems of
Science Fiction," by Gene
Wolfe (*The Writer*, May 1976)

As a salesman, [Gerard] O'Neill faithfully utters every shibboleth of the cult of progress. If we will just have the good sense to spend one hundred billion dollars on a space colony, we will thereby produce more money and more jobs, raise the standard of living, help the underdeveloped, increase freedom and opportunity, fulfill the deeper needs of the human spirit, etc., etc. If we will surrender our money, our moral independence and our judgment to someone who obviously knows better what is good for us than we do, then we may expect the entire result to be a net gain. Anyone who has listened to the arguments of the Army Corps of Engineers, the strip miners, the Defense Department or any club of boosters, will find all this dishearteningly familiar.

The correspondence between the proposed colonization of "the high frontier" of outer space and the opening of the American frontier is irresistible to Mr. O'Neill. I find it at least as suggestive as he does, and a lot more problematical. The American prospect after, say, 1806 inspired the same sense of spatial and mental boundlessness, the same sense of limitlessness of physical resources and of human possibility, the same breathless viewing of conjectural vistas. But it is precisely here that Mr. O'Neill's sense of history fails. For the sake, perhaps, of convenience he sees himself and his American contemporaries as the inheritors of the frontier mentality, but not of the tragedy of that mentality. He does not speak as a Twentieth Century American, faced with the waste and ruin of his inheritance from the frontier. He speaks instead in the manner of a European of the Seventeenth and Eighteenth Centuries, privileged to see American space and wealth as conveniently distant solutions to local problems.

That is to say that, upon examination, Mr. O'Neill's doctrine of "energy without guilt" is only a renewal, in "space-age" terms, of an old chauvinism: in order to make up for deficiencies of materials on earth we will "exploit" (i. e., damage or destroy) the moon and the asteroids. This is in absolute obedience to the moral law of the frontier: humans are destructive in proportion to their supposition of abundance; if they are faced with an infinite abundance, then they will become infinitely destructive.

—Wendell Berry, in *The CoEvolution Quarterly*, Spring 1976

I enjoyed *Watership Down* immensely, and read it through in two days—that's 477 pages in the Puffin edition. If a good book's good, a good *long* book's better! It is a tremendous story, and so well made, so brilliantly and yet soberly conceived and worked out, that I feel mean-minded stating any reservations or qualifications that might cool a prospective reader. And yet there is something about the book that bothers me. I'm not sure what it is, but I can point to certain manifestations of it, that seem to indicate a lack of balance somewhere very deep in the conception of the work. For instance—and above all—the role of women. Women *rabbits,* yes, to be sure. What do doe-rabbits do? They have baby rabbits, yes, to be sure. Many jokes on the subject. Do they do anything else? Well, not in the book. They are—like women in macho thrillers or sword-and-sorcery—objects: prizes of conquest, breeding-stock. One or two rise briefly as characters, equal for a moment to the vivid male characters, but they *do* nothing, and soon sink back into nameless passivity. Now I wonder, first, if this is accurate observation of rabbit behavior. The female of a social species is often more adaptable, shrewder, and more inventive (imaginative) than the male, since the raising of the young is a complex social act requiring real intelligence, whereas the procreative impulse of the male is a blinding compulsion, not requiring intelligent behavior, merely strength and active gonads. Would it really be the bucks who led a rabbit migration, or would it—as with wild cattle, deer, and elephants—more likely be the mature females of the group? But then, these rabbits are also seen as people, are humanized. Well, then, what is Mr. Adams saying about people? Why does he treat half of them as essentially subhuman, without wit or initiative?

The politics of the book reflect a similar bias, faintly. I find it rather dreary that the non-rabbit animal characters are "humorous foreigners" of the type dear to English cheap fiction decades ago. They're so funny, don't you know, they can't speak English properly! The satirical projection of a rabbit Police State is superb, and the description of its destruction is a marvelous stretch of suspense and strategy; but I find the rabbit Utopia that replaces it to be curiously unsatisfying. Everybody "knows his place" so well. It seems just a touch Victorian, for either rabbits or Utopia.

—Ursula K. Le Guin,
in *Hedgehog #1,* 1977

Behind my own work with the government are three basic imperatives with which I have been concerned since 1950:

to avoid nuclear war, not only year-by-year but for the long term;

to bring the annual growth rate of the world population to zero —not to 2 per cent or 1 per cent;

to avoid a transformation of our society into a system of social organization or government where individual values have no influence.

These are imperatives because their negatives are irreversible transformations, which will mean the end of our society, if not of human life. We can not see or plan beyond these catastrophes, which are thus in the nature of essential singularities. Any of the three could bring the world to a life among the ruins of a vaguely remembered past splendor of science, law and architecture. . . .

Zero population growth rate is necessary if we are to look more than a few decades into the future and to avoid making irrevocable choices. After all, a growth rate of 1 per cent per year, corresponding to the difference, I suppose, between 2.6 children per family and 2.0 per family, means a factor 3 in population in a hundred years, a factor 30 in three hundred years and so on. There is no long-term future for humanity unless the average population growth rate is strictly zero. . . .

There is also a great imbalance in the public reaction to many of these problems. For instance, the problem of nuclear reactor accident, or more particularly the possibility of terrorist attack against nuclear reactors, looms fairly large in the public press. At the same time, it is national policy expressed through the public health service that children no longer should be vaccinated against smallpox. But the smallpox virus persists; it is in storage in many places all over the world. When we have a population that is not vaccinated against smallpox, one terrorist distribution of this virus will kill not tens of thousands, but tens of millions or hundreds of millions of people in the U. S.

> —Richard L. Garwin, speech on
> acceptance of the Leo Szilard
> Award, April 27, 1976: quoted
> in *Physics Today,* February 1977

MOONGATE

It came with the moonlight over the cliff—
something so alien that it profoundly changed
everyone who experienced it, each in his
own very different way.

Kate Wilhelm

I

When anyone asked Victoria what the GoMarCorp actually did,
she answered vaguely, "You know, light bulbs, electronics, stuff
like that." When her father pressed her, she admitted she didn't
know much about the company except for her own office in the
claims department of the Mining Division. She always felt that
somehow she had disappointed her father, that she had failed
him. Because the thought and the attendant guilt angered her she
seldom dwelled on it. She had a good apartment, nice clothes,
money enough to save over and above the shares of stock the
company handed out regularly. She was doing all right. At work
she typed up the claims reports on standard forms, ran a computer check and pulled cards where any similarities appeared—
same mine, same claimants, same kinds of claims . . . She made

7

up a folder for each claim, clipped together all the forms, cards, correspondence, and placed the folder in her superior's in-basket. What happened to it after that she never knew.

Just a job, she thought, but when it was lunch time, she went to lunch. When it was quitting time, she walked away and gave no more thought to it until 8:30 the next morning. Mimi, on the other hand, boasted about her great job with the travel agency, and never knew if she would make it to lunch or not. Victoria checked her watch against the wall clock in the Crêpe Shop and when the waiter came she ordered. She ate lunch, had an extra coffee; Mimi still had not arrived when she left the restaurant and walked back to her office. "Rich bitch, couldn't make up her mind how to get to Rio," Mimi would say airily. "I'm sending her by dugout."

Late in the afternoon Diego called to say Mimi had had an accident that morning; she was in the hospital with a broken leg. "You can't see her until tomorrow. They've knocked her out back into last week to set it, so I'll come by later with the keys and maps and stuff. You'll have to go get Sam alone."

"I can't drive the camper alone in the mountains!"

"Gotta go. See you later, sugar."

"Diego! Wait . . ." He had hung up.

Victoria stared at the report in her typewriter and thought about Sam. He had worked here as a claims investigator eight years ago. She had been married then; she and Sam had developed a close nodding relationship. He was in and out for two years, then had grown a beard and either quit or been fired. She hadn't seen him again until six months ago, when they had met by chance on a corner near the office.

His beard was full, his hair long, he was dressed in jeans and sandals.

"You're still there?" he asked incredulously.

"It's a job," she said. "What are you up to?"

"You'll never believe me."

"Probably not."

"I'll show you." He took her arm and began to propel her across the street.

"Hey! I'm on lunch hour."

"Call in sick."

"I can't," she protested, but he was laughing at her, and in the end, she called in sick. When she told Sam it was the first time she had done that, he was astonished.

He drove an old VW, so cluttered with boxes, papers, magazines, other miscellaneous junk, there was hardly room for her to sit. He took her to a garage that was a jumble of rocks. Rocks on the floor, in cartons, on benches, on a picnic table, rocks everywhere.

"Aquamarine," he said, pointing. "Tourmaline, tiger-eye, jadeite from Wyoming, fire opal . . ."

There was blue agate and banded agate, sunstones, jasper, garnet, carnelian . . . But, no matter how enthusiastic he was, no matter by what exotic names he called them, they were rocks, Victoria thought in dismay.

When he said he made jewelry, she thought of the clunky pieces teenaged girls bought in craft shops.

"I'll show you," he said, opening a safe. He pulled out a tray and she caught her breath sharply. Rings, brooches, necklaces— lovely fragile gold chains with single teardrop opals that flared and paled with a motion; blood red carnelians flecked with gold, set in ornate gold rings; sea-colored aquamarines in silver . . .

A few weeks later he had a show in a local art store and she realized that Sam Dumarie was more than an excellent craftsman. He was an artist.

"You get off at noon on Good Friday," Sam had said early that spring. "Don't deny it. I lived with GoMar rules for years, remember. And you have Monday off. That's enough time. You and Mimi drive the camper up to get me and I'll show you some of the most terrific desert you can imagine."

"Let's do it!" Mimi cried. "We've both asked off until Wednesday. We were going to my parents' house for the weekend, but this is more exciting! Let's do it, Vickie." With hardly a pause she asked if Diego could join them. "He's a dear friend," she said to Sam, her eyes glittering. "But he wants to be so much more than that. Who knows what might develop out on the desert?"

Watching her, Victoria knew she was using Diego, that it was Sam she was after, and it didn't matter a bit. Hadn't mattered then, didn't matter now, she thought, driving slowly looking for a restaurant, remembering Diego's words:

"Get hungry, just pull over and toss a steak on the stove. Enough food for a week for all of us. Get sleepy, pull over, crawl in one of the bunks. That simple."

But there was no place to pull over on the highway, and no place to park and broil a steak. She spotted a restaurant, had dinner, and wished the motels had not had their no-vacancy lights on all down the main street of this small town. According to the map, she was about fifty miles south of Lake Shasta, and there would be camp grounds there, places to park and sleep. She climbed back inside the camper and started driving again.

Sam had given Diego explicit directions, and the more Victoria thought about them, and about the roads—everything from double green lines down to faint broken lines on the map—the more she wished she had taken Mimi's suggestion and called the Oregon state police. Sam had gone up to the mountains with friends who had left him there. The police could find him, she thought, or find his friends and locate Sam that way. They could give him a ride to the nearest town where he could rent a car to drive himself home. Sam would understand why no one had showed up at the appointed hour. And she knew she had refused that way out because Mimi had angered her finally.

"Why?" Mimi had asked petulantly. She was very lovely, her hair black and lustrous, her brown eyes large as marbles. "After all, if you haven't snagged him in six months, why do you think this weekend will do it?"

It was after twelve when she finally came to a stop, hit the light switch and rested her head for several minutes on the steering wheel. She had been up since six that morning, had worked half the day, and she felt as if she had been wrestling elephants all evening. She neither knew nor cared where she was, someplace near the lake, someplace where the traffic was distant and no lights showed. She hauled herself up, staggered through the camper to the bunks and fell onto one of them without bothering to undress. Presently she shifted so that the covers were over her instead of under her, and it seemed she had hardly closed her eyes before she was wakened by shouts.

Dazed, she pulled the shade aside. It was not yet light.

"This is a parking lot!" a man yelled at her. "Move it out of here."

It was bitter cold that morning and the sky was uniformly gray. She turned the radio on to the weather channel and nodded glumly at the report. Freezing level three thousand feet, snow in the higher passes.

All morning she crept along, sometimes in the clouds, sometimes in swirling snow, sometimes below the weather. At one o'clock she realized she had left the cold front behind her; she was east of the mountains, heading north in Oregon. The sun was brilliant, but the wind speed had increased enough to rock the camper, and she fought to hold it to forty miles an hour.

The rain forest had given way to pines on her left, and off to her right there was the desert. Later in the afternoon she turned east on U.S. 26, and after a few miles stopped at a rest area for lunch. This was the Juniper Wayside Park, a small plaque said, and went on to extol the virtues of the juniper tree. The trees were misshapen, no two alike. Some grew out sideways like shrubs, some were almost as upright as pines; none was over twenty feet tall. Beyond the small grove of junipers the ground was flat, brown, dotted with sagebrush and occasional clumps of wirelike grass. The wind screamed over the empty land. Shivering, Victoria got back inside the camper. She made a sandwich and studied the instructions Sam had written.

She had less than sixty miles to go; it was four-thirty. She should be there well before dark. A truck thundered past the park, and she jumped, startled. It was the first vehicle that had passed her since she had turned east. But, she thought, it proved other traffic did use this highway; she would not be totally alone on the desert.

When she started again, no one else was in sight. The road was straight as far as she could see in both directions, and it was a good road, but she had to slow down again and again until she was driving no faster than thirty-five miles an hour. Even at that speed the wind out of the northwest was a steady pressure against the side of the camper, pushing, pushing. When it let up, she rebounded. When it gusted, she was almost swept off the road.

To her left—she could not judge distance in this treeless country—there were hills, or mountains, and sharply sawed-off mesas. Now and then a pale dirt road appeared, vanished in the sagebrush. Her highway was sending out feelers, tendrils that crept toward the hills and never reached them.

Milepost 49. She shook her head. Those little roads were being swallowed by the desert. It was all a joke. Sam had not meant for them to drive on one of those go-nowhere roads. Milepost 50, 51 . . . She slowed down even more, gripped the wheel hard enough to make her hands ache. There was noplace she could stop on the highway, noplace she could pull over to consider. U.S. 26 was two lanes; there was no shoulder, only the desert. When Milepost 57 came, she turned north onto a dirt road. She felt only resignation now. She had to keep driving; the road was too narrow for two cars to pass. On either side there was only rock-strewn, barren ground, sagebrush, and boulders, increasing in size now. She could see nothing behind her except a cloud of dust. The sun had dipped behind the mountains and the wind now hurled sand against the windshield. The road curved and she hit the brakes, gasping. Before her was a chasm, a gorge cut into the land so deeply she could not see the bottom, only the far side where sharply tilted strata made her feel dizzy for a moment.

Some ancient river, she thought, had thundered out of the hills, an irresistible force that no rock could withstand. Where was it now? Gone forever, but its passageway remained. A mighty god, it had marked the land for centuries to come, its print cruelly raked into the earth. The forests it had nourished were gone; the bears and otters and beavers, all gone; the land was deserted, wailing its loneliness. She roused with a jerk. It was the wind screaming through the window vent. Soon it would be dark; she had to find a place where it would be safe to stop for the night.

She read the directions again before she started. Sixteen miles on this road, turn right, through a gate, a short distance to a second gate, twelve more miles. She glanced at the odometer frequently as she drove, willing the numbers to change. The cliffs on her left were already dark in shadows, and the gorge she cautiously skirted appeared to be bottomless. This narrow road had been blasted out of the mountain; it threaded upward in a series of blind curves.

Every step for six months, she thought, had led her to this: driving alone on the desert, miles from another person, miles from help if she should have an accident. Driving on a track that seemed designed to make any stranger end up at the bottom of a ravine.

She realized there was a wire fence on her right. She could not remember when it had first appeared. She had been climbing steadily, slowed to ten miles an hour on hairpin curves, with no attention to spare for scenery. Now the land was flattening out again. She almost cried out her relief when she saw the gate. She had to turn on the headlights to see how to open it: she drove through, got out and closed it again and stood looking at the western sky, streaked with purple, gold, and a deep blue that almost glowed. The wind stung her eyes and chilled her. She turned around to study the track ahead. It could not be called a road here, she decided, and knew she would not try to drive another mile that day.

"I'm sorry, Sam," she murmured, climbing back into the camper. She humped and ground her way only far enough from the dirt road not to be covered with dust if someone else drove by, and then she turned off the motor. Without that noise, it seemed that the voice of the wind intensified, filled all available space. She closed the vent tight, and the high-pitched wail stopped, but the roar was all around her. Now and then the camper swayed, and she thought perhaps she should move it so that the wind would not hit it broadside. She sat gripping the steering wheel, straining to see ahead, until she realized how dark it had become; she could see nothing at all with the headlights off. Night had come like the curtain on the last act.

She pulled the shades tight, checked the locks, and thought about dinner, decided it would be more trouble than it was worth. Instead, she looked in the liquor cabinet, chose Irish, poured the last of the coffee into her cup, filled it with the whiskey and sat on a bunk sipping it as she pulled off her shoes. Her shoulders and back ached from her day-long battle with the wind. When her cup was empty, she lay down and pulled the covers over her ears. The wind roared and the camper shook and she slept.

She awakened and sat up, straining to hear; there was nothing. The wind had stopped and there was no sound except her breathing. A faint light outlined one of the windows where she had failed to fasten the shade securely. Wearily she got up, not at all refreshed by sleep, and very hungry. She went to the bathroom, looked at the shower, shook her head, and went to the refrigerator instead. Food, then a cleanup, then drive again. As she sipped her second cup of coffee she opened the shade and looked out, and for a long time didn't even breathe.

It was not dawn; the brilliant light was from a gibbous moon that had never looked this bright or close before. She stared at the desert, forgetting her coffee, forgetting her fatigue. There was an austere beauty that would drive an artist mad, knowing the futility of trying to capture it. Not color; the landscape was re-

vealed with a purity of light and shadow from hard platinum
white through the deepest, bottomless black that seemed for the
first time to be a total absence of everything—color, light, even
substance.

Slowly Victoria pulled on her coat and stepped outside. The
sky was cloudless, the air a perfect calm and not very cold. The
clumps of sage were silver—surreal stage props for a fantasy
ballet; grasses gleamed, black and light. Nearby a hill rose and
she started to walk up it. From the top she would be able to look
out over the strange world for miles, and, she thought, it was a
strange world, not the same one that existed by sunlight.

She walked with no difficulty; every rock, every depression,
every clump of sagebrush was clearly, vividly illuminated. Light
always symbolized warmth, she thought, comfort, the hearth,
safety. But not this hard, cold light. She looked behind her at the
camper, silver and shining, beyond it to the pale road, farther to
the black velvet strip that was the gorge, the black and white cliffs,
the sharp-edged mesas . . . For a moment she felt regret that she
would never be able to share this, or explain it in any way; then
she turned and continued up the hill.

She saw boulders on the crest of the hill and went to them and
sat down. To the east the brilliant sky was cut off by high,
rounded hills; far off in the west the horizon was serrated by the
Cascade peaks. Closer, there were mesas and jumbled hills, a dry
wash that kept reversing its ground/figure relationship, now
sunken, now raised. She lost it in the hills and let her gaze sweep
the valley, continue to the dirt road she had driven over earlier,
the kinky black ribbon of the gorge . . . Platinum whites, silver
whites, soft feathery whites, grays . . .

Something stirred in the valley and she shifted to look. What
had registered before as a large shadow now had form, a hemi-
spherical shape that looked solid. Suddenly chilled, she pulled
her hood up and pressed back against the boulders. A patch of
pale orange light appeared on the shape and something crossed
before it, blocking the light momentarily. Then another shadow

appeared, another . . . The shadows moved onto the desert floor
where they reflected the moonlight just as her own camper did
and, like her camper, they were vehicles. Campers, trucks with
canopies, trailers, motor homes, station wagons . . . They lined
up in a single column and moved toward the dirt road, without
lights but distinct in the brilliant moonlight, too distant for any
noise to reach her. More and more of them appeared, bumper to
bumper, a mile of them, five miles, she could not guess how far
the column stretched. Now they were reaching the dirt road.
When the first one drove onto it, headlights came on; it turned
south, and she could see the taillight clearly. The next one followed, turning on lights when it entered the road. The third one
turned north.

"Of course," she breathed. "On 26 they'll divide again." Suddenly she began to laugh and she buried her face in her hands
and pressed her head down hard against her legs, needing the
pain. "Don't move," she told herself sternly. "They'll see you."
After a few minutes she looked up. The hemisphere was a shadow
again. The line of campers and trailers was halfway across the
valley. Down the road she could see many sets of rear lights.
Those turning north were hidden from view almost instantly by
the cliffs.

Moving very slowly she stood up, keeping close to the boulders. She began to pick her way among the tumbled rocks. She
had to stop often to fight off dizziness and the laughter that kept
choking her as she stifled it. She could no longer watch where she
was going, but groped and felt her way like a blind person. "The
birthplace of recreational vehicles!" she gasped once and nearly
fell against a rough boulder, then clung to it. "Biggest damn
mother of them all!" she sobbed.

She was running and couldn't remember when she had started
to run. They would train instruments on the surrounding hills,
she realized, and they would come to eradicate any witnesses.
They would have to. She knew she must not run over this ground,
knew it and ran blindly, stumbling, seeing nothing, falling again

and again. She screamed suddenly when something caught her arm and dragged her to a stop.

"Whoa now, honey. Just take it easy. You're pretty far from the nearest bus stop. You know?"

She struggled frantically and was held, and gradually she could hear the voice again. ". . . calm down. Steady now. Nothing's out here to hurt you. Coyotes, jackrabbits, seven head of the damnedest dumbest cattle . . ."

Then he was saying, "That's right, just take a look. Reuben's the name. Honey, you're as cold as a trout in snow water. Come on. That's the girl. Build up this little fire. Here, wrap yourself in this."

She was holding hot coffee, drinking it, and still he droned on, his voice warm and comforting, almost familiar. He was talking about cattle.

"Spotted them yesterday with the plane, but no way you're going to bring them in with no plane. Nope. Me and old Prairie Dog here"—a great pale dog lifted its head, then put it down on its paws—"we come up like we been doing forty years. Not him, acourse, he's only eight or nine, but only one way to get seven head a cattle back in the herd, and that's on a horse." He paused and leaned toward her. "You feeling a bit better now? Not shaking so hard?"

"I'm all right," she said. She glanced around. They were in a hollow with hills and boulders all around them. "How did you find me?"

"I was asleep," he said. "I heard this thing crashing all over the place and thought you was a coyote, to tell the truth. But old Prairie Dog didn't. He knew. Took me straight to you." He laughed, a deep growly snorting noise. "Thought at first I was still asleep and dreaming a pretty girl come to keep me company." He refilled her cup, felt her hand, then sat down again, satisfied. "You're okay, I reckon. Now you tell me what the hell you're doing out on the desert three o'clock in the morning."

He had been asleep; he could not have seen it, then. Victoria opened her mouth, looked at the fire, and instead of telling him about the thing in the valley, she said, "I woke up when the wind stopped and just walked out a little from my camper."

"An' saw something in the moonlight that scared the bejeesus outa you."

She looked at him quickly, but he was turned away, facing the cliffs.

"I know," he said, almost harshly. "When the moon's big and bright, you see things out there. It's when you start seeing them in daylight that it's time to hang up the saddle." He stood up. "You came through the gate back by Ghost River. Right?"

"I don't know the name. By the gorge."

"Not far," he said. "Key's in the thing?"

She nodded.

"I'm going to get it, bring it over here. You sit tight by the fire. Prairie Dog!" The dog jumped to its feet. "Come over here, boy, here. Stay, Prairie Dog." The dog sat down by Victoria. "He won't move till I get back. Won't be long." He took a step or two, then stopped. "Call it Ghost River 'cause nights like this some folks claim they can hear the water crashing down the rocks." Then he left and she was shivering hard again.

It wasn't like that, she wanted to cry out at his back. She had seen something! The dog put its head on her knee, as if in sympathy, and she whispered, "I did see it!"

The cowboy returned, took her firmly by the arm and led her out of the hollow, through a second gate. "That's a mighty nice machine, Miss. Very fine. Just lock up tight and get some sleep. Going to be fine weather tomorrow, you'll have a nice driving day."

He opened the door and almost pushed her inside. "I'll be right down there, but you'll be all right now. Just lock it up and get some sleep."

She snapped the door lock, heard a distant "Good night," and shrugged off her coat and let it fall. She kicked off her shoes and fell into bed again and had no memory of pulling up the covers.

"Why would I tell such a ridiculous lie?" Victoria cried.

"That's the right question," Sam said.

She had reached the designated spot at ten, and two hours later Sam had arrived. She had coffee and sandwiches ready, and as they ate she told him about Mimi's accident. Sam, she thought, had been impressed that she had driven here alone. Then she told him about the thing in the valley, knowing even as she started, while she still had time to back out, that she was making a mistake.

Sam started to unload his backpack, jerking things out with furious energy. He hadn't actually called her a liar. What he had said, snapped, was, "Story time's over."

"Why do you think I'd tell any lie at all?"

"Maybe to pay me back. I know what kind of a drive that was. When that front came through I was prepared to wait three, four days. I can imagine how it was, bumping over rocks, sliding down gullies, hugging the cliffs over a thousand-foot dropoff, hating me for getting you into this. Fix old Sam. Tell him this cockamamie story, watch his eyes bug. You tried. It didn't work. No amusing little anecdote to hand over to your pals. Sorry."

"I didn't lie to you." She tried to keep her voice calm and matter of fact, but she heard the indignation in every word.

"All right! You dreamed it then. Or hallucinated. You were stoned, or drunk. I don't care what you call it, it isn't true!"

"Because I didn't get an affidavit or photographs?"

"Christ! Victoria, look, I know this country. There is no little hill back there. There are cliffs and mesas and chasms. No little hills you can stroll up in the middle of the night. That's point one. Two: do you have any idea in the world how scarce water is out here, how far apart the wells are? Too goddamn far to take the old faithful dog along, you idiot! You carry water for your horse, for yourself, if you have the room. You don't carry water for a fucking dog! Your old pal the cowboy had a nice fire blazing away, coffee on! What in Christ's name was he burning? You expect me to believe anyone would waste water making coffee in the middle of the night, have a fire burning away while he slept? And the seven head of cattle. That area's fenced off to keep cattle the hell away from there. No water, larkspurs in the spring— that's poison, Victoria, like arsenic or ptomaine. There wasn't a gallant cowboy. No ghost river. There wasn't a thing spewing out campers!''

He hit his palm hard against the now empty pack. "Let's get started. I have two hundred pounds of rocks up there."

Angrily, in silence, Victoria pulled her pack on, adjusted the straps and waited for Sam to lead the way up the mountain. Much later it occurred to her that Sam's fury had been all wrong. If he had believed she was lying, or mistaken, he might have laughed, might have been contemptuous or scornful. But furious? Full of hatred? Why? She could feel the shivering start again deep inside. When she looked up, Sam was watching. He turned and walked on.

The afternoon was crystalline, the air almost still, the sun was warm on her back. Every step they took upward revealed more of the alien country. Land that had appeared flat and unbroken turned into a series of mesas with sharp edges; a black pit closed, became a barren lava flow; a cliffside of mud with a sparkling waterfall became brown jasper with a thick vein of blue agate. Deceptive, lying, deceitful land, she thought.

"Fifteen minutes," Sam said suddenly, and Victoria almost bumped into him as she rounded a boulder as high as a two-story building.

She sank to the ground thankfully. Her legs were throbbing, her thighs so hot she was vaguely surprised that steam was not rising from her jeans. Office work and a daily stroll to lunch had not prepared her for this.

Sam squatted beside her and handed her his canteen. "It isn't much farther," he said. He pointed down the cliff. "Look. Poison Creek. Dry now, but sometimes there's water. Alkaline. Tomorrow we'll drive by it. You can pick up thunder eggs."

"This is all very beautiful," Victoria said. "I never knew that before."

"It can be, if you accept its terms, don't try to make it be something else. It fights back and always wins."

"The eternal desert, like the eternal ocean?"

"Something like that."

But he was wrong, she knew. The desert changed; she could see the evidence everywhere. It would change again and again. She did not doubt that the desert would win in any contest, but it would win by deceit. It would lull with a beautiful lie and then strike out. "No one would really try to fight a place like this," she said. "Only a fool."

Sam laughed. "Down there in Poison Creek there's gold. You'll see it tomorrow. It's no secret. A grain here, a few there, shining, laughing. The desert's little joke. It would cost more to ship in water and equipment to get it out than it's worth even today, or tomorrow, or next year, no matter how high gold goes. God knows how many men have died or been wiped out, have gone crazy, trying to get rich off that gold. One way or another the desert kills them. The ones who last are those who can pick up a handful of the sand, look at the shiny grains and let it all sift back down to Poison Creek where it belongs, and then smile, sharing the joke. They're the ones who accept the terms." He stood up and offered her a hand.

"Can you do that? Leave it there, laugh at the joke?" Victoria asked. She tried not to grimace as her legs straightened out painfully.

"Sure. I'm not after gold. Come on. You're getting stiff. It's best to keep moving."

She wanted to ask him what he was after, but she knew he would not answer. The reason they always got along was that neither ever asked that kind of question. They liked the same plays, music, books sometimes, and could talk endlessly about them. They argued rather often about politics, economics, conservation, religion, but it all remained abstract, a game they played. No other lover had been willing to remain so impersonal, had kept himself as uninvolved as she was determined to remain. He had asked if she was still married and she had said no, and the subject had never come up again.

Never again, she had said after the divorce, and it had been fine.

She thought of the cruel, deliberately hurtful words she and Stuart had flung at each other, as if each of them had been determined not to leave the other whole, unscarred.

"You're some kind of creeping fungus!" he had yelled. "You're all over me all the time, smothering me, sucking the life out of me!"

She had believed she was a good wife; it had come as a shock to learn that her goodness was an irritant to him. She never lied, always did what was expected of her, never was late by a second, never demanded anything not readily and easily available. She had been like that all her life, and her father distrusted her, Stuart hated her. The only two people she had tried to please wholly, absolutely, had ended by abandoning her. Never again, she had thought, would she ask anything of anyone. Never again would she be willing to give anything of herself to anyone. If no one could touch her, then no one could hurt her. If she belonged to no one but herself, no one could abandon her again.

But, she thought suddenly, never again meant keeping such a distance that everyone else, every man, would forever be a stranger. And strangers could be dangerous, unpredictable. Sam's sudden rage and this return to affability made her uneasy. She knew it would be impossible to resume the careless relationship they had had only a day before. She tried to imagine herself again in his arms, giving and finding pleasure, and the images would not come.

She concentrated on climbing. When they got to the camp high on the mountain, Sam would not let her rest, but packed quickly and started down. "You'll freeze up, or get a charley-horse," he said cheerfully. "Then I'd have to backpack you out of here. I'll get the rest of this stuff tomorrow."

It was as if he had managed to erase everything she had told
him, as well as his own reaction, but she did not have enough
energy to worry any more about that. Doggedly she followed him
down the mountain, seeing nothing now but the ground directly
ahead.

She dreamed of a swarm of fireflies winking on and off in an
intricate dance that she could not quite follow. It had to be seen
from the center, she realized, and she began picking her way
carefully to the middle of them. Observing the rhythms from the
outside had been charming, but as she drew inward, she began
to have trouble breathing; they were using up all the air, sucking
the air from her lungs. Off and on, off and on, off . . .

She woke up; Sam was shaking her hard.

"You were dreaming," he said. "Are you okay?"

She tried to sit up and groaned. "What time is it?"

"Midnight. Hungry?"

When they came back with the rocks he had made dinner, but
she had been too tired to eat. She had stretched out on the bunk
and had gone to sleep instead.

"What you need," Sam said, "is a cup of soup, which I just
happen to have." He jammed a pillow behind her back and
stepped over to the stove. He made the camper seem very small.

"Haven't you been to bed yet?"

"Nope. I was reading and waiting for you to wake up, starving
and in agony. Soup first, then a rubdown, milk and aspirin."

"If you touch me, I'll die," Victoria said.

Sam laughed and dragged a camp stool to the side of her bed.
"I'll hold, you drink." After her first few sips, he let her hold the
mug of beef broth. "I've got this guaranteed snake-oil liniment,
made by the oldest medicine man in the West out of certified
genuine magic snakes. What we do, see, is haul off the jeans, pull
the cover up to your fanny and let me work on those legs. Ten
minutes, and you'll walk tomorrow. A miracle."

"Hah!"

"Word of honor. If you misuse this potion, use it for anything other than what old Chief Calapooia intended it for, you will call down on your head, heart, soul and liver the wrath of the sacred snake god who then will do certain very nasty things to you."

He kneaded and massaged her legs and rubbed the liniment on them until they glowed, then he covered her again, tucking the blanket in snugly; he brought her milk and aspirin, kissed her chastely on the forehead, and before he could turn off the lights and get himself in bed, she was sleeping.

When she woke up in the morning she could remember that during the night Sam had shaken her again, possibly more than one time, perhaps even slapped her. She must have had a nightmare, she thought, but there was no memory of it, and perhaps she had dreamed that Sam tried to rouse her.

She got up cautiously; while she ached and was sore from her neck down, she felt better than she had expected, and very hungry. There was a note on the refrigerator door. Sam had gone up the mountain for the rest of his gear.

After she ate she went outside; there was no place to go that wasn't either up or down. It was only nine-thirty. Sam would be four hours at least; if he had left at seven, she had an hour and a half to wait. Time enough to drive back to the gate, locate the hill she had walked up, look for the thing in the valley by daylight.

The keys were not in the ignition. Victoria found her coat at the foot of the bed and searched for the single key Diego had had made—one for her, one for Mimi, one for himself, so no one would ever be stranded outside if the others were delayed. She searched both pockets, then dumped the contents of her purse on the bed. No key. Growing angry, she stripped the bed and searched it, the space between the mattress and wall, the floor around it. Sam could not have known about the extra keys; he had been gone when Diego had them made.

She made the bed again, then found a book and tried to read, until she heard Sam returning.

"Why did you take the keys?" she demanded as he entered the camper.

He looked blank, groped in his pockets, then turned and opened the glove compartment and after a moment faced her once more, holding up the key chain. "Pains me to see them in the ignition," he said. "I always toss them in there."

Silently Victoria began to secure the cabinets, lock the refrigerator, snap the folding chairs into place. She had known he would explain the keys. He would explain the single key away just as easily. She did not bother to ask. Soon they were ready to leave.

They stopped frequently; in the dry Poison Creek bed they picked up thunder eggs and filled an envelope with sand that Sam promised would contain some grains of gold. Once they stopped and he led her up a short, steep cliff, and from there it seemed the entire desert lay at their feet—brown, greenish-gray, tan, black. There were no wires, no roads, no sign anywhere of human life. The vastness and emptiness seemed more threatening than anything Victoria had ever experienced.

There had been no horse, Victoria thought suddenly. She could see the cowboy again—not his features, she realized. She had not seen his features at all. She visualized the fire, but not what was burning; the moonlight gleamed on the dog's pale coat. And there was no horse anywhere. The sheltered depression had been bright; if a horse had been tethered there, she would have seen it. The cowboy would have taken it into shelter, not left it out in the brutal wind.

Sam pulled her arm and she stifled a scream. She had not heard his voice, had not felt his hand until he yanked her away from the edge of the cliff. He pulled her, stumbling and shaking, back to the camper.

Neither spoke of her near trance. Sam made dinner later, they played gin, slept, and, as before, she knew when she awakened that she had had nightmares. When Sam said he was taking her home, she nodded. She felt that the barren desolation of the landscape had entered her, that it was spreading, growing, would fill her completely, and the thought paralyzed her with dread.

II

Serena Hendricks met Sam at the back door of the ranch house.

"Stranger! Your beard is a bush! Does Farley know you're here?" She had the complexion of a Mexican, the bright blue eyes of her German mother.

Sam shook his head. "Where is he?"

"Out there. God knows. A hundred degrees! You know it's a hundred degrees? Gin and tonic. Lots of ice. Come on." She drew him into the house.

Serena's parents had worked on the Chesterman ranch, her father the foreman, her mother the housekeeper. Serena and Farley had grown up together and, Sam thought, they should have married, but had missed the chance, the time, something. She had married one of the hands instead and her three children ran around the yard whooping and playing rodeo, while Farley remained single.

Sam followed her to the kitchen. The air in the spacious ranch house was twenty degrees cooler than outside.

"We expected you and your friends back in April," Serena said as she sliced a lemon and added it to ice cubes in a glass. She pursed her lips, closed one eye and poured gin, nodded, added tonic, stirred, then tasted it.

"There were complications," Sam said. Sometimes he almost wished he had asked Serena to marry him ten years ago, back when anything was still possible. Serena rolled her eyes, drew him to a chair at the table, dragged another one close to it and sat down by him, her hand on his arm. "That means a woman. Tell me about it."

Sam laughed, gently put her hand on her own knee and stood up. "What I'm going to do is get my stuff from the camper, go upstairs and take a shower and a nap."

"Pig!" she yelled at his back. "You're all alike! Inconsiderate pigs! All of you."

When he brought his pack in she handed him a new drink. "Same room as usual. Supper's at six. Sleep well, dream happy."

Farley and Sam had been at U.C.L.A. together; they had climbed mountains together; they had lived through an August blizzard on Mt. Rainier together. Farley was slightly taller than Sam and leaner, and his hair was graying.

They sat on the wide porch drinking beer at midnight.

"You haven't seen her since then?" Farley asked.

"I guess neither of us wanted to. She quit her job, moved. Got another job. Dropped just about everyone we both knew." He finished the beer and put the can down. From far off there came a coyote's sharp, almost human coughing, yapping cry. He waited. There was an answering call. Then another. They were very distant.

"She must have had a good scare," Farley said. "There's no Reuben in the territory, you know."

"There's nothing like she said."

"There's something, Sam boy. There is something. And I don't know any way on God's earth for her to have known it. We used to have a hand called Tamale. An old Mexican, one of Serena's uncles. He died when I was five or six. It's been that long. He'd tell us stories. Superstitious old bastard. He told me about Ghost River, scared me shitless. Haven't heard that again since then. Until now when Reuben comes along and tells your friend the same thing."

Sam felt prickles on his arms. "So there was someone. Who the hell was he?"

"Reuben," Farley said. He stood up. "Can't take these hours any more. Must be age. You want to ride out with me in the morning? I'm making the rounds of the wells. Lundy's had bad water up the other side of Dog Mountain. I'm collecting samples to have tested."

Water, Sam thought later, sitting at his window staring out at the black desert. Water was the only real worry out here. Dog Creek irrigated Farley's wheat. Dog Creek determined if Farley would succeed or fail. Years when the snow did not come to the mountains, when the winds drove the sparse clouds over too fast to release their rain, when the summer started early, ended late, Farley watched Dog Creek, and the reservoir his father had dammed, like a woman watching a feverish child at the climax of a serious illness. The fear of drought accounted for the gray in Farley's hair. There were a dozen deep wells on the ninety thousand acres of his ranch, most of them pumped by windmills, a few of them close enough to the power lines to use electricity. The water was pumped into troughs. If one of the wells started pumping bad water, or no water, if one of the troughs was shot by a hunter, sprang a leak in any way, that meant disaster. Days, weeks went by between checks of the troughs. In this country a lot of cattle could die in that time.

And she thought he would swallow that silly story about a cowboy and his dog!

They drove the jeep cross-country to inspect the wells, and Farley drove places where Sam would not have attempted to go. At one o'clock Farley stopped and they sat on the ground in the shade of an overhanging cliff to eat their lunch. There was a valley below them; on the other side were more cliffs. Suddenly Sam realized where they were: this was the same valley Victoria had talked about, viewed from the other side.

"See that fence?" Farley waved his beer can toward the opposite cliffs. "Three hundred acres fenced off. Tamale brought me out with him once, when I was five. I rode all the way, still remember. I asked him why this piece was fenced off and he told me about Ghost River. Said the cattle heard the water sometimes and went off the cliffs trying to get to it. I believed him. Never gave it another thought for years. Then I was home from school one summer and Dad had me come out here to fix one of the gates. I knew by then cattle don't find water by sound, they smell it. I asked him about the three hundred acres. He said it always had been fenced because of the larkspurs that come up thick in there." He looked at the other side of the valley thoughtfully. "They do, too," he said after a moment. "Only thing is, they're on both sides of the fence and always were."

In the valley was a thick stand of bunchgrass, the sign of a well-managed range. No sage or gray rabbit grass had invaded there, no erosion scarred the land. No tracks flattened the grass, or made ruts in the earth. The valley was a cul-de-sac, a box canyon surrounded by cliffs. Where the valley narrowed, with a break in the cliffs, there was a drop-off of two hundred feet. The wire fence started at the gorge, crossed the ranch road, climbed the cliff, followed the jagged ridge around to the break. On the other side the fence resumed, still clinging to the crest, then turned, went down the cliffs again, recrossed the road and ended at the gorge, several hundred yards from the other section. The area enclosed was an irregular ellipse. The irregularities were caused by the terrain. Where heaps of boulders, or abrupt rises or falls, made detours necessary, the fence always skirted around to the outside.

Farley got back in the jeep. "Might as well finish," he said, and drove along the fence on the crest, then started the descent down a rocky incline, bumping and lurching to the two-track ranch road and the first gate. He drove fast, but with care and skill; turned around at the second gate and made his way forward, as Victoria had done.

"Probably stopped along in here," he said. "First curve out of sight of the road." The gorge was nearby, and there should have been a hill to the right, but the hill was nothing less than another steep cliff. Farley studied it a moment, motioned to Sam and started to walk. Unerringly he turned and twisted and took them upward. They reached the top with little trouble.

"She could have done it," Sam said, looking down at the valley again, across it to where they had been a short time before. He looked about until he saw the boulders she had mentioned, where she had sat down. They started toward them. They were on the ridge of an upthrust, picking their way over the weathered edges of crazily tilted basalt, which would remain when everything about it was turned to dust. In some places there was less than a foot of space between a sheer drop-off on one side and a slope almost that steep on the other.

"Her guardian angel sure was with her," Farley said as they drew near the boulders. One of the mammoth rocks was balanced on the edge of the crest.

"I don't believe any of this," Sam said angrily. He stopped. Ahead of them, lodged in a crevice, something gleamed in the sunlight. Farley took several cautious steps and picked it up. He handed it to Sam, a single key. Without comparing it, Sam knew it was a key to his camper.

They made their way among the boulders, through the only possible passage, and came out on top the ridge that now widened for several hundred feet. At the edge of it Sam could look down over the gorge; he could see the ranch road, and between him and the road there was a small sunken area, the sheltered spot where "Reuben" had taken Victoria. There was no sign of a campfire ever having been there. No sign of a horse, a dog, a camp of any sort. Silently the two men walked back to the road and the jeep.

Farley did not turn on the ignition immediately. "That was in April, three months ago. Why are you checking on it now?"

Sam looked at the gorge wall, imagined a river roaring below. "Mimi, the girl who was going to drive up with Victoria, came to see me last week. She and Victoria were friends, but Victoria dropped her too. Mimi thought something happened out here between Victoria and me, that I raped her, or tortured her, or something. She told me Victoria is sick, really sick, in analysis, maybe even suicidal. Whatever is wrong with her is serious and it started here."

"You *have* seen her?"

"Yeah. For half a minute maybe. She wanted to see me like a

rabbit wants to see a bobcat. Wouldn't talk, had to run, too busy to chat." He scowled, remembering the pallor that had blanched her face when she saw him. "She looked like hell."

"So you want to get her back out here to find out what she saw."

Sam grunted. After a moment he said, "I don't know what I want to do. I have to do something. I just had to check for myself, see if there's any way it could have been like she said."

· Farley put the key in the ignition. Without looking at Sam he said, "She could have gone back east, or to Texas, but she didn't. She could have taken an overdose, slashed her wrists, gone off the bridge. She could have really hidden, but she kept in touch with the friend who could get to you. She wants you to help her. And you owe it to her for losing your temper because she had the vision you've spent so many years chasing." He turned the key and started to drive before Sam could answer.

That night Sam said he would try to get Victoria to come back, and Farley said he would visit his parents in Bend to see if there was anything his father could or would tell him about the fenced-off acres.

Sam walked. If you really wanted to find a god, he thought, this was where to look. Such absolute emptiness could be relieved only by an absolute presence. Men always had gone to a mountaintop, or to the desert, in search of God. Not God, he thought angrily, peace, acceptance, a reason, he did not know what it was he sought on the desert. He would be willing to settle for so little, no more than a clue or a hint that there was more than he had been able to find. After he had quit his job with GoMar, he had tried drugs for almost two years. Drugs and a personal teacher of the way, and both had failed. He had found only other pieces of himself. He had turned to asceticism and study, had become a jeweler. He had fasted, had lived a hermit's life for a year, had read nothing, denied himself music, the radio, had worked, walked, waited. And waited still.

He was out of sight of the ranch buildings, the spacious house
with old oaks and young poplars sheltering it; the big barns, the
small bungalows some of the hands lived in, the bunk house,
machine shops . . . You stepped over a rise and the desert swallowed it all, just as it swallowed all sound, and existed in a deep
silence, broken only by the voices of those few animals that had
accepted its terms and asked for nothing but life.

And just having life was not enough.

He waited across the street from her apartment until she entered and, after ten minutes, followed her inside. When she
opened her door and saw him, she hesitated, then with obvious
reluctance released the chain to admit him.

"Hello, Sam." She walked away from him and stood at the
window looking out.

He remained by the door, the width of the room between them.
He was three months too late. In those months she had turned
into a stranger.

When they had returned to San Francisco in the spring, he had
taken her bags inside for her, and then left. She had not invited
him to stay, and he had not sat down as he usually did. "I'll call
you," he had said.

But he had let the days slide by, pretending to himself that he
was too busy sorting the material they had brought back, too busy
with an order from a small elite store in Palm Beach, too busy,
too busy. Every time he thought of calling, he felt an uprush of
guilt and anger. Finally, filled with a senseless indignation, as if
she were forcing him to do something distasteful, he dialed her
number, only to get a recording that said her number was no
longer in service. Furiously he called her office; she had quit, and
left no forwarding address.

Relief replaced the anger. He was free; he no longer had to
think about her and whatever had happened to her out on the
desert. He could get on with his own life, continue his own
search. But he could not banish her from his mind, and worse,

his thoughts of her were colored with a constant dull resentment that marred his memories of the good times they had had, that quieted his sexual desire for her, that distorted her honesty and humor and made her seem in retrospect scheming and even dull. Over the months that they had been separated the new image he constructed had gradually replaced the old, and this meeting was destroying that new image, leaving him nothing. He had to start over with her, falteringly, uncertainly, knowing that the real changes were not in her but in himself. There were intimate things to be said between them, but intimate things could not be said between strangers.

Everything Sam had planned to say was gone from his mind, and almost helplessly he started, "I treated you very badly. I'm sorry." His words sounded stiff and phony, even to him. She didn't move, and slowly Sam repeated his conversation with Farley, all of it, including Farley's explanation of his rage. "It's possible," Sam said, then shook his head hard. "It's true I *was* sore because you saw something I didn't. I can't explain that part. We both, Farley and I, want to find out what happened."

"It's true then!" Victoria said, facing him finally. She was shockingly pale.

Sam started to deny it, said instead, "I don't know."

"We have to go back there to find out, don't we?"

"You don't have to now," Sam said quickly. "I think it would be a mistake. Wait until you're well."

"Thursday," she said. When Sam shook his head she added, "You know I won't get well until this is over."

Color had returned to her cheeks and she looked almost normal again, as she had always looked: quick, alert, handsome. And there was something else, he thought. Something unfamiliar, an intensity, or determination she had not shown before.

"Thursday," Sam said reluctantly.

She had never been so talkative or said so little. Her new job, the people in office, the changing landscape, a grade school teacher, sleeping in the parking lot, how easy driving the camper was . . .

"Mimi says you're in analysis," Sam interrupted her.

"Not now," Victoria said easily. "She was more Freudian than the master. Treated my experience like a dream and gave sexual connotations to every bit of it. The thing in the valley became phallic, of course, so naturally I had to dread it. Reuben was my father firmly forbidding my incestuous advances, and so on. I took it for several weeks and gave up on her. She needs help."

Too easy, Sam realized. She was too deep inside; all this was a glib overlay she was hiding behind. After dinner, she took two pills.

"Something new?" Sam asked.

"Not really. I used them when Stuart and I were breaking up. They got me through then."

"Bad dreams?"

"Not when I take these," she said too gaily, holding up the bottle of pills. She had changed into short pajamas; now she pulled a book from her bag and sat on her bed. "My system," she said cheerfully, "is to take two, read, and in an hour if I'm still reading, take two more."

"That's dangerous."

"At home I keep them in the bathroom. If I'm too sleepy to get up and get them, I don't need them. Foolproof. Hasn't failed me yet. Have you read this?" She handed him the book.

"Stop it, Victoria. What are you doing?"

She retrieved the book and opened it. "It's pretty good. There's a secondhand book store near the office . . ."

"Victoria, let me make love to you."

She smiled and shook her head.

"We used to be good together."

"Another time. I'm getting drowsy, floating almost. It's like a nice not-too-high once it starts."

"And you don't dream? How about nightmares? You were

having three or four a night last time I saw you. So bad you
wouldn't even wake up from them."
    She had became rigid as he spoke. She closed the book and let
it drop to the floor, then swung her legs off the bed.
    "What are you doing?" He felt the beginnings of a headache:
guilt and shame for doing that to her, he knew.
    "Water. More pills. Sometimes I don't have to wait an hour to
know."
    Presently she slept, deeply, like a person in a coma. She looked
like a sick child with her brown hair neatly arranged, the covers
straight, as if her mother or a nurse had only then finished preparing her for a visitor. He no longer desired her. That sudden
rush of passion had been so sudden and unexpected, he had been
as surprised as she. He had not thought of her as a sexual partner
for months. Their sex had been good, but only because each had
known the other would make no further demands. It had been
fun with her, he thought, again with surprise because he had
forgotten. It had been clean with her, no hidden nuances to
decipher; no flirtatious advance and retreat; no other boyfriends
to parade before him hoping for a show of jealousy. If they
existed she was reticent about them, as she was about everything
personal. No involvement at all, that had been the secret of their
success.
    He had planned to surrender the camper to Mimi and Diego,
and share his tent with Victoria, out of sight and sound of the
others, with only the desert and the brilliant moon growing fatter
each night. Even that, showing her the world he loved so much,
would have been something freely given, freely taken, with no
ties afterward. They both had understood that, had wanted it that
way.
    He turned off the lights but was a long time in falling asleep.
    Toward dawn he was awakened by Victoria's moaning. He put
his denim jacket over the lamp before he turned it on. She had
the covers completely off and was twisting back and forth in a
rocking motion, making soft, incoherent sounds. As he drew near

to touch her, to interrupt her dream, she stiffened and he knew she had slipped into a nightmare like the ones she had had before. The first time he had shaken her, called her repeatedly, and after a long time she had screamed and gone limp. After that he had simply held her until it was over, held her and murmured her name over and over. She had not remembered any of the nightmares.

He slid into the narrow bed and wrapped his arms around her, whispering, "It's going to be all right, Victoria. We're going to fix it, make it all right again."

It went on and on, until abruptly she began to fight him. Then she wakened and, gasping, she clung to him as he stroked her sweaty back. He pulled the covers over her again.

"*Sh, sh.* It's over. Go back to sleep now. It's all right."

"No more! I want to get up!"

"You'll be chilled. No more sleep. Just rest a few minutes. It's too early to get up. Try to relax and get warm."

The drugs and the nightmares were battling for her; the nightmares waited for a sign of weakening in the pills, ready to claim her swiftly then.

What had she seen? What was she still seeing when her pink pills lost their effectiveness in the darkness before dawn?

"How sick is she?" Serena asked. She was watching Farley and Victoria going toward the reservoir for a swim.

Sam shrugged. "I don't know. Why?"

"I like her. I don't want to see her sick, maybe die. Farley likes her. Is she, was she your girl?"

"Not the way you mean," Sam said laughing.

"What other way is there?" Serena raised her hands and let them drop, expressing what? Sam always knew exactly what she meant, yet could never put it in words.

After Serena left him on the porch, he wondered how sick Victoria really was. After six days on the ranch, she was tanned, vivacious, pretty. Maybe she was sleeping better. Farley was keeping her busy riding, hiking, swimming, whatever they could find to do out in the sun and wind, and her appetite was good again. By ten or eleven she was ready for bed. And sleep? He wished he knew.

Farley sidestepped every question about what he planned to do. "Don't rush," he said. "She's terribly tired. Let's get acquainted before we dance. Okay?" He said he had learned nothing from his father.

"Aren't we even going out there?"

"In time, Sam. In time. She quit her job. She tell you that? She's in no rush. No place she has to go."

She hadn't told him, and it annoyed him that she had told a stranger. It annoyed him that Farley and Victoria were having long talks that excluded him, that Farley had announced their swim after Sam had said he was expecting a long-distance call. Most of all it annoyed him that Serena evidently thought of Farley and Victoria as a couple. An hour later, his call completed, he walked over to the reservoir, but stopped on the hill overlooking the lake. Victoria and Farley were sitting close together under a juniper tree, talking. Sam returned to the house.

It was not jealousy, he knew. It was the delay. Victoria had something, could show him something that he needed desperately. Every delay increased his impatience and irritation until he felt he could stand no more.

After dinner he said coolly, "Tomorrow let's ride over to the gorge area and camp out."

Victoria leaned forward eagerly. "Let's. Let's camp out."

Farley's face was unreadable. He watched Victoria a moment, then shrugged.

"In that case," Victoria said quickly, "I'd better wash my hair now and get plenty of sleep." There were spots of color in both cheeks and she looked too excited. She hurried to the door, said good night over her shoulder, and ran upstairs.

Farley leaned back, studying Sam.

"There's no point in putting it off any longer," Sam said. He sounded too defensive, he knew. Sullenly he added, "I'm sorry if I upset your timetable."

"Not mine. Hers. She thinks she's going to die out there. We had an unspoken agreement, a pact, you might say, to give her a vacation and rest before she had to face that valley again."

"You know that's crazy!"

"I don't know half as much as you do, Sam. I seem to know less all the time. I don't know what's in the valley, don't know what it will do to her to face it again. I don't know why you think you can use her to see it too. Nope. I don't know nearly half as much as you do."

Sam had risen as Farley spoke. "Back off, Farley. I said I'm sorry. Let's drop it."

Farley nodded and left the room.

Gradually the ranch lights went out, until only the dim hallway light in the main house remained; outside, the desert crept closer. From the porch Sam watched the darkness claim the barn area, the yard, the bungalows, until he could feel it there at the bottom of the porch steps. He had dug around one of the desert ghost towns once, where only a juniper mounting post remained. That was what the desert would do here if this small group of people let it.

The moon rose, a half moon. Enough, Sam thought. It was enough.

That was what the old Indian had said. Sam had driven three hours over New Mexico desert roads, gravel roads, dirt and sand roads, to find the shack. It had a tin roof covered with sagebrush. An Indian woman had admitted him silently; inside, the temperature was over a hundred degrees, cooler than it would have been without the sagebrush insulation, but stifling. On a straight chair before one of the two windows sat the Indian man, one arm swathed in bandages where the stump was still not healed. There was a roughly sawn table, two chairs and several stools, a wood-burning stove with a cast-iron pot on it, a rope-spring bed and several rolled-up pallets. The walls were covered with newspapers, carefully cut and pasted up so that the pictures were whole, the stories complete. From outside there was the sound of children's whispers, a faint giggle. The woman scowled at the window on the opposite side of the cabin, and the sounds stopped.

Sam had seen many such cabins, many worse than this one. He pulled the second chair around to face the man, introduced himself, sat down and drew out his report form. "I've been to the mine," he said. "What I need now is a statement from you so the company can process your claim."

The Indian did not move, continued to gaze at the desert.

"Sir . . ." Sam looked at the woman. "He was rambling when he was found. Did he suffer head injuries? Can he hear?"

"He hears."

Sam glanced at the preliminary report. There had been an explosion at the potash mine; an avalanche apparently had carried this man down a ravine where he stayed for two days before he was found. Two days on the desert, in the sun, no water, bleeding from an arm injury, possibly head injuries. "You haven't filed a claim yet," he said. He explained the company's disability pension, the social security regulations, the medical settlement. He explained the need for the claimant's signature before processing could begin. The Indian never stirred.

Sam looked from him to the woman.

"He won't sign," she said.

"I don't understand. Why won't he file a claim?"

"He says he should pay the company," she said, and although her face remained impassive, she spoke bitterly. "He says a man should be happy to give up an arm to see the face of God."

"He's crazy!" Sam looked at the Indian for the first time. He had been looking at a claimant, a statistic, one like many others he had seen before and recognized instantly. Now he studied him.

"You have a right . . ." he started, then fell silent.

The Indian shifted to regard him and Sam thought, He *has*

seen the face of God. Harshly he demanded, "Who's going to take care of your family? Hunt for them, earn money? Who will go up to the mountain to get firewood? You have only one arm!"

"It is enough," the Indian man said, and turned his gaze back to the desert.

Sam filled out the claim and the Indian woman signed it. He drove away as fast as the company truck could take him. That was the last case he handled; two months later he quit his job.

For seven years, he thought, he had searched for something that would give him what that son of a bitch had. They called him an artist now, and he knew that was a lie. He was a good craftsman, not an artist. He understood the difference. He was using the rocks he found, making something, anything that would permit him to survive, that would give him an excuse to spend days, weeks, months out on the desert. It amused him when others called him an artist, because he knew he was using a skill to achieve something else; he felt only contempt for those he fooled —the critics, the connoisseurs, the buyers.

He would have it, he knew, if he had to risk an arm, both arms, Victoria, Farley, anything else in the world to get it. He would have it.

III

Farley watched Victoria. She rode reasonably well, held her back straight and trusted her horse to know where to put his feet, but she would have to do a hell of a lot of riding before it looked natural on her. He planned to watch her and if she started to slump, or her hand got heavy on the reins, he would call a halt, walk her up a ridge or down a valley, anything to rest her without suggesting that that was his intention.

Watching Victoria, he thought of Fran, riding like a wild thing, so in tune with her horse, it seemed the impulses from her brain sped through its muscles, in a feedback system that linked them to create a new single creature. The last time she had come back, they had ridden all day.

When they stopped to water the horses at one of the wells on her father's land, he asked, "You aren't happy in Portland, are you?"

"I get so I can't stand it. Begin to feel I'm suffocating, there's no air to breathe, and a million bodies ready to smother me. So I come back and can't stand this either. Too much wind, too much sand, too much sun and sky and cold and heat. Too much loneliness. When I start wanting to scream I know it's time to go back to the big city. Heads I lose, tails I lose."

Fran was beautiful, more so now at thirty than she had been at fourteen, or eighteen, any of the lost years. He had loved her, and had left her when he went to school. A year later she had married a doctor from Portland. She had two children, and Farley no longer tried to sort out his feelings about her. When she came home they spent days together out on the desert. When she was gone they never corresponded.

"You should have told me you'd leave here with me," Fran said that day. She tossed rocks down a hole in the ground where an earthquake had opened a fissure ten thousand years before. "We could have made it work, half the time in town, half out here."

He shook his head. "Then we'd both be miserable, not just one of us."

"Aren't you miserable? Aren't you lonely? Is this goddamn desert all you really want out of life?"

He had not answered. His life was his answer. He had tried to live in town, during, immediately after his college days, and he knew the city would kill him, just as a cage kills. His mother was dying in Bend where she had to remain for daily cancer treatments. His father was dying, too. The small town of Bend was killing him. He was like a caged animal, the luster gone, the sheen, the joy of living, the will to live, all leaving him as surely as her life was leaving her.

Fran was gone the next day. He might see her again in a month, or six months, or never. He continued to watch Victoria.

They skirted an old alfalfa field; it looked as dead as the rest of the desert this time of year. Even the deer passed it up for the greener range high on the mountains. But if the winter rain didn't come, if the summer persisted into fall, into winter, the cattle, deer, antelope, rabbits would all be here grazing, and they would bring in the coyotes and bobcats. There would be some ranchers who would start yelping about varmint control, bait stations, traps, and he would try to talk them out of it, as he had done before. Farley knew they could never control the coyotes and bobcats; only water or the lack of water could do that. In the desert everything was very simple.

They had reached the trail leading up Goat's Head Butte, and he called a brief rest to water the horses. He and Sam had inspected this pump and well only last week.

"There are trees up there," Victoria said, pointing.

"Snows up there just about every year, not much, but enough to keep them more or less green," Farley said. "We'll take it nice and easy. It gets a little steep and narrow up there, and, you'll be happy to hear, cooler. I'll go first and lead one of the pack horses, then you, Victoria, then Sam with the other pack horse. Okay? Just give Benny a loose rein and he'll stay exactly where he knows he should."

They zigzagged for the last hour of the climb; the curves became tighter, hairpin turns joining rocky stairsteps that let them look directly onto the spot where they would be in a few minutes. Then suddenly they were on the top, a mesa with welcome shade and waist-high bunch grass for the horses. The grass was pale brown and dry, but good graze. A startled hen pheasant ran across their path into the grass, closely followed by a dozen or more half-grown chicks. A hawk leaped from a tall pine tree into the sky and vanished, gliding downward behind the trees. From up here they could see other trails, most of them easier, but Farley would not bring horses up through the sparse woods and grasses. Such life was too precious on the desert, and horses were hard on trails. He had chosen the north climb because it was barren and rocky, and would suffer little damage from their passage.

"Do we get off now?" Victoria asked. She sounded strained.
Sam was already dismounting. He gave Victoria a hand.
"Tired? Sore?"

"Tired and sore," she said, standing stiffly, hardly even looking
around. "And scared. My God, I've never been so scared in my
life! What if that horse had stumbled? We'd still be falling!"

Sam laughed and put his arm about her shoulders. "Honey,
you did beautifully. You came up like a bird."

"I was afraid to move! What if I had sneezed, or coughed, or
got hiccups? What if the *horse* had looked down?"

Serena had packed beef chunks and chopped vegetables, and
within an hour stew was ready. They ate dinner ravenously and
took coffee with them to the western end of the butte where they
sat on rocks and watched the sunset over the Three Sisters in
their chaste white veils.

No one spoke until the display was over and the streaks of gold,
scarlet, salmon, baby pink had all turned dark. The snow on the
Sisters became invisible and the mountains were simple shapes,
almost geometrical, against the violet sky.

"They look like a child's drawing of volcanoes," Victoria said
softly. Then: "Why do they call this Goat's Head Butte? It certainly looks like no goat's head I've ever seen."

"A mistake," Farley said. "The Indians called it Ghost Head,
the source of Ghost River. A U.S. Geologic Survey cartographer
got it wrong."

Victoria drew in her breath sharply. "It really is called Ghost
River!"

She sat between Sam and Farley. There was still enough light
for them to see each other, but shadows now filled the valley
below; the moon was not yet out. For what seemed a long time
no one spoke. Farley waited, and finally Sam said, in a grudging
tone:

"I didn't know it then, Victoria, or I wouldn't have said what
I did."

"Piece by piece it's coming together, isn't it?" she said. Before either of them could respond, she said, "We're too far away."

"What do you mean?" Sam asked.

Helplessly Victoria shrugged. "I don't know what I mean. I think you have to be closer to feel anything. I don't know why."

Sam stood up, but Farley motioned him back. He put his hand lightly on Victoria's arm. "Tonight we observe," he said matter of factly. "Tomorrow we'll crisscross the valley and tomorrow night we'll camp down there. Relax, Sam. Just take it easy." Without changing his tone of voice he asked, "Victoria, what did you see in that valley that night?" He felt her stiffen and tightened his clasp on her arm.

"I told you."

"No. You told both of us your interpretation of what you saw. You translated something into familiar shapes. If you ask a primitive what something is that he never experienced before, he'll translate it into familiar terms. So will a child."

"I'm not a primitive or a child!"

"The part of you that interpreted what you saw, that has been reacting with terror, that part is primitive. I'm not talking to that part. I'm talking to the rational you, the thinking, sane you. What did you see? What was the first thing that caught your attention? Not what you thought it was, just how it looked."

"A black dome," she said slowly.

"No. Not unless you could see the edges beyond doubt."

"A black shape, domelike."

"Let's leave it at a black shape. Are you certain it had a definite shape?"

"No, of course not. It was night, there were shadows, I was on the hill over it."

He was silent a few moments, and finally Victoria said, "It was just black. I remember thinking it was a shadow at first, then it took on shape."

Farley patted her arm. "Then?"

"There was a door, when it opened, a light showed . . . That's not what you want, is it?"

"Just how it looked, not what you thought it was."

"A patch of pale orange light. No. A pale glow. Orange-tinted. I thought of a door, the way light comes through an open door."

They worked on it painstakingly, each detail stripped of interpretation, stripped of meaning. Victoria began to sound tired, and Farley could sense restless small movements from Sam.

"I knew they were vehicles of some kind!" Victoria cried once. "They reflected light, they moved like automobiles—in a straight line, gleaming, and they turned on headlights at the road."

"But what you described doesn't have to be vehicles," Farley said. "What you said was clusters of gleaming lights, like reflections on metal."

"I suppose," she said wearily. "They were spaced like cars on a road, and they moved at the same speed, in a straight line, not up and down, or sideways, or anything. Like cars."

"And when they turned on lights, could you still see the reflections?"

She sighed and said no, she didn't think so.

"You're getting tired," Farley said gently. "We should get back to camp, get some sleep. One more thing, Victoria. Look down there now, the moon's lighting the valley, probably not as brightly as that night, but much the same as it was then. If you had been up here that night, Victoria, would you have been able to see what you saw?"

Farley still had his hand on her arm. The moon behind them made her face a pale blur; it was impossible to see her features clearly, but he felt a tremor ripple through her, felt her arm grow rigid.

"No!" The trembling increased. "We're too far away. You can't see the road from here."

"Not because we're too far to see it," Farley said. "The road's lower over there than the valley is."

"You mean I couldn't have seen it from the hill either?"

"No."

Victoria rose unsteadily and stared at the valley, turned her entire body to look at the cliffs surrounding it.

"What is it?" Farley demanded. "You've remembered something, haven't you? What?"

"This isn't the right place."

"It's the place. You were over there. You can see the boulders, the pale shapes near the end of the ridge. Below that is the ranch road where you parked. It's the right place."

"It's wrong! It isn't the right place! I was on a hill. It wasn't like that!" She closed her eyes and swayed. "I was on a hill, and I could hear . . . I heard . . ."

"You heard what? You heard something and saw something and smelled something, didn't you? What was it?"

She shook her head hard. "I don't know."

Farley made her face the valley again. "Look at it, Victoria. Look! You're hiding among the boulders on that ridge over there. You know they might see you. You keep in the shadows, hiding. Don't move! Don't make a sound! What do you smell? What do you hear?"

She moaned and he said, more insistently, "You smell something. What is it, Victoria? You know what it is, tell me!"

"Water!" she cried. "Water, a river, a forest!"

"You're running," Farley said, holding her hard. "You're on the hill and you're running. Your eyes are open. What do you see?"

She tried to push him away. "Nothing! I can't remember that part. Nothing!"

"Look at the ridge. Look at it! You couldn't run up there! There's no place to run!"

"It's not the same place! I told you, I was on a hill, there was grass. I ran until that man, Reuben, stopped me."

"You're terrified they might hear you. You smell the river and forest. You hear the rushing water. You run. Where are you running to? Why?"

"The trees," she gasped. "Bushes under the trees. I'll hide in the bushes, in the mist." She pulled harder, her voice rising in hysteria. "There isn't any forest or river! Let me go! Let me go!" She began to sag. "I can't breathe!"

Farley and Sam half-carried, half-led her back to the campfire, which had burned to a bed of glowing ashes. Sam built up the fire and Farley held a drink to Victoria's lips, keeping one arm around her shoulders. She sipped the bourbon, then took the cup and drank it down.

"Better?" Farley asked. She nodded. "Sit down. I'll get a blanket to put around you." Wordlessly she sat down by the fire. Sam was making coffee.

No one spoke until they all had coffee. Then Farley took Victoria's hand. "We have to finish it," he said.

She nodded without looking at him. "I'm crazy," she said. "I would have killed myself that night if that cowboy hadn't been there to save my life."

"You saved yourself," Farley said. "You panicked and you ran. You knew there was no forest, no river, no mist, but they *were* there. You invented Reuben, you projected him, because you couldn't resist the evidence of your senses. You had to have help and no one was there to help you, so you helped yourself, through Reuben."

"I'm going to bed," Victoria said dully. She made no motion to get up.

Farley was not certain if she could accept anything he was saying. He could not tell if she heard him. "You acted out of self-preservation," he said.

"It was all just a dream or a series of hallucinations," Sam said. His voice was hard, grating. His angular face looked aged; his full beard made him look Biblical, like an old bitter prophet.

"You can't regard it all as one thing," Farley said. "That's the mistake you made before, the same mistake the psychiatrist made, that if part of it was false, it all was. Obviously the cowboy figure is right out of romantic fiction, but that doesn't make the rest of it false. I wondered if Victoria rejected the truth because she was convinced the truth was impossible, and accepted instead the illusions that could have been possible." He paused, then added, "Both in what she saw in the valley, and again in the cowboy."

Victoria stirred and shook her head. "I don't understand anything," she said, but with more animation now, as if she were awakening.

"I don't either," Farley said. "But you did see something, and you smelled and heard Ghost River. I bet not more than a dozen people today know it was ever called that, but you renamed it. That's what I keep coming back to."

"That's crap!" Sam shouted. "She saw something and ran. Probably she stumbled and knocked herself out. You know you can't run over that country, not even in daylight. She dreamed the rest of it." He had risen to stand over Victoria. "The only important thing is what did you see in the valley?"

"Not what you want me to say!" Victoria cried. "It wasn't a god figure. Not a burning bush or a pillar of flame. Not good or evil. Nothing we can know."

Farley reached out to touch her and she jerked away. "You said we have to finish it. We do! I do! Sam, you wanted to know my nightmare. Let me tell you. I'm wearing tights, covered with sequins, circus makeup, my hair in a long glittering braid. Spotlights are on me. I'm climbing the ladder to the tightrope and there's a drum roll, the whole thing. I know I can do this, the way you know you can ride a bike, or swim, or just walk. I smile at the crowd and start out on the rope and suddenly there is absolute silence. I look down and realize the crowd is all on one side of the rope, to my left: no one is on the right side. The audience is waiting for me to fall. Nothing else. They know I'll fall and they are waiting. They aren't impatient, or eager, they have no feelings at all. They don't care. That's when I panic, when I realize they don't care. And I know I must not fall on their side. I try to scream for someone to open the safety net, for someone to take my hand, for anything. Then I am falling and I don't know which side I'm on. I won't know until I hit. That is what terrifies me, that I don't know which side I'll die on." Her voice had become almost a monotone as she told the dream. Abruptly she rose to her feet. "I'd like some more bourbon, please."

Farley poured it and she sat down once more and drank before she spoke again.

"I came back here to see which side of the rope I'll land on. The next time I'll finish the dream and find out."

Sam reached for the bottle and poured bourbon into his cup. "A lousy dream," he muttered.

"Indifference, that's what made it a nightmare. Their indifference," Victoria said quietly. She sipped at her drink and went on. "It's the same way we might break up an anthill and watch the ants scurry. Or how we tear a spiderweb and maybe see the spider dart away, or not. We don't care. We watch or not, it doesn't matter. Like the bank camera that photographs me when I go to the window. Me, a bank robber, someone asking for information, it doesn't matter, the camera clicks its picture." She was starting to slur her words slightly. Her voice was low, almost inaudible part of the time. "It . . . they watched me like that. They didn't care if I went over the cliff or not."

Farley felt the hair rise on the back of his neck and wondered if she realized what she was saying. She wasn't talking about the dream any longer.

"They didn't care if I went over the cliff. They didn't care if I stopped, or ran, what I did." She drained her cup, then set it down on the ground with elaborate care. "That's inhuman," she said. "Not like a god, the opposite of what it would be like for a god. Beyond all idea of good and evil. No awareness of good and evil."

Sam sighed and said, "She's drunk. She never could drink."

Victoria pushed herself up from the ground. She nodded. "I am," she said carefully. "I'll go to bed now." Both men rose. She looked at Farley. "I know why I'm here. I have to see where I land. And I know why Sam's here. He's looking for God. Why are you here? What is your noble cause?" She was taking care to pronounce each word, as if speaking a foreign language.

"You're too stinko to talk any more tonight."

"I can't talk, but my ears are not drunk. My ears are not blurring anything."

"Will you remember?"

She nodded an exaggerated yes.

"It's my land. Over the years twenty-five or thirty head of cattle have gone over that cliff. Two people have vanished in that area. My land. I have to know what's there. I put it off and pretended it was just a superstition, wiped it from my mind, but I can't do that now. You won't let me do it ever again." He paused, examining her face. "Do you understand that?"

"No, but I don't have to." She began to walk unsteadily toward the tent. "Because it's not true," she said, then ducked under the flap of the low tent.

It was true, though. He wanted to exorcise a devil, Farley thought, sitting down again. And Sam wanted to find God. All Victoria wanted was to learn the truth. They'd both use her, and through her they might find what they looked for. Across the fire from him, Sam sat brooding, staring into the flames.

"I want to stay up tonight," Sam said abruptly. "Just in case there is something down there."

Farley nodded. "We'll take turns. You want to sleep first?"

Sam shrugged, then wordlessly got up and went to his sleeping bag spread on the ground a short distance from the fire.

Farley sat with his back against a pine tree and watched the shifting patterns of light and shadow as the moon moved across the sky. From time to time he added a small stick to the fire, not enough to blaze much, just to maintain a glow to keep the coffee hot. A fire during a night watch was friendly, he thought, nudging a spark into flame.

What was he doing here? What he had answered was part of it. Maybe all of it. He didn't know. For hundreds of years people around this area had known this piece of land was strange, not to be trusted. The Indians had shunned it for generations. His father had known it was not safe for cattle or men and had fenced it off. Easier to cross off three hundred acres out of ninety thousand than to pursue a riddle that probably could not be solved anyway. He would have done the same if Sam and Victoria had not forced him to examine it. He was examining many things suddenly, he admitted to himself.

"You have so many books!" Victoria had exclaimed. "Did you major in geology?"

There were four shelves of geology books. "Nope. That's why I have to keep reading. Can't find the one I'm looking for, I guess."

"And that is?"

"Life and death, desert style. Something like that. Someone who can relate the earth cycles to life cycles. I'm not sure, that's why I keep reading and searching."

"You'll have to write it yourself," Victoria had said.

And Fran had asked, "Aren't you lonely?"

He was sure he was not lonely in the sense she meant, but there had to be more. A few months ago he had not known that. Every day he got up at dawn and worked as hard as any of the hands on the ranch, doing the same kind of work, doing more than any of them most days. Dinner at six, read, bed by ten. There were women in Bend, one in Prineville, all very casual, non-compelling.

He was evading again. Why was he here? He had come home because he could not live in the city. He had found strength in this harsh desert. But evil had followed him, had claimed his mother. Sometimes when the phone rang late at night, he found himself pausing, willing it to be his father telling him it was all over finally. Sometimes he found himself watching Serena playing with her children and he almost hated her for being able to find a good life so simply without any effort at all.

He could have married Serena. They had experimented with sex together; at the time they both had assumed they would marry when they were grown. Something in him had said no, and he had practically pushed her into the arms of Charlie Hendricks. And Fran. She would have gone to school with him. Their parents had expected it, and even discussed the financial arrangements. Instead he had decided he couldn't handle a bride and the university at the same time. Leave him alone, his mother had said, he'll find himself in school. But he had found nothing.

He had been drafted and at first he had believed he was finally going to do something worthwhile. He had discovered only despair and hopelessness. School again, sinking ever deeper, then the flight home to the safety of the land. Here, he had thought, was the only place he had been able to find any hope. Here nothing was unclean, nothing was evil. The coyotes, the bobcats, the summer frosts and the winter droughts all were proper here.

He had sought refuge in work on this healing land, only to learn that evil was here too. Not the land! he wanted to howl. And he knew this time there was no place he could go, no last refuge he could bury himself in.

Reluctantly, compelled by circumstances he could not understand, he accepted that finally, after years of flight, he would stand and confront the enemy.

IV

Victoria dreamed that her boss was coming, that he would rage at her for not doing her work better. "I'm doing the best I can," she cried. "Even a child could do it better," he stormed at her. And she woke up.

The light was as it had been the other night, perhaps not as bright, but almost. She didn't make any noise; she knew that either Farley or Sam would be up, and for the moment she didn't want to talk to anyone. She remembered the dream. No boss had ever raged at her in that way. A child could do it better, of that she was certain. Slowly she sat up and waited for the moment of terror to pass. It always overwhelmed her when she first awakened; then it receded, but never completely.

Now she could see Sam, a clear profile against the pale horizon. His full beard made his head look grotesquely oversized. He had aged. It was as if he had left Shangri-la and before her eyes were passing into the mundane world where age caught up. He looked old and tired. He looked frightened. She tried to imagine Farley frightened as Sam was, and somehow it was harder to picture him so. She didn't understand Farley. Something was driving him, and she didn't know what.

Something was out there that each of them needed to learn about. They had followed Farley's plan, had searched all day by sunlight, on horseback, then on foot, and had found nothing. But the moon changed the land; it made strange things possible.

"You should be sleeping," Sam said when she joined him.

"I know. The silence and the moonlight woke me up, I think. Has it been quiet all evening?"

"Yup. Not a thing stirring."

She sighed. "The desert is very beautiful at night, isn't it. That's a surprise. I'd read that, but it's like reading that the ocean is beautiful, or that the sunset is beautiful. It's meaningless until you see it. I can almost understand why Farley wants to stay here."

Sam laughed. "Nobody understands why Farley stays here. He's a hermit."

"Sam," she said, "after tonight, then what?"

He shrugged.

"I mean, what if nothing happens?"

"Then I come back tomorrow night, and the next night, and the next night."

"But what if nothing ever happens?"

"Vicky, don't talk about that right now. Let's watch the horse. Let's watch the desert. Watch the shadows on the face of the moon. They deepen as you watch. Let's not talk about anything else right now."

She sat down beside him. "May I smoke?"

Sam laughed irritably. "I wish you'd stayed asleep."

"I know. I'm just nervous. What if noth—" Suddenly she stopped. The horse had a listening attitude; its ears were straight up, poised. They were like the ears of a racehorse before the signal. It was sniffing the air. And now, coming from nowhere, Farley was there with them.

The three of them watched the horse as he sniffed the air and pawed. He was pulling at the tether, neighing. The other horses, hobbled on the safe side of the fence, answered sleepily. They weren't interested. Whatever it was that had wakened the one horse hadn't bothered them. Now he was acting wild, rearing.

Farley said, "You two stay here, I'm going to go get it." He ran to the gate and opened it very quickly.

Victoria closed her eyes. She didn't know what she expected, but she didn't expect him to return with the horse. Somehow that seemed too simple.

After a moment, Sam shook her and said, "Well, whatever it was we'll probably never know. That horse sure isn't going to tell us." Farley was standing before them with the horse. He led it to the others, hobbled it, and returned. He looked stunned, and bewildered, and he looked frightened.

"What was it?" Sam asked brusquely.

Farley said, "We—we'll all have to go across that fence and hear it. You can't hear it from here."

"The river!" Victoria cried.

Farley nodded. "You can hear the river over there."

For a moment no one moved as they listened to the still desert. Then they went through the gate together and stopped a few feet from the fence.

Victoria strained to hear, but there was nothing. Everything looked the same, yet different, the way it always looked unchanged even while changing. She thought Sam was cursing under his breath. He strode ahead, holding himself too stiff. Angry, she thought, and disappointed. Abruptly Sam stopped, gazing upward at the ridge.

"Farley, look!"

A woman had appeared on the ridge, making her way clumsily through the jumbled boulders. She glanced backward once and hurried even more. A flicker of light appeared around the rocks.

Victoria felt Farley clutching her arm too hard. "It's me," she breathed. His grip tightened.

The other Victoria ran wildly down the slope of a hill they

could not see. She was dashing panic-stricken through the air, and behind her, gaining on her, came the cloud of lights. The cloud flickered all about her, like a swarm of fireflies. The light did not illuminate, it obscured the racing figure.

Now she was coming down the ridge, drawing near the edge of the cliff, stumbling, falling, rising only to stumble again. Suddenly she flung herself down and drew up her legs in a tightly curled position. The swarm of cold lights settled over her, seemed to expand and contract with her breathing. Minutes passed. The expansion was less noticeable, the lights more compactly together. Suddenly the woman stirred and rose, moving like a sleepwalker. She looked straight ahead and started to walk slowly, carefully down the side of the mesa. The swarm of lights stayed with her, but she was oblivious of them. At the bottom she turned toward the ranch road where Sam's camper was parked. Moving without haste, she passed the camper, opened the gate, returned to the vehicle, got in and drove through. Ten or fifteen feet from the gate the light swarm stopped, hovered in air for a few moments, then streamed back up the cliff, like a focused light beam that could move around curves with ease.

Victoria felt the frozen, supporting rigidity leave her. She sank to the ground.

"Me too," Farley muttered, his arm still about her. They sat huddled together.

"I'm going over there," Sam said. He started in the direction of the camper, stopped after a dozen or so paces. He came back to them and also sat down. "Gone. It's not there."

Victoria freed herself from Farley's arm and stood up. "We have to go up to the ridge," she said. She felt almost detached.

"Okay," Farley said, "but first we go to camp and get flashlights and jackets. We may be out for hours, and it can get damned cold."

Impatiently Sam started back to camp; Victoria and Farley followed more slowly.

"Are you all right?"

"Yes." She really was, she realized. Since they had seen something, too, the strangeness must be in the land, in the valley, not in her; her relief made her almost giddy.

At the campsite, Sam already had his jacket on and his day pack slung over his shoulder. He handed Victoria her pack and tossed the third over to Farley, who knelt and started to rummage through it. Victoria snatched up her jacket. Farley moved to the big packs.

"Come on," Sam said. "You put flashlights in. I saw you do it." He turned and strode toward the gate again. Victoria hurried after him.

"I'm getting my camera," Farley called. "Be right with you."

"Ass!" Sam said. "Like a goddamn tourist."

The gate was still open and they left it that way for Farley.

"I think the best way up is—" Sam stopped, his hand on Victoria's arm. "Jesus!"

It was different. The crystalline light was changed: a pale mist dimmed the moonlight; the air was soft and humus-fragrant, the coolness more penetrating. To the right Ghost River thundered and splashed and roared. Victoria looked behind them, but the gate was no longer there. The ranch road was gone. Underfoot the ground was spongy; wet grass brushed her legs. She looked to the ridge that had become a wooded hill, and over the crest of the hill streamed the light swarm, winding sinuously among the trees toward her and Sam.

V

Farley hesitated at the gate, then left it standing open; the horses were safely hobbled, and a quick retreat might be necessary. He was carrying his camera, his pack over his shoulder, not strapped yet. He began to hurry. He hadn't realized the other two had gotten so far ahead of him.

"Sam! Victoria!" His echo sounded as dismal and lonesome as a coyote's call. He stopped to study the cliff up to the ridge, and he felt a chill mount his back, race down his arms. The cliff was almost vertical, the road they had been on was gone; ahead the cliff curved, and the narrow terrace ended dead against the wall. He backed up a few steps, denying what he saw. He strained to hear the river, and heard instead a low rumble, and felt the ground lift and fall, tilt, sink again; the rumble became thunder. He was thrown down, stunned. The thunder was all around him. Something hit him in the back and he pulled himself upright, only to find the ground really was heaving and the thunder was an avalanche crashing down the cliff all around him. Frantically he ran, was knocked down again, ran, fell, until he was away from the cliff. He stumbled to the horses, groped blindly to untie them, and he fell again and this time stayed where he fell.

He dreamed he and his mother were having a picnic at Fort Rock. The Fort was a natural formation, an extinct volcano, the caldera almost completely buried; what remained formed an amphitheater where he was on stage, she his audience of one. He recited for her and she applauded enthusiastically; he sang and danced, and when he made his last bow she came to him with tear-filled eyes and hugged him. She was very pretty, the wind blowing her hair across her face, her cheeks flushed under the dark tan, her eyes shining blue and happy. She opened a beach umbrella and they stayed under it out of the sun, while she read to him and he dozed.

He dreamed he was in the hospital. He had taken her place, had released her. People kept wanting to talk to him, kept wanting him to speak, but he wouldn't because then they would learn they had the wrong patient.

He woke up and felt a terrible confusion because he *was* in a hospital bed; his father was sleeping in an armchair at the window. For a long time Farley didn't speak, hoping that if he remained perfectly still he might wake up again in his own bed.

He studied the peaceful face of his father. The late afternoon sun gave his pale face a ruddiness that had faded months ago. His

father was fifty-seven and until recently had always looked ten
years younger than he was. Relaxed now, he looked as he had
when they used to go on all-day outings—like the trip to Fort
Rock . . . A memory stirred, a dream surfaced, and he realized
why his father was here, in his room, not in hers.

He started to get up, and grunted with pain.

"Farl! You're awake?" Will Chesterman moved with such
effortless speed that people often thought of him as a slow man,
very deliberate. He awoke, crossed the room and was leaning
over Farley all in one motion.

"Dad. How'd I get here? Mother?"

"No talking. Supposed to call the nurse the second you open
your eyes. No moving. No talking." He pushed a button on the
call box and after a moment of muted static a woman answered.
"My son's awake," Will said. The nurse said she would call the
doctor, to please keep Farley quiet . . .

"Tell me about Mother."

"We buried her yesterday."

Farley shut his eyes hard. "Christ! How long have I been here?
What happened?"

"Six days. Now, Farl, I'm not answering anything else, so just
don't bother. You got a concussion, ten broken ribs, dozens of
stitches here and there, and you are a solid bruise. Nothing seriously damaged. Now just shut up until Lucas gets here and goes
over you."

Then unabashedly he leaned over and kissed Farley on the
forehead. "God, I'm glad to see you back, son. Now just relax
until Lucas comes."

"I've been out for six days?"

"Awake and sleeping, not really out all that time. Lucas said
you might not recall much at first. Don't stew about it."

Farley started to speak and his father put his hand over his
mouth. "Any more and I'll go out in the hall."

Lucas Whaite arrived and felt Farley's skull, examined his eyes,
listened to his heart, checked his blood pressure, and then sat

down. "How much you remember now, Farley?"

"Being in here? Nothing. Or coming here."

"You remember what happened to you?"

"We camped out, by the gorge near the old road . . ." Suddenly it was all there. "Are they all right? There was an earthquake. Were they hurt bad?"

The doctor and Will exchanged glances. Will said slowly, "Listen, son. There wasn't any earthquake. You were talking about it before, and we checked. Farl, someone came damn near to beating you to death. Looks like they used four-by-fours on you, then left you for dead. Was it Sam Dumarie and the woman with him? What for, son?"

"Where are they?"

"Wish to God we knew."

Farley groaned and turned away. "They're missing? Is that what you mean?"

"No one's seen them since you all rode out together last week. The horses came back around noon Sunday and some of the hands scattered to look for you. They found you at the campsite, more dead than alive. Should have died too, I guess, out there in the sun bleeding like a stuck pig. Your friends were gone, their day packs and yours gone with them, nothing else. And they haven't lighted yet. Now you tell us what the hell happened."

Farley told them. Then a nurse came with his dinner and Lucas said he should eat and rest, and no more talk. He left, taking Will with him. The next day Lucas took out forty-nine stitches, from both legs, his back, his side and right arm. "Been run through a goddamn mangle," he grunted. "Boy, there ain't no way you're going to lay where you ain't on something that's going to hurt."

"Where's Dad? What's he doing about Victoria and Sam?"

Lucas lighted his pipe. "He's sleeping, I hope. Told him we had hospital business to attend to this A.M."

"You don't believe me, do you?"

"Farley, I delivered you, took out your appendix, named your diseases as they appeared, wrote your prescriptions for ear drops, cough syrup, stitched you up from time to time. I know you don't lie, son. But I also know there hasn't been any earthquake in this whole territory for years. It's the concussion, Farley. Funny things happen when the brain gets a shock like that.''

"You believe Sam Dumarie could do all this to me and be able to walk away afterwards?"

Lucas tapped out his pipe and stood up. He lifted Farley's right hand and held it so Farley could see the knuckles—unmarked, normal. "No," he said slowly, "you'd have him in worse shape. We all know that. But he's gone, the woman's gone, and you're in here. Listen, son, I've held Tom Thorton off long as I can. Maybe there was a landslide, or maybe you fell off a cliff, but there wasn't any earthquake, and he'll know that just as sure as I do. Maybe you plain can't remember yet. I'll back you up on that. But no earthquake.''

Over the next two days Tom Thorton, the sheriff, questioned him, a state trooper questioned him, the search was resumed in the desert, and no one was satisfied. Farley told Tom Thorton he had been caught in a landslide and Thorton came back with a map for him to pinpoint the exact location.

This was how it had been with Victoria, Farley thought. No one had believed her and she had come to doubt her sanity. Thorton returned again looking glum.

"Look, Farley, I was over every inch of that ground. There ain't been no slide or anything at all out there. You sure of the place?"

"You calling me a liar, Tom?"

"Hell no! But a man can make a mistake, misremember. I been reading about concussions. Down in San Francisco they been using a medical hypnotist, helping people remember things better. I been thinking—"

"No," Farley said. "Why would I be lying, Tom?"

"I been thinking," Tom Thorton said. "We all know this Dumarie's been digging around them mountains for years. What's he looking for? He makes fancy jewelry, right? So what does he need? Gold! Silver! What if he found it on your land and took you out to show you, and you gave him an argument about it, being's it's on your land and all. Gold comes between brothers, fathers and sons. So he waits till your back is turned and knocks you over the head with a rock, then he takes you over by the gorge and rolls you down the cliff, him and that girl with him. He doesn't want you found anywhere near the gold."

"Jesus Christ! Just go out there and find them, will you, Tom? They're both dead by now, but they're out there, somewhere near the gorge, or down in it, or in the fenced-off valley."

The next day Lucas reluctantly agreed to let Farley go home. It had been ten days since they had made camp by the ranch road at the Ghost River gorge. On the way home Will drove by the small cemetery. It was wind-scoured; clumps of junipers, small groves in the barren land, were the only signs of the care given the burial ground where Farley's grandparents lay near Farley's uncle and a cousin; where his mother now was.

Standing at her grave by his father, Farley said, "I'm sorry I wasn't with you."

"I know. That last night she dreamed of you. She told me. You sang and danced for her, recited some poetry. She said she held her umbrella over you so you wouldn't get sunburned. The dream made her happy. She died without pain, smiling over her dream."

Both men became silent; the wind whispered over the tortured land.

Farley sat on a rock, aching, hurting, unwilling to move again soon, and watched Fran ride up. She made it look so easy, he thought, remembering how Victoria had sat in the saddle climbing Goat's Head Butte.

Fran waved, but didn't urge her horse to quicken its gait; it was too hot to run a horse on the desert. She stopped near his jeep in the shade of a twisted juniper tree, tied her horse, then joined him inside the fenced area. No one ever brought animals inside if they could help it.

"They all said you look like hell," she said cheerfully, surveying him. "They're right."

"You just happened to be passing by?"

"I came when . . . I've been home awhile, thought I might as well hang around to see you. Want to talk about it?"

He didn't know if she meant his mother's death, or the landslide he had dreamed up for the sheriff. "No."

Fran nudged him over and sat by him. The sun was low; long shadows flowed down the gorge like cool silent lava.

"It was here, wasn't it?" Fran asked. She lighted a cigarette and pocketed the match. "Serena said you came out here right after breakfast. Been here all day?"

He stared morosely at the gate standing open. Here in the hot still afternoon it was just another ranch gate; no way it could vanish with a twist of the head.

"We all think you were lucky. If you hadn't been separated from them you'd be gone too."

Farley turned to look at her. "Tell that to Tom Thorton. And my father."

"We aren't a bunch of superstitious Indians," she said, "afraid of a curse on the land, or land claimed and held by a god. Tom will never admit anything so irrational, but he went over this whole area with half a dozen men at least twice. The rest of it, searching the desert, the bulletins, that's all for show. Your father, my father, if they knew we were sitting here, well, they'd probably lasso us and haul us out."

"Aren't you afraid to be in here?"

"Not during daylight."

Farley laughed and pulled himself off the rock, wincing as he moved. "And I was going to invite you to come back with me tonight."

Fran caught his arm as she rose. "You're not serious! Why? What good can it do if you disappear?"

"I don't know. That girl asked for help, and I told her to trust me. Now she's gone. I can't pretend it never happened."

Fran shook her head impatiently. "When you were found, they thought you were dying, because they couldn't wake you up. Dad heard about it and called me. He doesn't approve, of course. We've had scenes. But he called me." She glanced at him, then looked out over the gorge. She was speaking almost dispassionately. "I was having a dinner party, people were just arriving, and I forgot them. Forgot my husband, my children, my guests, everything. I got in the car and left, didn't change clothes or pack. I just left. I outran a police car coming over Santiam Pass." She shuddered briefly. "Then they wouldn't let me see you. They wouldn't even let me look at you. It's a scandal, how I showed up late at night in a long dress, made a spectacle of myself." She lighted another cigarette. "Edward came down. It was all very loud and nasty. He's always known, but it was so discreet, he didn't have to admit it. I believe in your earthquake. It's shaken my world apart. I don't want you dead. I don't want you just gone, like your friends."

"It wouldn't work," Farley said. "You wouldn't stay here with me. I can't leave."

"Won't," she said; she dropped her cigarette and rubbed it out with the toe of her boot with exaggerated care. "Won't, darling." She shook her head at him. "Forever in love with the unattainable. It's the poor lost girl now, isn't it? Now you can live the ideal romantic dream, never have to make any tough choices. Come here and mope, prowl these hills all night and finally one day your horse will come in alone and you'll have exactly what you're after. Complete nonexistence." She strode away from him.

"What will you do?" Farley called after her.

Without turning she waved. "Probably go home and fuck the devil out of my husband and talk him into moving to San Francisco, or Hawaii." She yanked her horse's tether loose and swung herself into the saddle smoothly. "And you can follow your goddamn Pied Piper right into the side of the cliff!" She rode away at a hard gallop.

Tom Thorton was waiting for him when he got home. He charged off the porch, stopped when he saw Farley's face, and said, "Good God! You look like old puddled candlewax."

Farley concentrated on climbing the steps to the porch. Will stood watching.

"You eat anything today?" he asked quietly.

Farley sat down without answering, and presently Serena appeared with a tray. He drank the cold beer gratefully, then ate. He wanted a shower and clean clothes, but not enough to climb the stairs to the second floor.

"You can search those rocks till Doomsday. Won't find anything," Tom said. "I've been over that piece of ground three times myself."

Farley grunted. "That's the place. I'll find something."

Will opened a bottle of beer and poured it, watching the head form. "You came to the hospital and asked me about that piece of land," he said. "I told you it was poisoned, as I recall. When my father came out here in eighteen-ninety or about then, there were stone markers down there, put there by the Bannock Indians. They were still thick then. No one ever said how the Indians read the stones, but they did. Little piles, like dry walls, here a heap, a mile away another heap, and so on. Anyway, over the years Pa got to be friends with some of the renegades, sheltered them, hid them when the army was on their tail, and they warned him about that three hundred acres. One of them took him all around that piece and told him to keep clear of it. From nineteen hundred two when he actually homesteaded until nineteen twenty-four when he bought the west quarter, including that piece, two Klamath Indians disappeared over there; six or eight white men vanished. Course some of them could have just wandered on, but he didn't think so. Several dozen head of cattle went in and never came out. Soon as he got that land, he fenced it, been fenced ever since. Even so in nineteen twenty-nine two white men went in looking for oil and they vanished, left their truck, their gear, everything." He drank and wiped his mouth.

"Tom's been over it three times. I've been over it a hundred times or more."

"Why didn't you get help? People with equipment? Scientists?"

Will laughed, a short bark like a coyote's. "In nineteen fifty when the hunt was on for uranium, we had a couple of geologists here with their geiger counters, stuff like that. They heard me out and we went over. Nothing. They moved on. Who's going to believe you, son? You tell me. What's there to believe? How does it fit in with anything else we know?"

"We found something," Farley said angrily. "I heard that river! I smelled it!"

"And you're damn lucky to be sitting here talking about it," his father said quietly. "You're not the first to go in and see or hear something and come out again. But you're the first since my father began keeping a record in nineteen hundred two."

"Victoria came out."

"But she's not around to tell anyone."

Tom Thorton stood up then. "Whatever you say here don't mean I buy it. I can't put that kind of stuff in a report. People don't get swallowed up by the desert. And that girl's father is coming over here tomorrow. He says he's going to make you tell him what you've done to his daughter. I think you better have something ready to tell him. And you better be here. I've had my fill of him; I tell you that."

Farley hadn't gone back to the gorge. When he made a motion towards the steps, his father had said very quietly that he would knock him out and tie him to his bed first, and Farley knew he could do it. He had gone upstairs and to bed. Now, waiting for Victoria's father to arrive, he was glad he had slept. He felt better and stronger, and at the same time much worse. It was as if his emotions, his mind had taken longer to wake up than his body.

He felt deep shame over his treatment of Fran; his father's grief and loneliness was a weight he wanted to share without knowing how. Most of all he kept remembering Victoria's trust in him, her faith. The past few days all he had been able to think of was getting back to the gorge, finding something, anything. Not enough, he knew now.

He needed to think, to plan. Whatever was in the valley was pure malevolence; it could kill, had tried to kill him, had tried to drive Victoria over the edge of the gorge. He no longer believed in the earthquake he had experienced. It was as false as Reuben. You couldn't believe anything you saw, felt, heard, experienced in there; and that made the problem impossible, he thought. If observers could have watched him that night, what would they have seen? He felt certain now that they would have seen him tumbling over the ground, falling repeatedly, running frantically, just as he had seen Victoria running and falling. But, he thought with a rising excitement, then she had risen, had ignored the lights and, like a sleepwalker, had simply left the area. That was the starting point. The clue to her escape that night lay in that action: she had walked away like someone in a trance, or asleep.

His thoughts were interrupted by the appearance of an automobile, or the cloud of dust from a car, at the top of the hill overlooking the ranch buildings. The car came down too fast, screamed around the curve at the bottom of the hill; the dust cloud increased.

"You want me out here?" Will asked from inside the screen door.

"No point in it. I'll talk to him." Farley watched the car careen around the last curve, screech to a stop. The driver was a thin, balding man wearing a pale blue sports coat, white shirt, tie, navy trousers. He made Farley feel hot. He went down the steps to greet Victoria's father.

"Mr. Dorsett? I'm Farley Chesterman."

The man ignored his hand and walked quickly to the shade cast by the house. "This is where she came to spend a week? In this hellhole?"

"You might as well come up and sit down," Farley said. He

went up the steps and sat in one of the canvas chairs. "You want a drink? Beer, Coke, anything? That's a long hot drive."

"I don't want anything from you," Dorsett said shrilly. "I just wanted to see for myself. A pack of lies, that's all I've had from your sheriff. Nothing but a pack of lies. You don't look like someone almost dead to me. And this sure as hell doesn't look like any resort hotel where my girl would spend even five minutes, let alone a week. I want to know what happened up here, Chesterman, why my girl came here, what you've done to her."

Farley told him the official story of the campout, the landslide. "I was found and taken to the hospital. They haven't been found yet."

"I'll take that beer," Dorsett said, wiping his forehead with his handkerchief.

Farley went in for it and when he came back Dorsett was sitting on the porch.

"Why did your sheriff send people poking around in my affairs? What's any of this got to do with me?" The belligerence was gone from his voice.

"I don't know. I guess he's trying to account for the fact that Victoria and Sam weren't found."

"Ha! Because she's just like her mother—follow anyone who whistles."

"It's hard to believe they'd leave anyone hurt, not try to help."

"Didn't her mother leave me in a jam? She ran off with one of my buyers, vanished without a word, nothing. Left me with a two-year-old baby girl. What was I supposed to do with a *girl*?"

"Did you ever find her?"

"I didn't look! She found *me* a couple years later when lover-boy ran out of cash and things got tough." He drank his beer and stood up. "As for Victoria, she'll show up again. If you have any pull with that sheriff of yours, just tell him to keep his goddamn nose out of my business. I haven't seen her and don't expect to. I wasn't sure if it was just him, or if you were making insinuations too. Now I know. If it's a shakedown, he's bucking the wrong man. I didn't get where I am today being intimidated by two-bit politicians. You tell him, Chesterman."

Farley didn't stand. Dorsett regarded him for a moment, turned and went back to his car. He drove away in a cloud of dust as thick as the one he had brought with him.

Victoria had said her mother died when she was a baby. Maybe she did, Farley thought.

Farley lay on his back, his hands under his head, on top his sleeping bag, and listened to his father and Tom Thorton exchange stories. Tom was talking about his dude-rustling days for Leon Stacy, before he had been elected sheriff twelve years ago.

"He says to me right off, 'Mr. Thorton, I don't know a damn thing about horses, trails, desert country, nothing else I should know. All's I know is Egypt, history, pyramids, anything you want to know, I can more'n likely tell you. Now if I agree not to treat you like an ignorant slob because you don't know shit about my specialty, will you agree not to treat me like one because I don't know yours?' " Thorton poured himself more coffee from the thermos. "Real fine fellow. Teaches at the University over at Eugene. Came back every year, still does, more'n likely. Nice wife, kids. Questions! Never heard so many questions. And they all listened to the answers. Fine people."

Farley counted stars, lost track, and went over the steps again. In the valley there was enough dynamite to blow up ten acres. On the ridge was the detonator. He had already cut the fence up there, made a four-foot opening. They could step through, observe whatever was in the valley, get out, and set off the explosives. On the cliff and at the bottom gate there were powerful searchlights. "It *will* work," he told himself again.

But there was nothing to blast. Halfway through their second night the men had seen nothing, heard nothing. The horse tethered fifteen feet inside the area remained quiet.

"Three nights," Will had said. "If there's nothing for three nights will you give it up? Admit there's nothing you can do."

He had been so certain. Victoria hadn't waited. Her first night, there it was. When they came again, it was right there. He got up, walked to the gate and watched the horse a few minutes. The starlight was so bright that if it acted up, they would be able to see it. He sat and poured coffee.

"You should get some sleep," he told Will.

"Intend to. Want to check the ridge again first?"

Farley shrugged. "No point. Not until the horse tells us."

Tom Thorton unrolled his sleeping bag. "Call me at three." He grunted several times, then began to snore softly.

"Me too," Will said. "If there's a sound, anything . . ."

"Sure, Dad."

The night remained quiet and Farley didn't bother to awaken either of the men. At dawn his father got up first, grumbled, and roused Tom, and when their relief came, two ranch hands who would guard the dynamite during the day, they returned to the house where Farley went to bed.

The third night was the same.

"Farl, that was the agreement," Will said stubbornly. "You agreed."

"I didn't. I didn't say I would or wouldn't. I'm taking the camper up there and staying a few more nights. I'll hang around during the day. You won't have to send anyone up to relieve me."

"It isn't that, and you know it. If it was this easy don't you think someone would have done it years ago? That thing comes and goes when it gets ready. It might be quiet up there for months, years. You planning to wait it out?"

"Yes!" Farley stamped from the room, up the stairs. He began to throw his clothes into a pack.

His door opened and Serena slid inside and shut it. "Farley, why are you carrying on like this, giving your father more grief? What's the matter with you?"

"I'm crazy! Haven't you learned yet? I'm crazy! Get the hell out of here, Serena."

"You're crazy all right. Driving off Fran, driving your father

beyond what he can endure. Why don't you stop all this foolish-
ness and help your father now that he needs you."

"I can't help him."

"You can! Just let yourself instead of rushing off after ghosts
all the time."

"There's something out there, Serena! I know because it almost killed me! Do you understand that? It almost killed me!"

"And it will kill you the next time! You think your father can
stand that?" Serena's voice rose.

"You don't understand."

"*I* don't understand? You're the one who doesn't understand
anything, Farley Chesterman! Right through the years everyone
else's had enough sense to leave it alone."

Farley indicated the door. "Beat it!"

"You pig! You don't care, do you?"

"*All right!* There's something out there! A devil. You understand devils, you Catholic bitch! There's a devil out there and I'm
going to get it off this land! That's what I have to do!"

"If there's a devil, it's not out on the desert! You're carrying
it around with you all the time!"

"Shut up and get the hell out of here! What gives you the right
to—"

There was a knock on the door. This time it was Will, who stuck
his head into the room and said mildly, "I thought you two gave
up screaming at each other ten, fifteen years ago."

Serena gave Farley one last furious look and ran from the
room, down the stairs. Will regarded his son for a moment, then
closed the door gently.

"Bitch," Farley muttered, and sat down on the side of his bed,
suddenly shaking. *Bitch, bitch, bitch.*

Although the sheriff had collected Victoria's belongings to
have them delivered to her father, no one had known what to
do about Sam's camper, and it was still parked in the side
yard. Farley loaded it, checked the water and food, added
coffee to the stores, and left, driving slowly, unwilling to add

to the coating of dust on everything in the valley.

At the gorge he told the two hands they could go back to the ranch. He chose a spot near the gate where the camper would have shade during the hottest part of the afternoons; then he climbed the cliff to check the detonator, and to scowl at the cul-de-sac below where something came and went as it chose.

His ribs ached abominably, and his head throbbed; fury clouded his eyes, blurring his vision. Somewhere down there, within the three hundred acres, he knew, the bodies of Victoria and Sam lay hidden. The packs they had carried, his pack and camera, it was all in there, somewhere. Unless, he thought, they had fallen over the gorge and the rushing river had carried them miles downstream. The desert shimmered with heat waves, and in the distance a cloud of dust marked the passing of a jeep or truck—it was impossible to see what had raised the cloud. No other life stirred in the motionless, hot afternoon; no sound broke the silence, and even the colors had taken on a sameness that was disturbing, as if a patina of heat had discolored everything, obscured the true colors, and left instead the color of the desert—a dull, flat dun color that was actually no color at all.

But he had smelled the river, he told himself, and then as if he needed more positive affirmation he said aloud, "I smelled the goddamn river, and I saw the earth move. I felt the rocks of the earthquake!"

And for the first time he wondered if that was so, if he really had smelled the river, really had been in an earthquake. And he wondered if maybe he *was* crazy. In the intense heat of the desert in August, he had a chill that shook him and raised goosebumps on his arms and made his scalp feel as if a million tiny things were racing about on it.

VI

Victoria watched the swarm of lights with rising panic, until Sam tugged her arm; then they both started to run blindly down the hillside. The lights swirled about them and Victoria stumbled, was yanked forward, stumbled again, and they both stopped, and now Sam was trying to brush the darting specks away.

The lights hovered around Victoria, blinding her momentarily, then left her and settled around Sam, who fell to his knees, then all the way to the ground, and rolled several times before he became quiet. Victoria could no longer see his body under the pulsating lights; instead, it was as if the shape was all light that gave no illumination, no warmth, but swelled and subsided rhythmically.

Victoria knelt beside him; they mustn't be separated, she thought. She reached for him, hesitating when her hand came close to the mass of lights; she took a deep breath, reached through and touched and held his arm. The lights darted up her hand, paused, flowed back down and rejoined the others. Presently Sam stirred. There was a tightening in his muscles, a tensing before he started to sit up. The lights dimmed, moved away from him a little distance, and he got up shakily, Victoria still clutching his arm.

"Are you all right?" she asked.

"Yes. I think so." His voice was hollow, distant.

He began to walk aimlessly, as if unaware of her; she held his arm tightly and kept up. Tree frogs were singing, and there was a chirping call of a night bird, and, farther away, the roar of the river. A pale moth floated before her face; a twig snapped. A large animal scuttled up a tree, as if in slow motion. A sloth! she realized. It turned its head to look at her, then humped its way upward until it was out of sight in the thick foliage.

Still the lights hovered about Sam, not pressing in on him as they had done at first, but not leaving him either, and she remembered watching herself—the other woman—surrounded by lights, walking as if in a trance out of the fenced-in area. She began to direct their steps, keeping parallel to the wild river, and suddenly the lights stopped, as they had done before. She and Sam had crossed the dividing line. She jerked Sam to a halt and stared in disbelief. The soft moonlit rain forest continued as far as she could see. She turned, but the lights were gone. Hesitantly she took a step, and they surged toward her from the tree-covered hill. She darted back across the invisible line, and they vanished.

"Sam, sit down a few minutes. Rest. It's all right now," she said. Sam obeyed. Victoria began to arrange stones and sticks to indicate the beginning of the three hundred acres. She made a short wall, only inches high, a marker, not a barrier. Sam was still blank-eyed.

For a long time neither of them moved. Not until she began to shiver did Victoria realize how cold the night air had become. Reluctantly she stood up to look for sticks to build a fire. Hypothermia, Farley had said, could strike any time, summer or winter. She had watched him put several thick fire-starting candles in each pack. Deliberately she thought about the candles, not about Farley, who must be dead or lost.

After a smoldering start, the fire began to blaze. Victoria was still nursing it when Sam suddenly jumped up and shouted, "Come back! Wait for us!"

Victoria hurried to him and grasped his arm. "Who, Sam? Who did you see?" She peered into the forest.

"The Indian. Where is he? Which way did he go?"

"There isn't any Indian." But perhaps there was. He might have seen her fire, might have been attracted by the smoke.

"There was an Indian, Victoria! With one arm. He was taking me somewhere. You must have seen him!"

Abruptly Sam stopped and rubbed his eyes hard. "I saw something," he muttered more to himself than to her. "A path, a path of glowing light, and the Indian motioned me to follow him away from it. The path was the wrong way, that's it. It was the wrong way, and he was going to take me the right way. With one arm! You must have seen him too!"

She shook her head. "He's like Reuben. Your Indian, my Reuben."

For a moment she thought he was going to hit her. Then he

slumped and his hands relaxed. "What happened?" he asked dully.

"I don't know. The lights came down the hill; you fell down, just like I did that other time. When you got up you were walking like someone in a trance, and I brought us out here." She stopped while Sam turned to stare at the forest all around them. "I thought it would be like the other time, that I would go back out, be where our camp was, but . . ." When she stopped there was only the sound of the river, a constant muted roar in the background. "I made a line to show where the gate was," she said, indicating it.

Sam hesitated only a moment, then took her hand and started over the stones. More afraid of being separated than of whatever lay on the other side, she yielded and they moved into the strange area once more.

This time everything was different. The trees were skeletal, bone-white under the brilliant moon. No grass had grown here for many years; the ground was barren and hard, littered with rocks that made walking difficult. The wind was piercing and frigid; it was the only sound they could hear—a high wail that rose and fell and never stopped entirely. Suddenly Sam yanked her arm hard and she felt herself being pulled backward, back over the wall that no longer existed. She fell heavily.

Sam knelt by her and held her. "I'm sorry," he said. "Are you okay? I didn't want to hurt you. The lights were coming down the hill. I couldn't let them swarm over me again."

"I know," Victoria said. "I had nightmares about them."

"I didn't see them the first time," Sam went on. "I saw a path, wide, easy, glowing. I knew it led to . . . to . . . I don't know what I thought it led to. It terrified me and I wanted to get on it, follow it home, all the time thinking it would kill me if I did. Then I saw the Indian, and I knew he knew the way. I know that Indian. He *does* know the way."

"We can't be separated," Victoria said. "Farley was separated from us. He must be in there somewhere, lost, maybe he fell over the gorge. Maybe they drove him over the gorge. . . ."

"*Sh.*" Sam's hand tightened on her arm. "Maybe he just came out somewhere else, like we did."

Victoria looked around. Everywhere it was the same, dead trees, no signs of life, and the bitter wind that tore through her jacket. "The fire's gone, the wall I made is gone. My pack. We can't put anything at all down and expect it to stay. We can't leave each other even a second, or one of us might vanish."

Sam nodded. "It's too damn cold," he said slowly. "Every time we've gone in and out, it's been different. Different climates, different scenery. Times." He stopped and when he spoke again, his voice was strained. "We're yo-yoing back and forth in time! That's it, isn't it! Come on, once more."

Victoria's ears were hurting from the cold and her toes were starting to go numb. "We should count our steps or something," she said. "The wall won't be there, no point in making another one. But we have to know how to get out again."

Sam nodded, and hand in hand they started forward. There was no sense of transition, nothing to indicate change, but one moment they were in the frozen air, and then the air was balmy and sweet smelling, not from a rain forest this time, but from thick lush grasses that crowded down the hillsides, and from tangled vines, creepers, dense bushes that made nearly impenetrable thickets to their right. The river was there, not a furious roar of a cascade, but rushing waters singing over rocks.

"Here they come," Sam muttered. "Out!"

The lights were coming in an elongated cloud, head-high, straight down the hill toward them. They took several steps, and the lights were no longer there. They had crossed the boundary.

They made a fire and huddled close together. "We need shelter," Sam said finally. "The moon's going down. While there's still enough light we have to arrange something." By the time the moon vanished over the mountains in the west, Sam had made a lean-to with the mylar space blanket from his pack, attaching it from bushes to the ground, and Victoria had gathered armloads of grass that made their mattress. They wrapped Victoria's jacket around their legs, and Sam's around their torsos, and after a long time they fell asleep in each other's arms.

"We can't stay here!" Victoria cried late the next afternoon. They had bathed in the clear river, had portioned out their scant rations, had hunted for berries to supplement their food, and now the sun was setting and she was hungry and tired.

Sam was standing just beyond their marker stones, facing the hill. Together they had explored the hill, the valley, the entire area repeatedly. They had crossed and recrossed the barrier without effect; nothing had changed.

"It's not evil, not malevolent," Sam said softly. "This must be what happened to the others who disappeared. They weren't killed at all, just put out somewhere else, away from harm."

They would starve, Victoria thought dully. Grazing animals would find this a paradise, but not humans.

"Once more," Sam said abruptly and started up the hill again. Victoria didn't follow this time. There wasn't anything up there, nothing in the valley. It didn't show itself by daylight, she thought, and suddenly realized that the only times anything had happened, there had been brilliant moonlight. She started to call Sam to tell him, but he was nearly to the top out of hearing.

When Sam came back it was twilight. "Think of the power!" he said exultantly. "It's showing us what we can have. How many of those who vanished realized what was being offered? They probably came out and ran as far and as fast as they could and died out there on the desert, or in the cold, or of starvation. But the power's there, down in that valley, waiting for anyone who has nerve enough to accept it. It's ours, Victoria! Yours! Mine!"

He wasn't hungry, he said, wasn't tired, just impatient. "There's a secret we haven't learned yet, about how to call it, how to make it manifest itself. We'll learn how to summon it."

He began to stuff things back into his pack. "Come on. I'm going to wait for it this time down in the valley. Hurry up before it gets too dark."

"It won't be there," Victoria said. "It's never there until after the moon is up. Both times the moon was up."

"Coincidence. Come on. The point is we don't know why it decides to come and when it will decide again. I intend to be there when it does, with you or alone."

They climbed the hill in the deepening, silent dusk, shadows moving among shadows.

"Unlimited power," Sam said hoarsely. "Omnipotent. It can move back and forth in time the way you cross a street."

But it was not omnipotent, Victoria protested silently. It was stopped by the invisible barrier. It had no power to control, only to observe. An observer, she thought, that's what it was, no more than an observer. It came only when the moon cleared the cliffs that were the eastern boundary of the valley, not when it wanted to. She had been able to get out in the right time, the right place once; it could be done again, if only she could remember how she had done it then. They were descending the hill now; it was a gentle slope, covered with waist high grass, no rocks, nothing to impede their progress. They might have been out for an evening stroll—if only she were not so hungry and so tired.

"You want to think of it as some kind of mechanism," Sam went on, "subject to the same laws and limitations that restrict all the machines you're used to. It isn't like that. It's an intelligent being, a godlike being, testing us, for some reason we can't begin to grasp."

Each time they had talked about it, he had refused to hear anything she said. Now she shrugged and they finished their walk into the valley.

"Where was it?" Sam demanded. "Exactly where?"

"I don't know. Everything is changed again. The center I think, but I don't know. Remember, we can't believe anything we see or feel in here. Your Indian, my Reuben, the dog, none of it was real."

He was no longer listening. He considered the valley for a few moments, selected a spot and spread his blanket on the ground.

"Here," he said. "We'll wait here. Don't speak now. Just concentrate on it, call it. Okay?"

Helplessly Victoria sat down also. The Indian and Reuben were the clues, she thought. "Sam, before we start concentrating, just tell me one thing. When your Indian was guiding you, why were you zigzagging?"

"We were making our way among the rocks and boulders," Sam snapped. "Now just shut up, will you? Go to sleep if you can."

"But . . ."

Sam caught her wrist in a tight grip and she became quiet. After a moment he released her and they sat side by side in silence.

But there weren't any rocks or boulders then, she had started to say. Not for her, she corrected. They had been together and still had seen different worlds.

Sam had invented the Indian, just as she had invented Reuben; if she had not interfered, would Sam's Indian have led him to the safety of his own time? It was as if within each of them there existed a core of consciousness that would not be fooled by the shifting scenery, a part of the mind that knew where they belonged and how to get back to it. *Come back!* she wanted to cry. *Reuben, Indian, anyone. Please come back!*

The night had become very dark, and it was too hazy to see the stars. Maybe it would be too cloudy for the moon to light the valley later, she thought. What if there were weeks of cloudy weather? They would die. The land would change, the forests grow, fall, be buried in rocks from earthquakes and landslides, and somewhere deep in the earth their bones would lie never to be discovered.

In a little while she put on her jacket, and still later she stretched out on the blanket and dozed. She was awakened by an exclamation from Sam. She sat up. The valley was moonlit again, brilliant, sharply defined, and Sam was walking away from her, his arms outstretched, oblivious of her, of the need to stay together.

"Sam!" she cried, but he didn't pause. From the corner of her eye she caught the flash of light coming down the hillside. She recoiled as the light dots touched her. Momentarily Sam was covered with them, a glowing crucifixion, and then he was gone.

"Sam!" She scrambled to her feet, and ran toward him, where he had been, and stumbled over rocks that had not been there only moments before. In panic she looked behind her: the blanket was gone, the pack; the valley was barren, with scattered clumps of desert grasses. In the distance there was a flare of light, and she thought of volcanoes, of earthquakes, and even as the thought formed, the earth shook beneath her, and she threw herself down, holding her breath. "No!" she said against the ground. "No!" She closed her eyes hard.

She didn't open them again until she could smell forests and leaf mold and pungent odors of mushrooms and mosses and ferns. She was wet from the grasses under her. Very slowly, concentrating on forests, she got up. She could see only a few feet in any direction because of the trees, and she no longer knew the way out of the valley. She walked, accompanied by flickering lights which she ignored, and then she heard someone else walking through the forests.

"Sam!" she called. "Farley!" There was instant silence and she held her breath, remembering the sloth she had seen before. There might be bears, or wolves, or wildcats . . . She eased herself around a mammoth tree, darted from its shelter to another one, then to a third, and was starting to skirt it when across an open area, she stood face to face with an Indian, a young man, not the one-armed Indian Sam had talked about. He looked as frightened as she, and the unquiet lights were hovering about him. Before he could move, she ran, and could hear him running behind her. Suddenly before her there rose a rock wall, the cliff, and she turned to see the Indian no more than twenty yards away. She watched, frozen, until he had taken several more steps, almost leisurely, and the lights that had been with him vanished. The barrier, she realized, they had both crossed the barrier without knowing it. She darted back toward the trees, and after only a few paces, the forest was gone, and the valley was frost rimed, blasted by an icy wind shrieking like a witch.

She stopped, backed up until she felt the cliff behind her, then stepped forward again, into a different time, with warmer air and junipers and grass. Now she sank to the ground and sat, hugging her legs hard, keeping her eyes wide open.

A flash of light caught her eye and she watched the swarm settle over something small, possibly a mouse; it moved erratically, stopped, moved again, and the lights withdrew, flowed back through the valley, up the cliff and disappeared.

She stared. *Up* the hill? She had assumed they came from somewhere near the center of the valley. She got up and began to walk toward the cliff. She could think only: there must have been a time before it was like this. Momentarily she was aware of a kaleidoscopic effect, of moving through layers of time, of ceaseless change. She paused, closing her eyes, then moved on.

A knoll rose like a gentle swell before her, and she began to ascend. When she stopped, it was because standing before her, filling her field of vision was a glowing shape that was indefinable. Smaller shapes, higher than she, glided over the ground toward her, came to rest in the air a short distance away. They were oval, or nearly so, glowing as the lights glowed, without illumination; behind the glowing surfaces she could almost see other shapes, darker shadows. She blinked rapidly, but was unable to resolve the shadows within the ovals. From one of the shapes there came a swarm of the restless light dots, a cloud large enough to envelop her completely. She did not flinch when the swarm settled over her like a suffocating net.

She was aware that the large oval shape was sinking into the ground, and distantly she thought: they are placing it now, without trying to understand who they were or what they were placing. She was aware when the motion of the oval stopped, and she thought: they realize they already have me, wherever they store information—computers made of glowing dots?, an information pool in the ground? wherever. She was aware of a heavier blanket

of lights all over her, inside her, draining her, using up the air so
that she could no longer breathe.

"God Almighty!" She heard the voice, opened her eyes.

"Reuben!" He stood before her with his hands on his hips.

"You again? The little lost girl again. What in hell are you
wandering out here for this time?"

"I've lost a friend. I'm looking for him."

Reuben scowled. "Bearded fellow? Some kind of religious
nut?"

Victoria nodded. "Is he still in the valley?"

"Come on, I'll take you to him. Can't understand why in tarna-
tion this part of the world is worse than a big city suddenly,
people wandering about all night where they got no business
being."

Victoria knew she didn't have to hold his hand, knew he would
not leave her until she was ready. They started down the steep,
dangerous cliff.

A motion caught her eye. Across the valley, silhouetted against
the sky, she saw a man's figure, and recognized Farley. He was
climbing down the opposite cliff. The lights flashed toward him
and he turned and scurried back up. She took a step toward him
and he was gone. In the valley she could make out boxes.

Concentrating on them, she let Reuben lead her across the
valley until they stood before the boxes.

Dynamite! Farley was going to blow up the valley!

And somewhere within a few feet of where she stood, in another time, Sam sat and waited for something he could not even
name. She blinked hard and saw Sam, almost hidden by the high
lush grass. He was sitting crosslegged, his hands on his knees,
staring ahead fixedly; he was covered with lights. He wouldn't
hear her, see her, be aware of her at all, she knew; but the blast?
Would the blast jolt him back into his own time?

She hurried back up the cliff that became a gentle slope under
her feet. The large oval had not moved, was still partially in the
ground; around it there were now a dozen or more of the smaller

ovals. She stopped and was aware that from all sides the lights were streaming toward her. Before they reached her, she realized that she had lost them before; she had moved from one time to another and left them behind. Now she felt almost a physical assault as they touched her, thicker and thicker clouds of them settling over her, then entering her, becoming part of her.

She visualized mushroom clouds and lasers; moon-landing vehicles and satellites; the skyline of New York and a hologram of a DNA model; computers that extended for city blocks deep underground and missiles in their silos; undersea explorer crafts and a surgeon's hands inside a chest cavity mending a faulty heart . . .

A core sample, she thought, taken through time, to be collected at a later date, to be wandered through by beings she could not even see well enough to know what she had seen.

And when they came to collect their sample, a great gaping wound in the earth would remain and the earth would heave and tremble and restore equilibrium with earthquakes and volcanoes.

Her head felt hot, throbbing; it was harder and harder to hold the images she formed. If only she could rest now, sleep a few minutes, she thought yearningly, just let it all go and sleep.

Reuben's grumble roused her again. "This is going to take a hell of a long time if you lollygag like that. Come on, get it over. I got me a sleeping bag and a fire and I sure would like to get back to them sometime before morning."

She thought of men aiming polarized lights that were indistinguishable from moonlight, calling forth the lights that streamed out into nets that would contain them. She thought of men excavating the hillside, studying the energy source they found. She thought of low white buildings hugging the hills, high-voltage fences outlining the enchanted three hundred acres.

The large oval shimmered and started to rise. The small ovals clustered about it.

Victoria felt leaden, unable to move. She looked down at herself and saw that the lights no longer surrounded her, but had become part of her; she was filled with light.

"Give me your hand," Reuben said patiently. "Telling you, honey, it's time."

He led her to the boulders where she looked down at the valley and waited for the shifting landscape to become the right one, with high grass and the figure of a man, sitting, waiting.

The lights were streaking back now from the valley, the hills, abandoning the objects they studied. Farley would see them and know it was time.

Sam waited. As random images formed, words sounded in his inner ear, he acknowledged and banished them. He might wait all night, all the next day, forever.

He no longer knew how long he had been there; he felt no discomfort or sense of passing time. When he heard his name called from behind him, up the hillside, he denied it, but the call came again and he turned to see.

And now his heart thumped wildly in his chest and he was overwhelmed by exultation and reverence. With tears on his cheeks, he extended his arms and moved toward the figure that burned and was not consumed by the flames, that was light and gave no light, that was motionless in the air above the slope he started to climb.

"My God!" he whispered, and then cried the words. "My God! My God!"

Victoria felt a wrench when the lights flowed out of her. She swayed and groped for the boulder; her head felt afire, and a terrible weakness paralyzed her; her vision dimmed, blurred, failed.

"Let's get the hell outa here," Reuben said, and his hand was warm and firm on her elbow as he guided her, blind now, up the slope that was rocky and steep.

The blast shook them, echoed round and round in the valley, echoed from the gorge walls, from rocks and hills and sky. It echoed in Victoria's head and bones. She found herself on the ground. The noises faded and the desert was quiet, the air cool, the sky milky blue with moonlight.

She waited for a second blast, and when none came, she pulled herself up. She was on the gorge side of the cliff, protected by the ridge from the force of the explosion. Slowly she began to pick her way up the cliff. At the top she paused.

Across the valley, on the cliff opposite her, she could see Farley in the moonlight. His gaze was upward, intent on the sky. Victoria thought: He has seen evil depart on giant bat-wings, recalled to hell from whence it came. She smiled slightly.

Midway down the cliff she could now see Sam getting to his hands and knees, shaking his head. He stood up slowly. And he, she thought, had come face to face with his god.

They made a triangle, three fixed points forever separated, forever bound together by what had happened here.

Farley had seen her, was waving to her. She waved back, and pointed down toward Sam. No one would believe them, she knew, there would be endless talk, and it wouldn't matter. They would reappear together and stay together, as they had to now, and the talk would subside, and people would even come to regard them as inseparable, as they were. She thought she heard a growly whisper, "No more little Miss Goody?" She laughed and held out her hand to Sam, who was drawing close; he was laughing too. Hand in hand they picked their way down the cliff to join Farley at the gate.

THE NOVELLA RACE

We looked terrific in the stadium, holding our
quill pens, clothed in azure jumpsuits with the flags
of our countries over our chests. . . . No one
read what we wrote, but a lot of people enjoyed our
public displays. At least one writer was
sure to crack up before the Games were over,
and occasionally there was a suicide.

Pamela Sargent

Anyone who wants to be a contender has to start training at an
early age. Because competitions are always in Standard, my parents insisted that I speak Standard instead of our local dialect. I
couldn't use an autocompositor. We never owned a dictator either. "You'll only have a typewriter during the race," my mother
would say. "You'd better get used to it now."

I had few friends as a child. You can't have friends while training in writing, or any other sport for that matter. The other kids
plugged in, swallowed RNA doses, or were hypnotized in order to
learn the skills they would need as adults. I had to master the
difficult arts of reading and writing. At times I hated my typewriter, the endless sentence-long exercises, and the juvenile competitions. I envied other kids and wished that I too could romp
carelessly through life.

Some people think being an athlete keeps you in shape. Every-

85

one *should* take a few minutes each day to sit down and think. But competitive sports usually damage the body and torment the mind. A champion is almost always distorted in some way.

As I grew older, I noticed that others simply marked time. They were good spectators, consumers, and socializers, but they went to their graves without attempting anything extraordinary. I wanted a gold medal, honor, and fame. Even when I wanted to quit, I knew I'd gone too far to turn back.

By the time I was sixteen I knew I was neither a sprinter nor a distance runner. My short stories were incomplete and I did not have the endurance for the novel competition. Poetry was beyond me, although my grandmother had taken a bronze medal in the poetry race of 2024. I would have to train in the novella.

My parents wanted me to train with Phaedon Karath, who had won four Olympic gold medals before turning professional, thus disqualifying himself from further competition. Karath was hard on his trainees, but they did well in contests. I would have preferred going to Lalia Grasso, whose students were devoted to her. But those accustomed to her gentle ways often messed up during races; they did not develop the necessary streak of cruelty nor the essential quality of egotism.

Everyone knew about Eli Shankquist, her most talented trainee and a three-time Pan-American gold medalist as well. During the Olympic race, the only one that matters, he became involved with the notoriously insecure Maliah Senbok. Touched by her misery, he spent a lot of time encouraging her. And what did he get? He didn't finish his own novella and Senbok took a bronze. A lot of spectators sympathized with Shankquist, but most writers thought he was a fool.

None of Karath's students would have been in such a fix. So I sent off my file of fiction and waited long months for an answer. Just before my seventeenth birthday, a reply arrived on the telex. Karath wanted a personal interview. I left on the shuttle the next day.

Karath lived in a large villa overlooking the Adriatic. As I
entered, I looked around the hallway. Several green beanbag
chairs stood next to heavy Victorian tables covered with illuminated manuscripts. Colorful tapestries depicting minstrels
and scribes hung on the walls. The servo, a friendly silver ball
with cylindrical limbs, ushered me to the study.

The study was clean and Spartan. To my right, a computer
console stood next to the wall. To the left, a large window overlooked the blue sea. Karath sat at his glass-topped desk, typing.
He looked up and motioned to a straight-backed wood chair. I
sat down.

As I fidgeted, he got up and paced to the window. I had seen
him on the screen a few times but in person he seemed shorter.
He was wiry, with thick dark hair and a small hard face. He
looked, I thought apprehensively, like a young tough, in spite of
his age. I waited, trying to picture myself in this house, typing
away, making friends, workshopping stories, getting drunk, having an affair and doing all the things a writer does.

Karath turned and paced to the desk. As he picked up a folder,
which I recognized as my file, he muttered, "You're Alena Dorenmatté."

I tried to smile. "That's me."

"What makes you think you belong here?"

"I want the best training in the novella I can get."

"That's a crock of shit. You want to fuck and get drunk and sit
around thinking artistic thoughts and congratulating yourself on
your sensitivity. You won't sweat blood over a typewriter. You
want to be coddled."

He threw my file across the desk. It landed on the floor with
a *plop*. I picked it up, clutching it to my chest.

"Let me fill you in, Dorenmatté. There's nothing but cow pies
in that file. Understand? I don't think you could win a local."

"I won a local last year, I placed first in the BosWash." He
couldn't have reviewed my citations very carefully. "Why'd you
ask me here anyway? You could have insulted me over the relay."

"Maybe the truth wouldn't sink in over the relay. I like to say what I think face to face. You're not a writer. Your stories are nothing but clichés and adolescent tragedy. You can't plot and you can't create characters. You have nothing to say. You'd make a fool of yourself in Olympic competition. Cow pies, that's what you write. Go home and learn how to socialize so you don't ruin your life."

My face was burning. "I don't know why anybody trains with you. If the other trainers were that mean, no one would ever write again."

He flew at me, seized the file, and tore it in half, scattering papers over the floor. Terrified, I shrank back.

"Let me tell you something, Dorenmatté. A writer doesn't give up. He takes punishment, listens to criticism, and keeps writing. If he doesn't make it, it's because he wasn't any good. I don't run a nursery, I train writers. Now get out of here. I have work to do."

I stood up, realizing that I couldn't respond without bursting into tears. Grasping at my last threads of dignity, I turned and walked slowly out of the room.

I could have applied to another trainer. Instead I moped for months. At last my father issued an ultimatum: I would have to move to a dormitory and learn to socialize or enter a competition.

Even my parents were deserting me. I moved out and rented an apartment in Montreal. I stayed inside for weeks, unable to move, barely able to eat. One night I tried to hang myself, but I could never tie knots properly and only fell to the floor, acquiring a nasty bruise on my thigh. Fate had given me another chance.

I had forgotten that the PanAmerican Games were being held in Montreal that year. Somehow, even in my hopeless state, they drew me. I found myself entering the qualifying meet in paragraphs. I lugged my typewriter to the amphitheater and sat with a thousand others at desks under hot lights while the spectators came and went, cheering for their favorites. Several writers made use of the always-popular "creative anguish" ploy, slapping their foreheads in frustration while throwing away wads of paper. Ramon Hogarth, winner of the West Coast local, danced around his desk after completing each sentence. My style was standard. I smoked heavily and gulped coffee while slouching over my machine. Occasionally I clutched my gut in agony, drawing some applause.

I qualified for the semifinals and was given a small room filled with monitoring devices. The judges, of course, had to watch for cheating, and spectators all over the hemisphere would be viewing us. I tried to preserve my poise at the typewriter, but gradually I forgot everything except my novella. I wrote and rewrote, rarely taking breaks, knowing that I was up against trained contenders. Whenever I became discouraged, I remembered the mocking voice of Phaedon Karath.

I made it to the finals. I recall that I envied the short-story writers, who had a four-month deadline, and pitied the novelists, who had to suffer for a year. I can remember the times when my words flowed freely, but there were moments when I was ready to disqualify myself. I agonized while awaiting the decision and wondered if I could ever face another race.

I placed sixth. Delighted, I got drunk and daringly sent off my sixth-place novella to Phaedon Karath. A few days later, his reply appeared on my telex: STILL COW PIES BUT IMPROVEMENT STOP COME TO ITALY STOP SEE IF YOU CAN TAKE REAL WORKOUT STOP.

At the villa I had to work on sentences for months before I was allowed to go on to paragraphs. Karath insisted on extensive rewriting, although constant rewriting could kill you off in competition as easily as sloppy unreworked first drafts. He rarely praised anyone.

We workshopped a lot, tearing each other's work apart. Reina Takake, a small golden-skinned woman who became my closest friend, used to run from the room in tears. The more she cried, the more Karath picked on her. We would spend hours together planning tortures for him and occasionally writing about the tortures in vivid detail.

At last Reina packed and left, saying good-bye to no one. Karath told us of her departure during a workshop, watching us with his gray eyes as he said that Reina couldn't cut it, that she had no talent, and that it was useless to waste time on someone who couldn't take criticism.

I hated him for that. I stood up and screamed that he was a petty tyrant and a sadist. I told him he had no understanding of gentle souls. I said a few other things.

He waited until I finished. Then he looked around the room and said, "The rest of you can continue. Dorenmatté, step outside."

Trembling, I followed him out. He led me down the hall and stopped in front of my room. He turned, grabbed me by the arms, and shoved me inside. I stumbled and almost fell.

"Stay in there," he said. "You're not coming out until you finish a specific assignment."

"What assignment?" I asked, puzzled.

"The novella you're going to write, and rewrite if necessary. You'll write about Takake and about me if you like. Do it any way you please, but you have to write about Takake. Now get to work."

He slammed the door quickly. I heard him turn the lock. I screamed, bellowed, and cursed until I was hoarse. Karath did not respond.

I spent a few hours in futile weeping and a few days in plotting an escape. Food was brought to me, occasionally with wine; the upper door panel would open and the amiable servo would lower the food into my room. At first I refused it but after a few days I was too hungry to resist.

I soon realized I'd never get out of my windowless room until I wrote the novella. I took a bath, then bitterly went to work. At first I rambled, noting every passing thought, incorporating some

of the paragraphs Reina and I had written about torturing
Karath. But soon a particular plot suggested itself. I outlined the
story and began again.

I worked at least a month, maybe more, before I had a draft to
show Karath. Oddly enough, I could not sustain my anger at him
nor my grief at Reina's departure. I understood what had happened and what I had felt, but these events and feelings were
simply material to be shaped and structured.

I gave my final draft to the servo and waited. At last the door
opened. I made my way downstairs to Karath's study.

He sat behind his desk perusing my novella. I cleared my
throat. His cold eyes surveyed me as he said, "It isn't bad, Dorenmatté. It wouldn't make it in a race, but there might be some hope
for you." As I basked in this high praise, he threw the manuscript
at me. "Now go back to work and clean up some of your sentences."

A year later I took the gold medal in the PanAmerican Games.

But it was Olympic gold I wanted, the high point for a champion. There would be publicity, perhaps other competitions if my
health held out. But contests were for the young. Eventually I
would become a trainer or sign contracts with the entertainment
industry; gold-medal winners can get a lot for senso plots or
dream construction. Maybe novelists can do serialized week-long
dreams and short-story writers are better at commercials, but you
can't beat a novella writer for an evening's sustained entertainment. Since practically no one reads now, except of course the
critics, most of them failed writers who write comments on our
work for each other and serve as judges during competitions,
there isn't much else a champion can do when the contest years
are over.

The Olympics! Karath rode us mercilessly in preparation for
them. He presented countless distractions: robots outside with
jackhammers, emotional crises, dirty tricks meant to disorient us,
impossible deadlines.

Two years before the Games, which like the ancient Olympics are held only every four years, I had to enter preliminaries. I got through them easily. The night before I left for Rome, Karath and the others workshopped a story of mine and tore it to shreds. I recall the hatred I saw in the faces of my fellow trainees. None had qualified this time, although all had won locals or regionals. They would undoubtedly gossip maliciously about me when I left and point out to each other how inferior my work really was.

I arrived in Rome the day before the opening ceremonies. The part of the Olympic Village set aside for writers was a scenic spot. The small stone houses were surrounded on three sides by flower gardens and wooded areas. Below us lay all of Rome; the dome of St. Peter's, the crowded streets, the teeming arcologies. I wanted to explore it all, but I had to start sizing up the competition.

I sought out Jules Pepperman, who had been assigned a house near mine. I had met him at the PanAmerican Games. Jules was tied into the grapevine and always volunteered information readily.

He was a tall slender fellow with an open, friendly personality and a habit of trying to write excessively ambitious works during competition, a practice I regarded as courting disaster. It had messed him up before, but it had also won him a gold in the Anglo-American Games and a silver in the PEN Stakes. I couldn't afford to ignore him.

His house smelled of herb tea and patent medicines. Jules had arrived with every medication the judges would allow. I wondered how he endured competition, with his migraines and stomach ailments. But endure it he did, while complaining loudly about his health to everyone.

I sat in his kitchen while he poured tea. "Did you hear, Alena? I'm ready to go home, I'm sick of working all the time, the prelims almost wiped me out. There's this migraine I can't get rid of and the judges won't let me take the only thing that helps. And when I heard . . . you want honey in that?"

"Sure." He dropped a dollop in my tea. "What did you hear?"

"Ansoni. He's so brilliant and I'm so dumb. I can't take any more."

"What about Ansoni?"

"He's here. He's competing. Haven't you heard? You must have been living in a cave. He's competing. In novella."

"Shit," I said. "What's the matter with him? He must be almost sixty. Isn't he ineligible?"

"No. Don't you keep up with anything? He never worked professionally and he wasn't a trainer."

I tried to digest this unsavory morsel. I hadn't even known that Michael Ansoni was still among the living. He had taken a gold medal in short-story competition long ago and gone on to win a gold eight years later in novella, the only writer to change categories successfully. I couldn't even remember all his other awards.

"I can't beat him," Jules wailed. "I should have been a programmer. All that work to get here, and now this."

I had to calm Jules down. I didn't like his writing, which was a bit dense for my taste, but I liked him. "Listen," I said, "Ansoni's old. He might fold up at his age. Maybe he'll die and be disqualified."

"Don't say that."

"I wouldn't be sorry. Well, maybe I would. Who else looks good?"

"Nionus Gorff." Gorff was always masked; no one had ever seen his face. He had quite a cultish following.

"Naah," I responded. "Gorff hates publicity too much, he'll be miserable in a big race like this."

"There's Jan Wolowski. But I don't think he can beat Ansoni."

"Wolowski's too heavyhanded. He might as well do propaganda."

"There's Arnold Dankmeyer."

I was worried about Dankmeyer myself. He was popular with the judges, although that might not mean much. APOLLO, the Olympic computer, actually picked the winners, but the judges' assessments were fed in and considered in the final decisions. No one could be sure how much weight they carried. And Dankmeyer was appealingly facile. But he was often distracted by his admirers, who followed him everywhere and even lived in his house during races. He might fold.

"Anyway," I said, "you can't worry about it now." I was a bit insulted that Jules wasn't worried about me.

"I know. But the judges don't like me, they never have."

"Well, they don't like me either." I had, in accordance with Karath's advice, cultivated a public image with which to impress the judges. My stock-in-trade was unobtrusiveness and self-doubt. I would have preferred being a colorful character like Karath, but I could never have carried that off. Being quiet might not win many points, but there was always a chance the judges would react unfavorably to histrionics and give points to a shy writer.

"At least they don't hate you," Jules mumbled. "I need a vacation. I can't take it."

"You're a champion, act like one," I said loftily. I got up and made my departure, wanting to rest up for the opening ceremonies.

We looked terrific in the stadium, holding our quill pens, clothed in azure jumpsuits with the flags of our countries over our chests. The only ones who looked better were the astrophysicists, who wore black silk jumpsuits studded with rhinestone constellations. They were only there for the opening ceremonies; their contests would be held on the Moon. At any rate, the science games didn't draw much of an audience. Hardly anyone knew enough to follow them. And mathematicians—they were dressed in black robes and held slates and chalk—were ignored, even if they were gold medalists. The social sciences drew the crowds, probably because anyone could, in a way, feel he was participating in them. But we writers didn't do so badly. No one read what we wrote, but a lot of people enjoyed our public displays. At least one writer was sure to crack up before the Games were over, and occasionally there was a suicide.

We marched around, the flame was lit, and I smiled at Jules. At least we were contenders. No one could take that away.

The race began. I worked methodically, meaning that I used my own method. During the first two weeks I wrote nothing. I saw a lot of Rome. A wisp of an idea was forming in my mind, but I wasn't ready to work on it.

Jules was slaving away. He would creep along slowly and finish a draft, then take a week off during which he would feel guilty about not working. He had to rewrite a lot. "Otherwise," he had told me, "I'd be incomprehensible."

During the second month, I met Jan Wolowski while taking a walk. He was too intense for my taste. He was always serious, even at parties, and he had no tolerance for the foibles of writers. He was also dogmatic and snobbish. But he *was* competition.

I said hello and we continued walking together. "How you doing?" I asked, not really wanting to know.

"Still taking notes and working out my plot."

"I hate making notes. I like to write it as it comes. But I don't have a chance anyway." That last line was part of my self-depreciation routine, but on some level I believed it. If I really thought I was good, some part of me was sure, I would lose.

"I wrote a good paragraph this morning," he said. "I have my notebook with me. Want to hear it?"

"No." Wolowski liked to read to other competitors. It would bore, exasperate, or demoralize them. He read me his paragraph anyway. Unfortunately, it was good.

We passed Dankmeyer's house. He was holding court at a picnic table with his admirers, some fettucini, and plenty of wine. Dankmeyer could turn out a novella in a week, so he was able to spend most of his time garnering publicity.

"Did you ever meet Lee Huong?" Wolowski asked as I waved to Dankmeyer, hating his courtier's guts.

"No."

"You should. She may be the best writer here."

"I never heard of her. What's she won?"

"Nothing, except a bronze in the Sino-Soviet Games years ago. She's close to forty."

"Then she can't be that great. At that age, she ought to quit."

We passed Ansoni's house. All the shutters were closed. I had heard he slept during the day and worked at night.

"I mean," Wolowski continued, "that she's the best *writer*. If people still read, they'd read her. I've read her best stuff and it wasn't what she wrote in contests."

We stopped by a café and sat down at a roadside table. I signaled to a servo for a beer. The man was trying to disorient me. I knew these tricks. "Better than Ansoni?" I asked.

"Better than him."

"Bullshit. I don't believe it." I looked around and saw some spectators. They grinned and waved. A boy shouted, "Go get it, Dorenmatté!" It was nice to have admirers.

I spoke to Lee Huong only once, two months before the end of our race, at a party for the short-story medalists.

The party was held in an old villa. The dining room was filled with long tables covered with platters of caviar, various fruits, suckling pigs, standing rib roasts, and bowls of pasta. I settled on a couch and dug in. Across from me, Jules was flirting with the silver medalist in short stories, a buxom red-haired woman.

Benjamin MacStiofain sat next to me and grimly devoured a pear. "These Olympics are disgusting," he muttered. "What's the use? We come here, we agonize, we break our hearts, then someone wins and everybody forgets about it. I hate it all. This is my last competition." MacStiofain always said every meet was his last.

"I heard Dankmeyer finished his novella already."

MacStiofain's mustache twitched. "Did you have to tell me that?" He got up and wandered away morosely.

Then I saw Lee Huong. She drifted past, dressed in what appeared to be white pajamas. Her small light-brown face was composed; her almond eyes surveyed the room benevolently. It was eerie. This late in the race a writer might be depressed, anxious, fatalistic, or hysterical, but not calm. It had to be a tactic.

She nodded to me, then sat down on the couch. I nodded back. "Is this your first Olympic contest?" she asked.

I said it was.

"It means little."

"You're absolutely right," I replied. "It means nothing . . . if you're a loser." I was being crude. But Lee Huong only smiled as she got up and walked away. Maybe she knew something I didn't know.

I remembered what Wolowski had said. What if he was right about Huong? If she was the best, it meant that inferior writers defeated her regularly. And if that was true, it might mean that inferior writers beat better ones in all contests. MacStiofain, I recalled uncomfortably, believed that APOLLO picked the winners at random, although the human judges might give you an edge. The Olympic committee had denied this, but we all knew that MacStiofain's sister had taken a gold in cybernetics. She might have told him something.

I had lost my appetite during these ruminations, so I got up and made a show of leaving, waving to Jules and telling him that I was heading back to work. This obvious maneuver almost always succeeded in making the writers who remained feel guilty. Karath's classic move, bringing his typewriter to parties and working in the midst of them, was one I greatly admired but could never emulate with conviction.

On my way back, I saw Effie Mae Hublinger sitting on a stone wall with a few spectators. Her game was being just folks, nothin' special 'bout me, jes' throwin' the ol' words around, but at heart Ah'm jes' a li'l ol' socializer. Anyone who believed that about a writer deserved to be fooled, or worse yet, put in a story as a character.

The last month was pressurized. Anyone who could spare the time was playing dirty tricks. Wolowski, who admittedly was erudite, lectured to anyone he saw on the subject of our ignorance and lack of real ability. This upset a few writers, but only encouraged Jules, for some strange reason.

MacStiofain finally cracked. In a show of poor sportsmanship, he duked it out with a novelist. The day after that brawl, he was disqualified for taking unauthorized drugs.

They had to drag him away. The robopols put him in a straitjacket while he screamed that someone had planted the drugs, but we knew that wasn't true. At any rate, we all calmed down a bit, since a formidable contender was now out of the race.

Lee Huong kept her equilibrium. That drove Effie Mae Hublinger crazy. With a few of her friends, she camped out on Huong's front step for three days, creating a ruckus. This infantile tactic only lost Hublinger time she could have spent on her own novella.

Someone visited Jules and managed to swipe his medicines, unnoticed by the monitors. Even Jules, angry as he was, had to admire such skill and daring. But it was Dankmeyer who created a classic new ploy. Two weeks before the end of competition he handed in his novella.

Jules, hysterical by then, relayed this news to me. He was having trouble with his ending. He stomped around my workroom, talked himself into utter panic, talked himself out of it, then went back to his house. Even Ansoni had been thrown off balance by that trick. Everyone had always waited for the deadline, revising and polishing. Dankmeyer would be famous. He topped off his stunt with a nervous collapse, which would help with the judges.

The day before the deadline, Rigel Jehan left without finishing his novella and was disqualified. Poor Rigel, I thought, glad he was gone. He could never finish anything during the big contests.

And then the deadline arrived. We handed in our manuscripts and carefully avoided each other while awaiting judgment. I went on a drunk in Rome. I came to in an alley with a large bump on my head, no money, and a hangover. I suppose it's all grist for the mill.

The closing ceremonies were held two years after the start of the Games. It took that long for some of the races to be completed. The economists, in gold lamé, sashayed around the arena, drawing a few cheers. The anthropologists topped them, weaving in and out, then dancing a nifty two-step in their robes and feathers. I wore my bronze medal proudly as I strutted with the others, our quill pens held high. There was, after all, no shame in being defeated by Ansoni, although it irked me that Dankmeyer had taken the silver. He had recovered nicely from his nervous breakdown and was casting friendly glances at me with his sensitive brown eyes. I ignored him.

I returned to Karath's villa after that. He congratulated me but got down to essentials quickly. I had only a couple of months to train for the next Olympic prelims.

Then disaster struck. I had no words left. At first I thought it was only exhaustion. I grew listless. I put the cover over my typewriter, then hid it under my desk, where it reproached me silently. The other trainees whispered about me. I had to face the truth: I had a writer's block. I might never write again. No one ever discussed writer's block, considering it indelicate, but I knew others had gone mute.

Karath was kind and sympathetic, although he knew I could not remain at the villa; he had to worry about contagion. He was too courteous to ask me to leave. I left by myself, one cold cloudy morning, not wanting to see the other trainees gloat, and took a shuttle to New Zealand.

Blocked and miserable, I shut myself off from all news. I received a few kind notes, which I did not answer; nothing is worse than the pity of other writers. Yet even in that state I had to view the next Olympics.

Reina Takake took the gold; I found out she had gone back to Karath after I left. I watched her receive it, hating her, hating my former best friend more than I had ever hated anyone. That did it. Hate and envy always do. Something jogged loose in my brain and I started writing again. Let's face it, I'm not fit for anything else. I only hope I can be a contender once more.

BRIGHT COINS IN
NEVER-ENDING STREAM

A purse that always has one more coin in the
bottom of it, no matter how many you take out—that
was what Matthew Quoin had been offered in a dubious
transaction a long time ago. And how could
a man ever lose by such a bargain as that?

R. A. Lafferty

People sometimes became exasperated with Matthew Quoin, that
tedious old shuffler. Sometimes? Well, they were exasperated
with him almost all the time. It isn't that people aren't patient and
kind-hearted. All of them in our town are invariably so. But
Matthew could sure ruffle a kind-hearted surface.

"Oh, he is so slow about it!" people said of him. That wasn't
true, Matthew's fingers flew lightninglike when he was involved
in a transaction. It was just that so very many movements were
required of him to get anything at all transacted.

And then the stories that he told about his past, a very far-
distant past according to him, were worn out by repetition.

"Oh, was I ever the cock of the walk!" he would say. "I left a
trail of twenty-dollar gold pieces around the world three times,
and that was when twenty dollars was worth something. I
always paid everything with twenty-dollar gold pieces, and there

was no way that I could ever run out of them. Ten of them, a
hundred of them, *a thousand of them,* I could lay them out whenever they were needed. I had a cruse of oil that would never be
empty, as the Bible says. I had a pocketbook that would never be
without coin. I was the cock of the walk. Plague take it all, I still
am! Has anybody ever seen me without money?"

No, nobody had. It was just that, of late years, it took Matthew's
money so long to add up. And often people had to wait behind
him for a long time while he counted it out, and they became
sulky and even furious.

When people became weary of listening to Matthew's stories
(and of late years he could feel their weariness for him like a hot
blast) he went and talked to the pigeons. They, at least, had
manners.

"The bloom is off the plum now," he would tell those red-
footed peckers, "and the roses of life have become a little ratty
for me. But I will not run out of coin. I have the promise that I
will not. I got that promise as part of a dubious transaction, but
the promise has held up now for more years and decades than
you would believe. And I will not die till I am death-weary of
taking coin out of my pocketbook: I have that promise also. How
would I ever be weary of drawing coins out of my pocketbook?

"This began a long time ago, you see, when the pigeons were
no bigger than the jenny-wrens are now. They had just started
to mint the American twenty-dollar gold piece, and I had them
in full and never-ending flow. I tell you that a man can make an
impression if he has enough gold pieces. Ah, the ladies who were
my friends! Lola Montez, Squirrel Alice, Marie Laveau, Sarah
Bernhardt, Empress Elizabeth of Austria. And the high ladies
were attracted to me for myself as well as for my money. I was
the golden cock of the golden walk.

"You ask what happened to those golden days?" Matthew said
to the pigeons, who hadn't asked anything except maybe, "How
about springing for another box of Crackerjacks?"

"Oh, the golden days are still with me, though technically they are the copper days now. I was promised eight bright eons of ever-flowing money, and the eighth of the eons could last (along with my life) as long as I wished it to last.

"And, when the first eon of flowing money slipped into the second, it didn't diminish my fortune much. It was still an unending stream of gold. Now they were five-dollar gold pieces instead of twenty-dollar gold pieces, but when there is no limit to the number of them, what difference does that make? I would take one out of my pocketbook, and immediately there would be another one in it waiting to be taken."

"I suppose I really had the most fun when I was known as the Silver Dollar Kid," Matthew Quoin told them. He was talking to squirrels rather than pigeons now, and it was a different day. But one day was very much like another.

"I never cared overly for money. I just don't want to run out of it. And I have the promise that my pocketbook will always have one more coin in it. I liked the sound of silver dollars on a counter, and I'd ring them down as fast as one a second when I wished to make an impression. And they rang like bells. I was in my pleasant maturity then, and life was good to me. I was a guy they all noticed. They called me 'Show Boat' and 'the Silver Dollar Sport.' I always tipped a dollar for everything. That was when money was worth ten times what it is now and a dollar was really something. What, squirrels, another sack of peanuts, you say? Sure I can afford it! The girl at the kiosk will be a little impatient with me because it takes me so long to get enough coins out, but we don't care about that, do we?"

The fact was that Matthew Quoin, though he still commanded a shining and unending stream of money, had a poor and shabby look about him in these days of the eighth eon. As part of an old and dubious transaction, he had the promise that he could live as long as he wished, but that didn't prevent him from becoming quite old.

He had a grubby little room. He would get up at three o'clock every Friday morning and begin to pull coins one at a time (there was no possible way except one at a time) out of his pocketbook. It was one of those small, three-section, snap-jaw pocketbooks such as men used to carry to keep their coins and bills in. It was old, but it was never-failing.

Matthew would draw the coins out one at a time. He would count them into piles. He would roll them into rolls. And at eight o'clock in the morning, when his weekly rent was due, he would pay it proudly, twenty-seven dollars and fifty cents. So he would be fixed for another week. It took him from three until eight o'clock every Friday morning to do this; but he cat-napped quite a bit during that time. All oldsters cat-nap a lot.

And it didn't really take him very long (no more than five or six minutes) to draw out enough coins for one of his simple lunch-counter meals. But some people are a little bit testy at having to wait even five or six minutes behind an old man at the cashier's stand.

"I was known as the Four-Bit Man for a few years, and that was all right," Matthew Quoin said. "Then I was known as the Two-Bit Man for a few other years, and that was all right too." This was a different day, and Matthew was talking to a flock of grackle-birds who were committing slaughter on worms, slugs, and other crawlers in the grass of City Park. "It didn't begin to hurt till I was known as the Dime-a-Time Man," Matthew said, "and that stuck in the throat of my pride a little bit, although it shouldn't have. I was still the cock of the grassy walk even though I didn't have as many hens as I had once. I had good lodgings, and I had plenty to eat and drink. I could buy such clothes as I needed, though it flustered me a bit to make a major purchase. We had come into the era of the hundred-dollar overcoat then, and to draw out one thousand coins, one by one, with people perhaps waiting, can be a nervous thing.

"I began to see that there was an element of humor in that dubious transaction that I had made so many years ago, and that part of the joke was on me. Oh, I had won every point of argument when we had made that deal. The pocketbook was calfskin, triple-stitched, and with German silver snat-latch. It was absolutely guaranteed never to be clear empty of coin, and it should last forever. Each coin appeared in the very bottom of the pocketbook, that's true, and the contrivance was rather deep and with a narrow mouth, so it did take several seconds to fish each dime out. But it was a good bargain that I made, and all parties still abide by it. The Dime-a-Time years weren't bad.

"Nor were the nickel years really. There is nothing wrong with nickels. Dammit, the nickel is the backbone of commerce! It was in the nickel years that I began to get rheumatism in my fingers, and that slowed me down. But it had nothing to do with the bargain, which was still a good one."

When the penny years rolled around, Matthew Quoin was quite old. Likely he was not as old as he claimed to be, but he was the oldest and stringiest cock around.

"But it's all as bright as one of my new pennies," he said to a multitude of army caterpillars that was destroying the fine grass in City Park. "And this is the eighth and final eon of the everflowing money, and it will go on forever for me unless I tell it to stop. Why should I tell it to stop? The flow of money from my pocketbook is as vital to me as the flow of blood through my veins. And the denomination cannot be diminished further. There is no smaller coin than the copper penny."

It didn't go all that bright and shining with Matthew Quoin in the penny years, though. The rheumatism had bitten deeper into his hands and fingers, and now his lightning fingers were slow lightning indeed. The "time is money" saying applied to Matthew more explicitly than it had ever applied to anyone else, and there were quite a few slownesses conspiring to eat up his valuable time.

And every time that prices went up, by the same degree was he driven down. After five years in the penny eon he was driven down plenty.

"If it takes me five hours just to draw out and count the money for my week's rent, then things are coming to an intolerable stage with me," he said. "Something is going to have to give."

Something gave.

The government decreed that, due to the general inflation of the economy and the near-worthlessness of the one-cent piece, or penny, that coin would no longer be minted. And, after a cutoff date in the near future, it would no longer be legal tender either.

"What will I do now?" Matthew Quoin asked himself.

He went to talk to the people at the Elite Metal Salvage Company, Scavenger Department.

"How much a pound will you give me for copper pennies?" he asked.

"Two cents a pound," the man said. "There hasn't been very much copper in copper pennies for years and years."

"There is in these," Matthew said. "They follow the specifications of the earliest minting." He showed several of them to the man.

"Amazing, amazing!" the man said. "They're almost pure copper. Five cents a pound."

"I don't know whether I can live on that or not," Matthew Quoin said, "but I've no choice except to try."

Matthew Quoin changed his life style a bit. He gave up his lodging room. He slept in a seldom-flooded storm sewer instead. But it was still a hard go.

A nickel a pound! Do you know how many pennies, pulled out rheumatically one by one, it takes to make a pound? Do you know how many nickels it takes now just to get a cup of coffee and an apple fritter for breakfast? Matthew Quoin had started at three-thirty that morning. It would be ten o'clock before he had enough to take to the Elite Metal Salvage Company to sell for legal tender. It would be ten-thirty before he had his scanty breakfast. And then back to the old penny-fishing again. His fingers were scabbed and bleeding. It would be almost midnight before he had enough (yes, the Elite Metal Salvage Company *did* do business at night; that's when they did a lot of their purchasing of stolen metal) to trade in for supper money. And that would represent only one hamburger with everything on it, and one small glass of spitzo. But Matthew would never be clear broke. He was still cock of the walk.

"Now here is where it gets rough," Matthew Quoin said. "Suppose that I give up and am not able to live on the bright flow of coins, and I die (for I cannot die until I do give up); suppose that I die, then I will have lost the dubious transaction that I made so long ago. I'll have been outsmarted on the deal, and I cannot have that. That fellow bragged that he'd never lost on a transaction of this sort, and he rubbed it in with a smirk. We'll just see about that. I've not given up yet, though I do need one more small morsel of food if I'm to live through the day. Do you yourself ever get discouraged, robin?"

Matthew Quoin was talking to a lone robin that was pulling worms out of the browned grass that was beginning to be crusted with the first snow of the season. But the robin didn't answer.

"You live on the promise of spring, robin, though you do well even now," Quoin said. "I also have a new promise to live for. I have been given a fresh lease on life today, though it will be about seven years before I can put that lease into effect. But, after you're old, seven years go by just like nothing. A person in the Imperial Coin Nook (it's in a corner of the Empire Cigar and Hash Store) says that in about seven years my coins will have value, and eventually he will be able to pay a nickel or dime or even fifteen cents for each of them. And that is only the beginning, he says: in fifty years they may be worth eighty cents or even a dollar each. I am starting to put one coin out of every three into a little cranny in my sewer to save them. Of course, for those seven years that I wait, I will go hungrier by one third. But this promise is like a second sun coming up in the morning. I will rise and shine with it."

"Bully for you," the robin said.

"So I have no reason to be discouraged," Quoin went on. "I have a warm and sheltered sewer to go to. And I have had a little bit, though not enough, to eat today. I hallucinate, and I'm a trifle delirious and silly, I know. I'm lightheaded, but I believe I could make it if I had just one more morsel to eat. This has been the worst of my days foodwise, but they may get a little bit better if I live through this one. It will be a sort of turning of the worm for me now. Hey, robin, that was pretty good, the turning of the worm. Did you get it?"

"I got it," the robin said. "It was pretty good."

"And how is it going with yourself?" Matthew Quoin asked.

"There's good days and bad ones," the robin said. "This is a pretty good one. After the other robins have all gone south, I have pretty good worm-hunting."

"Do you ever get discouraged?"

"I don't let myself," the robin said. "Fight on, I say. It's all right today. I'm about full now."

"Then I'll fight on too," Matthew swore. "One extra morsel would save my life, I believe. And you, perhaps, robin—"

"What do you have in mind?" the robin asked.

"Ah, robin, if you're not going to eat the other half of that last worm—"

"No, I've had plenty. Go ahead," the robin said.

THE SYNERGY SCULPTURE

There were spheres and cubes and pyramids, and
some of these were continuing to develop, twisting
upon themselves in a complex fashion. At one
point, hanging from a bent limb, a transparent green
teardrop had grown stalactites and stalagmites
of shimmering yellow. . . .

Terrence L. Brown

"It's the latest thing, John," said Mary James to her husband.
"Why, Jim and Elsie have had theirs for two weeks, and the
Martins have ordered theirs. We simply must have one—and
think of how much fun it will be to watch it grow."

John James scanned the brochure his wife offered him. In
large, brightly colored letters, it proclaimed the desirability of
ordering "your Synergy Sculpture" today.

"I don't understand what it does," he said.

"Look here, silly," said Mary, pointing to a paragraph headed
"HOW IT WORKS." "See, we tune it to our thought waves, we plug
it in and then we watch it grow." A vengeful look came into her
eyes. In a moment she added a smile. "I'll bet we can grow a
better one than Jim and Elsie, even if they are two weeks ahead
already."

"Have you read this?" John asked, pointing to the brochure.

Mary nodded. "Well, it says here: 'The Synergy Sculpture is not a toy. It is a *sensitive scientific instrument* designed to aid couples and groups in *becoming more aware of their emotional interactions.* The Synergy Sculpture measures emotional interactions among the two to ten people to whom the unit is tuned—not individual emotional states. It has been used successfully by *hundreds of psychotherapists throughout the world* as a monitor of the growth of couples and groups toward emotionally mature relationships!"

"So?"

"So, what do we need it for? Don't you think I'm emotionally mature enough for you?"

"Oh, that's not the point, and you know it."

John shrugged. "So the thing measures our vibes," he said, "and grows."

"Right," said Mary enthusiastically. "And the better the vibes between us, the more complex, colorful, and beautiful it gets."

"What happens if our vibes aren't so good?"

"You're always pessimistic." She sighed. "If we fight, then it stops growing. If we continue fighting, then it starts to wilt, to die. But that won't happen," she added quickly. "We love each other, right? So the sculpture will pick that up, and in no time it'll be bigger and better than anyone else's."

John gave in. "We might as well get one, I guess. Maybe we'll learn something." If they failed, they could always hide the thing in the closet.

The Synergy Sculpture arrived four days later. It was a glass case three feet square and four feet tall. The mechanism itself was encased in the bottom six inches, and this portion was opaque. On the back face were an on-off switch, the power cord, and inputs to tune the mechanism. The sculpture itself would grow in the three and a half foot volume enclosed by clear glass.

The salesman who brought the sculpture also brought the leads which he used to tune the mechanism to John and Mary. It was a simple procedure. He attached the electrodes to both for a few moments, and that was it. The sculpture was now sensitive to any interaction between John and Mary.

"That's all there is to it," the salesman said, as he wrapped up the leads and prepared to leave. "The sculpture should begin to form within an hour. The mechanism itself is guaranteed for five years, although it may need periodic sensitivity adjustments. If there seem to be any problems, just give me a call. The manual explains what the various shapes of sculpture mean in terms of your relationship. Remember, if you turn it off, or unplug it, the sculpture will disintegrate, and you'll have to start all over. I hope you enjoy it. Good-bye."

As soon as the door closed behind the salesman, Mary turned to John and flung her arms about him.

"I love you," she said.

"Want it to get a good start, huh?" said John, laughing.

"Why not? Can you think of a better way to get it going?" She smiled coquettishly at him.

"No, I guess not."

An hour later the sculpture had indeed begun to grow. John and Mary sat before it in dim light. On the left side five small mounds had erupted. They were reddish, and had begun to sprout small tendrils of green. On the other side a single stalk of pink had risen about two inches high. It was round and had sprouted limbs that made it look vaguely like a cactus.

"If we let anyone see this, they'll know what it is we do all the time," said John.

"What do you mean?"

"Well," said John, waving his hand at it, "pink and red are the colors of passion, aren't they?"

"They must be," said Mary, with an exaggerated sigh. They both laughed, and cuddled even closer.

Two days later the sculpture was about eight inches tall at its highest point and was growing steadily. It was also becoming more complex. At first it had been growing mostly in treelike forms—the manual said this was a normal beginning, but primitive if it got no further. Now it was beginning to generate a wide variety of color, and was generating more complex and beautiful shapes. There were spheres and cubes and pyramids, and some of these were continuing to develop, twisting upon themselves in a complex fashion. At one point, hanging from a bent limb, a transparent green teardrop had grown stalactites and stalagmites of shimmering yellow. The central stalk of the cactuslike form had shot up to a height of six inches; then the tip of it had opened and curved outward in an unbroken film which descended to encase the entire structure. In all, it was impressive, although small compared to the volume it had to grow in.

John was the first home from work that evening. He immediately undressed and headed for the shower; it had been a long, hard day. John was a computer programmer at the university. The system had been down most of the day, and of course, he had had an extra heavy schedule as well. The result was a day of frustration at being unable to run programs, and anger at people who didn't understand that there was nothing he could do about it, and would not leave him alone to do what he was paid for— programming.

He heard Mary come in and call hello. He pretended not to hear. After his shower, he put on his robe and slippers and joined Mary in the living room. She was examining the sculpture.

"Did you look?" she asked excitedly. Without waiting for him to answer, she turned back to the sculpture. "See? This blue globe is turning in on itself again. Now there's the flowerlike thing within the globe within another globe. The manual says the more complex they get, like that, the more emotionally mature the relationship is."

She looked back at John, who had collapsed into an easy chair. His eyes were closed.

"Did you hear me?" she asked, after a moment.

"I heard, I heard."

"Well, did you see what I'm talking about?"

"No, I *didn't* see what you're talking about." He slumped further into the chair. "And I can't say I really care, at the moment."

"What got into you?"

"I had a bad day."

"So you bring it home and snap at me?"

"Where else am I supposed to bring it? I suppose it should magically go away when I step in the door?"

"Lower your voice," she said.

"Why should I? It feels good to shout now and then."

Mary looked back at the sculpture. The colors seemed paler. Then she noticed that the double-globed flower was changing.

"John, look." The note of concern in her voice made him open his eyes. He went over to the sculpture and knelt beside her.

The double-globed flower was fading to a murky white color; then, while they watched, the whole thing—the two outer globes and the flower—distorted, seeming to melt like hot wax. But it didn't drip, just melted into itself and was gone. The whole sculpture seemed to have lost some of its brightness.

"It's so sensitive," John said. "We destroyed it with our argument." He turned to Mary. "I'm sorry, honey. I should have thought before I snapped at you."

"It's okay, I understand."

They kissed gently, and hugged each other. Then they glanced at the sculpture to see if it had regained its brightness. It had, a little.

"See, it's already helped us make our relationship more mature," said Mary.

By the following evening, the sculpture had regained most of its lost brilliance, although it had not yet begun to grow again.

Mary was late getting home, and John felt a knot growing in his stomach as he waited for her. When she finally arrived, forty-five minutes late, it was obvious that she was upset. She muttered something as she stalked through the living room.

"Bad day?" asked John.

"Those crazy asses," she exploded. "They can't make the hardware to the right specifications, so the interface doesn't work, and then they blame my design." She threw up her arms, then crossed them, and stood looking out the window.

John got up and went to her. "Relax, Mary. It's not your mistake and they'll see that."

"When?" she asked, raising her voice. "And why should I relax?"

John put his arms around her, but she pulled away.

"Stop it! I'm in no mood to be soothed and placated."

"Now who's bringing it home?" asked John.

She turned then, and they both looked at the sculpture. It was already beginning to lose its recently regained brilliance.

"John, I'm sorry," said Mary, turning to him. "You're right, it's stupid of me to do that, especially when I tell you not to."

In answer, John leaned over and kissed her lightly.

"Love me," she whispered.

The knot in his stomach had grown tighter; now he was the one who was not in the mood, but he forced himself to participate. His performance was at least satisfactory; he could tell because the sculpture was regaining its glow.

It was three days later, and Mary had taken the afternoon off. She made herself a sandwich for lunch, and sat at the kitchen bar eating it. The kitchen was a mess, the counter tops were piled high with dirty dishes, the floor hadn't been swept in a week, a bag of groceries had not been put away as yet.

It was a depressing sight, and it made her headache worse. She rarely got headaches like this one. The pain started at the top of her forehead, and then progressed in both directions until it circled her head. And then it didn't stop developing, but changed from just spreading to growing in intensity. It had been bothering her for the last two days, and was the reason she had taken the option of this afternoon off. Now, after looking at the mess in the kitchen, she wasn't sure that she would be able to relax.

She left the kitchen and went into the living room. Things weren't a lot better there. Miscellaneous stuff was strewn all over the room. It had a quite lived in look. She ignored it, ignored the kitchen, and spent the first part of the afternoon reading. She finally dozed off, and was sleeping when John got home from work.

Mary had been sleeping so soundly that she had to claw herself back to clear thinking. She was fully awake when John returned to the living room and sat stiffly in a chair. He seemed tense to her.

"Hi," she said softly.

"For having the afternoon off, you didn't accomplish much," he said, with an edge to his voice. He swung his arm to encompass the room. "This place is a mess. And the kitchen's worse."

"Well, I'm sorry," she retorted, hotly. "It so happens that I was tired and had a headache."

Their eyes met, and there was a flash of non-verbal communication between them. They both looked at the sculpture. It hadn't begun to dim as yet. They were silent a moment. Then Mary got up and went over to where John sat. He smiled, although the tenseness didn't seem entirely gone. She sat in his lap and they kissed. Turning her head awkwardly and laying her cheek against his, she got a glance of the sculpture. It was still brightly colored.

"I'll get started in a minute," she said. She got up and went to the bathroom. She took three aspirin. Her headache was back, with a vengeance.

It was Sunday afternoon. John and Mary had spent Saturday working together on projects around the house. It had been an amiable day, and the sculpture was glowing brightly, and had added some new complexities. That morning they had sat together before it and marveled at what their relationship had created.

Mary was sitting contentedly, reading. John got up and

switched on the TV. It was time for the football game.

"Must you, John?" Mary asked, looking up.

"It's an important game," he explained.

"But why do you want to spend time listening to that hollering and screaming when we can spend a quiet afternoon together doing something we both enjoy?" She punctuated her words with a sidewise glance at the sculpture.

That was enough. John turned the TV off. He was irritated, but didn't show it outwardly. He sat quietly, doing nothing, but inside he was restless, and his stomach knotted. A few minutes later, he went to the bathroom and had diarrhea.

Mary was home first from work on Monday. She slumped into a chair and took time to try to relax. A few minutes later John arrived.

"What's for dinner?" he asked.

"Nothing," she replied. "I'm not cooking tonight."

"It's your turn," he replied.

"I don't care." She felt irritable, wished that he would leave her alone.

"Mary, we can't afford to go out again. You know that." He caught her eyes, and then glanced to the sculpture. Her eyes followed his. It hadn't started to dim yet.

"You're right, of course," she said, getting up. She tried to control her irritability. She kissed him. "What would you like?"

Before she started dinner, she went to the bathroom and took four aspirin. Her headache was back. She scratched her arm; she seemed to be developing a rash.

It had been a month since the synergy sculpture arrived. It was now just over two and a half feet high at its highest point, and it shone sharply with brilliant colors. Although it had many different attachment points at the base, these had all grown together at some point, making the sculpture a single structure. It was extremely complex, and difficult to describe. All possible geometrical shapes seemed to be incorporated within it somewhere, giving it its complexity. But somehow the shapes molded into one another to give an appearance of regularity where there should be chaos, with the result that the overall design was pleasing to the eye. The colors, which melted and flowed into each other, enhanced this beauty. It was a sculpture to be proud of.

John and Mary sat before it holding hands.

"Did you talk to Jim Anderson today?" Mary asked.

"Yes, and he said that next Thursday was fine. He said for us not to worry about dessert. He and Elsie will bring something."

"They don't have to do that."

"I know, but he said they wanted to, so I didn't argue."

They were silent a moment, watching the sculpture.

"Ours is better than theirs," said Mary.

"It is," agreed John. Then, "I wonder if they fought just before we got there Tuesday night? Their sculpture seemed dull."

"I know. I wondered that, too. Wait until they see how bright ours is."

"If it stays this bright."

"Of course it will. We don't fight."

"I guess you're right."

It was Tuesday night.

"We've got to get the cars ready for winter," said Mary.

"What?" asked John, looking up from his reading. John was tired; he had a crop of new students, and they seemed more incompetent than the last bunch.

"Antifreeze, snow tires, you know," answered Mary.

"Do we have to talk about it now?" said John, testily.

"It has to be done," persisted Mary. She glanced at the sculpture.

"You're right, of course. I'll get some antifreeze tomorrow and see about having the tires changed." He forced a smile. The knot in his stomach had changed to a pain, and the diarrhea had been worse. He would have to see a doctor about it. Now the pain came back, worse than before.

It was Wednesday night.

Mary was tired; it had been a long day, and she had spent most of it convincing her supervisor that indeed, it was poor manufacturing of the hardware and not her design that was causing the malfunction of the interface. She had finally won, but in all, the fiasco had cost her nearly two weeks' work.

John arrived and immediately began to clean up around the house. Knowing part of this was her responsibility, but not feeling then that she wanted to take it, Mary was irritated, but she held her tongue. She ate listlessly of the tuna casserole he prepared; she didn't like tuna casserole, and he knew it. After dinner she sat down to watch TV. She didn't want to have to think hard enough to read.

John sat down close to her and watched with her for a few minutes. Then he turned to her and blew in her ear.

"Let's make love," he whispered. He kissed her neck.

"I'm tired," she said, turning away.

"Come on, think what it'll do to the sculpture."

She agreed.

Afterward, she lay with her head on his chest.

"We have to plan things for tomorrow night," said John.

"Please, John, must we, right now?"

"I think we should," he said, glancing to where the sculpture glowed in the darkness.

"Okay," she agreed, then. "But first I've got to go to the bathroom." In the bathroom she took four aspirin—that's all there were left. Her head felt like it would explode. Absently, she scratched her arm, then looked at it. It was a fiery red. She would have to see a doctor about the rash and the headaches.

It was Thursday evening. Jim and Elsie Anderson arrived on time. John ushered them into the living room. Mary and he had dimmed the lights and pulled the synergy sculpture out from before the window so that it took up a central space in the room. John and Mary were quite proud of the sculpture. It was now nearly three feet high, very complex, and quite brilliant. As near as they could determine from using the rating scale in the manual, their sculpture indicated that their relationship was ninety-five percent ideal.

"Wow," said Jim Anderson as he caught his first glimpse of it. From behind him, John grinned widely at Mary.

"Ohhh," cooed Elsie. "It's so bright." Mary grinned back at John.

John mixed drinks for them all, and then they sat, surrounding the synergy sculpture as though it were a fireplace.

"Look here," said Elsie, pointing. "I've never seen a shape like that before."

"It looks almost like a Klein bottle," said Jim, gazing closely to where Elsie pointed.

"What's a Klein bottle?"

"A three dimensional Moebius strip," he explained. He pointed to another shape. "And this one is a torus."

"The colors," exclaimed Elsie, "they're just . . . just breathtaking."

Mary and John beamed with pride. It seemed that the sculpture pulsed as a result. But perhaps that was just their imaginations.

"We're quite proud of how it turned out," said Mary.

"But, of course, it's still growing," added John quickly. He gestured, "See? It's got probably six inches left to take up." He smiled widely.

"Well, yours is certainly more spectacular than ours was," said Elsie.

"Was?" asked Mary.

"Oh," she said coyly, "didn't Jim tell you? Ours was mistuned and something was wrong with the sensing unit. We had it taken in for repairs the day after you saw it."

Covertly, John nudged Mary, and they both giggled inwardly.

After the Andersons had left, Mary said, mockingly, "Oh, didn't you know, ours was mistuned. Why I'm sure it would have been as good as yours if only we hadn't got a lemon." They both laughed loud and long over that.

The next day, John only worked in the morning. He was caught up with his work and had no labs, so he came home unexpectedly. He made a stop along the way and picked up two tickets for the theater that evening.

Mary also found that her work load was light, and she too took off early. One of the other engineers in her office was trying to get rid of two tickets to the football game that evening. Mary took them off his hands, expecting to surprise John with them.

They arrived home together. Inside, they both spoke simultaneously.

"I've got two tickets to the theater," said John.

"I've got two tickets to the football game," said Mary.

"What?" they both said, again at the same time.

They were both immediately angry. John spoke.

"You mean you bought tickets without checking with me first?"

"Me? What about you?" she shouted back.

John felt his stomach tighten and his bowels loosen.

Mary felt her head begin to throb and her arm begin to itch.

Then, at the same time, they both looked at the sculpture. It seemed to them that it began to dim. Again, they spoke simultaneously, although in lowered tones.

"Okay, let's go to the theater," said Mary.

"Okay, let's go to the football game," said John.

The sculpture began to glow again.

"What do you mean, the headaches and the rash are psychosomatic, Doctor?" said Mary. "That can't be. My husband and I have the most beautiful, most complex synergy sculpture on the block."

"Ulcerative colitis, and a stomach ulcer?" asked John unbelievingly. "Are you sure, Doctor?"

The Memory Machine

The Great Modesty Sweepstakes

This anthology is the fourth in a distinguished series by the editors, in which . . . the combination of little known masterpieces by outstanding writers in the field of horror have [*sic*] earned both the acclaim of the critics and the support of the readers. . . .

Sam Moskowitz is known as a researcher and scholar in the field of the fantastic and has authored many basic books on the history of science fiction. . . .

Alden H. Norton is a veteran editor of such nostalgic fantasy magazines as *Astonishing Stories, Super Science Stories, Famous Fantastic Mysteries* and *Fantastic Novels,* who has a weakness for this type of material.

> —"Editors' Note" in *Horrors*
> *in Hiding,* edited by Sam
> Moskowitz and Alden H. Norton

Harrison is one of the few writers of today who maintain the old grim jesting vigour of yesterday; ever since "Deathworld," the last of the great ASF serials, which began appearing in the

121

January 1960 issue, he has been a favourite on an imposing scale.

—*The Astounding-Analog
Reader, Volume Two,*
edited by Harry Harrison
and Brian W. Aldiss

DAW Books is a new publishing company designed for one specific purpose—to publish science fiction. That is our only directive. DAW Books derives its name from the initials of its publisher and editor, Donald A. Wollheim, who has been in the forefront of science fiction all his life. As a fan, as a writer, as an anthologist, and for the last three decades as the editor whose work has most consistently found favor in the eyes of those who spend their money for science fiction in paperback books.

Donald A. Wollheim is those readers' best guarantee that behind every book bearing his initials is the experience and the work of someone who likes what science fiction readers like, and who will do his best to give it to them. . . .

—D. A. W.
"A Statement to Science
Fiction Readers," in an
early DAW book

I tried to argue him out of his foolish stand, but he was adamant. I was positive that Pan Dan Chee liked me; and I shrank from the idea of killing him, as I knew that I should. He was an excellent swordsman, but what chance would he have against the master swordsman of two worlds? I am sorry if that should sound like boasting; for I abhor boasting—I only spoke what is a fact. I am, unquestionably, the best swordsman that has ever lived.

—John Carter, in *Llana
of Gathol,* by Edgar
Rice Burroughs

But No Flowers on Mother's Day

Eddore was—and is, huge, dense, and hot. Its atmosphere is not air, as we of small, green Terra know air, but is a noxious mixture of gaseous substances known to mankind only in chemical laboratories. Its hydrosphere, while it does contain some water, is a poisonous, stinking, foully corrosive, slimy and sludgy liquid.

And the Eddorians were as different from any people we know as Eddore is different from the planets indigenous to our space and time. They were, to our senses, utterly monstrous; almost incomprehensible. They were amorphous, amoeboid, sexless. Not androgynous or parthenogenetic, but absolutely sexless; with a sexlessness unknown in any Earthly form of life higher than the yeasts. Thus they were, to all intents and purposes and except for death by violence, immortal; for each one, after having lived for hundreds of thousands of Tellurian years and having reached its capacity to live and to learn, simply divided into two new individuals, each of which, in addition to possessing in full its parent's mind and memories and knowledge, had also a brand-new zest and a greatly increased capacity.

—*First Lensman*, by
E. E. Smith, Ph. D.

Also Known as Redneck Delight

Their courses were built into their guidance system, in a way that nobody had figured out; you could pick a course, but once picked that was it—and you didn't know where it was going to take you when you picked it, any more than you know what's in your box of Cracker-Joy until you open it.

—*Gateway*, by
Frederik Pohl

If Only We Could Train Ours Like That

Outside in the growing darkness the animals were on their nightly peregrinations, moving in from the woods, beginning to circle the house. The dogs could sometimes be seen from the house, running in packs wild as wolves. Cats bristled and spat in the hedges when they went out to the privy or to fetch more wood for the dying fire.

—*Comet,* by Jane White

Spawning God Knows What Tufts and Armpits

Her eyes had been enlarged, and her naturally small chin further diminished, in accordance with the fashion dictates of the time, even as Hagen's dark eyebrows had been grown into a ring of hair that crossed above his nose and went down by its sides to meld with his moustache.

—"To Mark the Year on Azlaroc," by Fred Saberhagen, in *Science Fiction Discoveries*

THE BIRDS ARE FREE

"Your techniques of shivering and coughing are
quite good. Your technique of throwing out all your
food, while a bit drastic for my taste, may well
be warranted here. However, your technique of falling
senseless to the ground and then lying there limp,
while your consciousness retreats into an imaginary
world, is inefficient in the extreme."

Ronald Anthony Cross

The last night we spent in the high country, we climbed up to the
top of one of those large flat buttes and sat near the edge. From
there we watched the campfires come on, one by one, all around
the great lake and for miles and miles along the road leading to
it. The effect was of a large number nine of fire, and the festival
of Our Lady of the Lake was begun.

After a while the master broke the silence. It was not often that
he did so, for he spoke only when necessary. In fact, he was
meticulous about the expenditure of energy in any form.

He was a delicate little man with hair and beard like white puffs
of cloud floating away from his face and dissolving into the air.
Spry as an elf. And he was old, so old; no one knew how old he
was, but there was something about him all the same that was
frightening, a certain austerity, or sharpness, a quality of power.
When he spoke, you listened.

He raised his hand to be sure he had my attention, then he spoke in a high, shrill voice.

"I know you are excited. Nevertheless, you must use all your power to listen with a calm mind. Do not add anything or subtract anything. I have arranged what I wish to say to you into a list for your convenience.

"One. We will go to the festival.

"Two. You will fight for the championship.

"Three. We will gain the prize money.

"Four. If you are alert, you will have the opportunity to learn much."

Stunned, I waited for him to continue, but he sat quietly, looking into my eyes, smiling in his strange, distant manner, his hands now folded in his lap.

His eyes closed. Perhaps he meditated; perhaps he slept.

"I never dreamed," I stammered. "I mean, we haven't been to a city in five years, to win the purse, to fight for the championship of Our Lady; I never dreamed that when I spent those years training in the martial arts, that I was training for this."

He opened his eyes and held out his arm to silence me.

"I find it necessary to speak again," he said. "This time when I finish speaking, you must, unless I request you to answer, remain completely silent in contemplation of what I have just said. This rule should apply in your relationship with intelligent people throughout your life and, should some theory such as reincarnation prove correct, throughout your future lives as well.

"I have asked you to listen carefully to what I say. Neither add nor subtract from it. At no point did I say, for instance, that all your training in the martial arts was toward the goal of defeating this champion. To carry it further, at no point have I suggested that your training in the martial arts had any goal whatever. It is an example of your adding to my teaching, to infer that you are being trained for something, when for all I have told you, you may be just expending energy in one form as opposed to expending it in a different manner. Your habit of adding to everything

is your only obstacle in life. You must let go of it."
  He closed his eyes. Now I thought perhaps he had gone to
sleep. My mind was filled to the bursting point with myriads of
conflicting, agitating thoughts, visions, conjectures.
  I took my blanket from my pack and lay down on it. Gradually
my thoughts, locked in their death-struggle of duality, sank under
a wave of weariness, into another dimension, where they fought
on as my dreams. The last thing I saw, as I drifted off to sleep,
was the image of the old man, sitting crosslegged before the fire,
erect as always, relaxed as always: asleep, I wondered, or meditat-
ing?
  I seemed to be struggling against something in vain. Perhaps
I had been tied up. I looked down at my wrists, and sure enough,
long, indistinct hemp ropes trailed away from my wrists into
smoke. I began to jerk at them frantically, but I could not get
loose. Something struck me across on the shoulders and I came
awake with a terrible start.
  It was just before dawn, and the master was standing over me
with his staff raised, ready to strike me again if necessary. He
looked furious, but I suspect that was only to impress me with my
failure.
  "You should be discouraged from taking inferior action in your
dreams, as well as in your waking life," he had told me once. Also:
"Your dream dilemmas are the result of lack of awareness, the
same as your waking dilemmas."
  Now, with the rim of the sun beginning to rise over the edge
of the distant, flat-topped mountains, with the first bright flashes
of gold and purple, we stood in the position of commencement
of the early-morning form. Then we began to move slowly and
carefully through the form, oiling our joints, limbering up our
muscles, our sense of balance, our basic techniques; preparing
our bodies for any movement they might be required to make
later in the day; also measuring the wind currents, the altitude,
adjusting to the resistance of today's particular ocean of air.
  I became aware, for instance, of a slight southeast wind, which

made it necessary to adjust the natural inclination of my body a few degrees from time to time. It would be well to keep an eye on it during the day. The footing was excellent, a trifle uneven, but for the most part solid and sure, with little mounds and hollows supplying good purchase.

As we completed the form, I shivered in the early-morning chill. I noticed out of the corner of my eye that the master was smiling happily. He considered shivering, like sneezing, an efficient, enlightened technique of adjustment to changes in the environment.

"If something harmful gets into your nose, why, blast it out with all your might. What a thrill of survival this gives!"

As for shivering, I have seen him take off his shirt in the iciest weather, and tremble until his outline blurred, then stop and examine the color of his skin for a certain pink hue, which he took to mean that his blood was circulating more swiftly, and the adjustment was taking place successfully.

The yawn, however, he considered as a more or less desperate attempt to adjust the oxygen level of the body by gulping it in hysterically.

"Breathe deeper in the first place, you fool, instead of waiting until you've almost passed out," he said.

Sickness and fainting he viewed as the result of refusal to adjust to the environment. Once, when a young woman had fainted with illness in a rainstorm, he remarked to her casually as she began to revive, "Your techniques of shivering and coughing are quite good. Your technique of throwing out all your food, while a bit drastic for my taste, may well be warranted here. However, your technique of falling senseless to the ground and then lying there limp, while your consciousness retreats into an imaginary world, is inefficient in the extreme. I suggest you abandon it and concentrate your efforts more in the area of crying out for help, or perhaps even merely moaning for sympathy."

We came down a narrow dirt path, moving fast, I waving my arms, he his staff, to adjust our balance; the old man leading the way, hopping and prancing from rock to rock, shortcutting the

path wherever he could, until we landed on flat ground at the
bottom, with a minor army of little stones and pebbles following
us.

Here we caught our breath, deliberately (under his critical eye)
breathing in huge gulps of air, ending with shallow, swift hyper-
ventilation.

Then we proceeded leisurely along the road that led to the
great lake.

At first I thought there were many-colored flags waving in the
wind. The voices were like the plaintive cries of gulls. Then I
began to recognize, with my eyes: silk scarves, turbans, bright
yellow turmeric-dyed cotton robes waving in the wind. With my
ears: "Fresh fruit, wine, beer, meat—step this way, gentlemen—
fish, I have fish." And later with my nose: strong perfume,
strong wine, human sweat. And with some other sense I felt an
all-pervading spirit of drunkenness and exhilaration, the raw
soul of festival. What faces, I thought, what bodies. With a
giddy flush I pushed the whores away from me, the bold ones
who strove to push their ripe breasts up against my bare chest
and shoulders; but gently, gently, for the daughters of our
golden lady are sacred.

Ancient ruins lined the roads. They were chipped and broken,
filled with rubble, and yet they stood, they still stood.

"What do they suggest to you, master?" I gestured toward the
broken buildings.

He shrugged noncommittally. "Things change; life goes on."

"Could we have built them, could we possibly have built
them?"

"Why not?" He increased his stride a trifle, to discourage my
questioning.

The crowds became thicker, the voices louder, brasher. Suddenly we beheld an incredible sight: the street of the trappers and
sellers of wild birds.

A fusillade of color, a blaze of song. Endless rows of woven
straw baskets of beautiful birds.

Their calls filled the air: some sharp and grating, some clear, some full, and some sad and distant as a dream.

"I've never seen such a beautiful sight," I said.

Something strange was in the master's expression, something I had never seen before.

"You know not how to look," he said, "and nothing I can teach will ever show you how to look at these exotic birds, these beautiful free spirits sold into slavery, betrayed by the caretakers of this beautiful planet, Earth."

Now we continued in silence, into the crowd.

We passed by the park of the temple of Our Lady. The groves of trees were etched clear, but strangely two-dimensional against the oncoming night. It was as if the light were being drained from the sky swiftly and suddenly; the torches were lit, the lamps of colored paper hung, the dancing and drinking had begun in earnest.

It was well after dark when at last, in the heart of the city, we asked directions to the cheaper inns and restaurants, frequented by gladiators.

The next morning I fought my preliminary bout. I almost felt sorry for him. He pawed the air helplessly, frantically. His balance was absurd. I avoided him until he tired somewhat, and swatted him a few light blows, careful not to bruise my knuckles; I was saving my kicks for someone else.

The crowd went wild. It was easy to see I was to be their favorite.

I was tall and fast. A smooth classical boxer, and quite handsome, I thought to myself. But I was young, oh I was young.

"Not a bruise on me." I was jumping up and down, swatting invisible flies in the air. "I can't lose, I just can't lose, with a teacher like you how could I?"

But he was paying no attention to me. To my annoyance I saw that he was staring fixedly at something beyond me. I turned, and caught my breath.

"What a freak," I said.

He was a short man, a broad man, a mutant. He had reddish

skin and dark curly hair. His face was jagged and lonely, somber and strong, his bone structure grotesquely thick and square. His arms were short and muscular, all four of them. His eyes were used to pain.

Now I noticed the girl at his side. The astonishing contrast somehow seemed right: the princess and the caveman, Beauty and the beast. It was one of those paradoxes which forever seem to remind us that we didn't invent the world out of our logical mind, that it invented us out of the unfathomable depths of its crazy nature.

No problem there, I thought. The mutant moved in a surly, awkward manner, bobbing and weaving like a duck. He took too many blows to get inside, where he could work his short arms, and yet he was impressive in his clumsy way. He was thorough and decisive, and he was accurate with his hands.

"He can't even kick," I said. "He's already got his face bruised up and it's only the first prelim."

The old man shook his head. For the second time that day he said, "You know not how to look."

The days of the festival fell by, light and swift. I won my preliminaries effortlessly, careful not to take any chances or injure my hands. Each night after a simple meal and a short walk, I went to bed early, my frantic mind filled with the color and excitement of festival.

The night of the semifinal a change was made in the schedule. The two finalists were given the next day off to rest for the final event, a brutal fight in a roped-off area, broken into rounds and rest periods, but fought to the finish. We would wear no padding on hands or feet. I would bruise my knuckles on that one, I thought to myself.

That night I went after dinner to the tavern where the gladiators went to drink and whore. A glass of wine or two wouldn't harm me, with a day off before the fight, or so I told myself.

I saw them in the tavern, through the frenzied dancing couples, by the light of colored lanterns. She held a glass of red wine to her lips; she touched her hair; she smiled at something he said; and seeing me, was it because of seeing me? her smile blossomed. I should like to think that even if she gave her smiles freely, in that one instant, in the Tavern of the Red Lion, she smiled for me alone, before she looked away.

He was drunk, mean drunk. How grotesque he appeared in the muted light of the glowing colored lanterns! He was so broad and so short. The features of his face, already distorted by his twisted genes, were now beaten and bruised, swollen and lumpy. He had not won by the easy road I had taken, but he had won all the same.

When I sat down at their table his head was resting in his arms. He was either singing or crying in a low groaning tone.

"Well, since it's me and you for the purse, I don't see why we can't be civil about it. I'd like to buy you and your lady a drink or two. I'd like to be friends."

He raised his broad ugly face from his arms, and now I saw, with a suppressed shudder, a second pair of hands tensed gripping the table.

"You know how I beat them, pretty boy, how I'm going to beat you?" He spoke so quietly that I could barely hear him.

And now he held out his four arms in the air for my inspection.

"I beat them with these short thick arms, you think. But you're wrong, I beat them because I was born mean. I was born to be hit and hit back. I beat them because I was born a mutant, and I hate every normal son of a bitch alive.

"And do you know, pretty boy, I hate you most of all. Because she smiles for you. Because they all smile for you, when they're laughing at me, when they're frightened of me."

He was speaking softly, almost in a whisper; it was hard to follow him over the raucous dance music in the bar.

She held one of his arms, pleading with him in a soft, worried voice, until suddenly he slapped her viciously across the face.

Her eyes grew even larger in shock; her mouth was open and round, as if to say, "Oh," with a thin trickle of blood from her ripe lower lip, to match the tears which slowly spilled and glistened on her cheeks.

His head slowly sank down, into the tangle of his arms, and he began to mumble once again to himself, in the darkness he had created.

She touched my arm as I rose to leave.

After the fight, when I recreated it in my mind, it seemed that I had done everything with genius. I easily stayed away from him in the early rounds, while he threw frustrating, exhausting punches into the empty air; my footwork was superb. He was even easier to hit than I had imagined. I had my best round in the sixth, when I began to land a series of hard high kicks; it must have seemed only a matter of time until he sank under a sea of blows and exhaustion. At the end of the round they gave me a standing ovation; I already knew I had lost the fight.

I remember the relentless expression in his eyes, the inexhaustible energy expressed by the slope of his shoulders, the opening and closing of his four hands, as he sat across from me in his corner between rounds.

Later, when I could see anything, I could see her. There were many people in the ring but I could see her form, first as a misty ghost in a cloud of pain, then clear; like an angel she was etched against the sky, while I lay on the ground, on my back, defeated.

"He's all right," she said. "Oh, thank the Goddess, he's all right."

And then she was gone, and there was the old man, methodically cleaning my face with a wet cloth, his expression as calm and distant as ever.

"You fought very well," was all he said.

Later that night I was awakened by a pounding on the door. I dragged my aching body out of bed, and through my swollen eyes I made out the form of one of the boys who worked at the tavern across the street.

"The old man's in the tavern and he's pushing the mutant hard, looking for trouble," he told me.

For a while I just stood there, and thought about going back to bed and pretending it was all a bad dream. I felt as if I had been trampled by a horse. Then I ran down the stairs and across the street.

"You're not actually much of a fighter," was the first thing I heard as I opened the door. "You're too stupid," the old man continued loudly. "Oh, it's all right in a ring where they keep inside the rules and someone tells you what to do. But outside the ring you're too stupid to adjust adequately to your environment."

The girl had one of the mutant's four arms, struggling with him, no doubt to save the life of a worthless old fool. The other people in the tavern were silent with shock. They didn't know the old man.

"If you want to wager your purse," he went on, "against this modest purse of mine, and learn, as well, as valuable a lesson as you have taught my young protégé, I will show you the difference between the martial arts and playing games in the ring. I must warn you, though, it will be rough."

The mutant hurled the girl aside and lurched to his feet. He fumbled at his belt and threw his purse on the counter where the old man had set his.

"Where? Where do you want it, old man, here or outside?"

The old man sprang to the counter, scooped up an enormous pitcher of wine and threw it on the mutant's feet, which were, I noticed, encased in new sandals made of slippery leather. Then he tossed a bowl of pepper in his face.

It was brutal and quick. The mutant was coughing and choking from the cloud of pepper, slipping and sliding on the wet floor in his wet shoes, while the old man hopped about like a cricket. He was in rare form, and he fought a brutal fight.

He snatched up a tall stool and prodded the mutant gingerly a couple of times with it to put him further off balance, and then quite suddenly, he struck him a terrible snapping blow on the knee. Almost before the mutant struck the ground, the old man dropped the stool, sprang to him and snatched one of his four wildly flailing arms out of the air. This he whipped viciously in a circle, then let go, and ran back to pick up his stool again.

"Have you had enough," he asked cheerfully, "or must I strike you again with this stool?"

The mutant sat up with an expression of agony. I don't think the leg was broken, but I know the arm was. His other three hands were clenched into fists, his short, massive arms pulsing with muscle. My God, I thought, he's going to try to fight on.

I suppose I intended to come between them, somehow to stop them, and all she saw was me running to aid the old man. I don't know. I only know the mutant's woman lunged at me from the side, and I felt a sharp pain in my arm.

She held the dagger high to show me my own blood.

"I'll kill anyone who touches him. I'll kill you both. Take the purse and get out. Get out." And it seemed to me, with all the pain I felt, the pain from the knife wound, the aching from my beating, the agony of being misunderstood, that on some deeper level of my being I felt a thrill of giddy awe. Somewhere inside my mind the puzzle fell in place, and I knew fully, for the first time in my life, woman in all her mysterious glory.

From then on my memories are like disjointed dreams. My mind was swimming from loss of blood, exhaustion, the beating in the ring, or just the confusion of too much color and too much noise.

Someone, I don't know who, tied up my arm with a scarf; the wound was shallow but painful.

With a strange urgency, I followed a form through the streets. At times I vaguely knew who I followed, at others he was only a shadow. And yet I found him where I somehow knew I would find him, all alone in the middle of that street. The cages were open, empty. Some of the astonished merchants were still counting their coin.

"Is the money all gone, old man?"

Later on, when I thought about him, I liked most to remember him then. He seemed filled with an inexpressible mixture of wild joy and grief. His eyes, I realized with astonishment, were filled with tears. It was the only emotion I had ever seen him show.

"The birds are free," was all he said.

Moments later he seemed to have forgotten them, and he reminded me in his dry voice about the list he had given me.

"The festival's over: one, we went to the festival; two, you fought for the championship; three, we gained the purse; four, if you were alert you should have learned much; of course, the mutant learned much also, I didn't foresee that," he said, apparently worried by this lack of foresight.

When we came to the edge of the city, where the fires died out, where the music of the people gave way and the music of crickets held forth, he turned toward the mountains; but I was young, and I had caught my first glimpse of woman in all her glory.

The last time I saw him, he was moving up the mountain as slender and spry as a youth, and I remember with some bitterness and with some sadness that he never looked back to where I watched him from the road.

A RIGHT-HANDED WRIST

If thy right hand offend thee . . .

Steve Chapman

Artie stood at the staple press in the warehouse, yanking open cardboard boxes and loading them on the press, folding in the bottom flaps; then he slammed down his shoe on the trigger pedal, the pneumatic armature banged the pedestal and rammed brass prongs through dusty cardboard. *Pshkkk.* In the warehouse, Artie was standing, folding the flaps, pressing down his dusty shoe on the leaky pedal, holding each box while the machine slammed in staples, throwing the stiff boxes onto a pile. *Pshkkk.* Artie was standing up, stapling boxes at the warehouse, holding down the bottom flaps while the pneumatic press blew dusty air in his face and rammed staples through cardboard. *Pshkkk.* Artie stood working in the warehouse, throwing empty boxes onto a pile.

The portable radio that hung from the New Kid's belt announced his approach. Artie looked up at him, strolling down the H-500-H-900 aisle. His eyes, under a red bandana, shot to Artie before he even got to the concrete column at the end of the aisle.

He ducked under the steel beams of the shelf and stepped right over to Artie, slinging a pink sheet from inside his belt. The Kid rattled the paper and said, "Your phone's ringing."

"Why is it my phone?"

"You work here."

"You also. You answer it. I answered it twice today. You know what it said? It tapped."

"Bad connection?"

"A tapping noise. You listen."

"Maybe it's Morse code."

"I happen to know Morse code."

The Kid hooked a strand of hair out of his mouth and pushed it over his ear, grinning. "Skilled labor. Am I ever suitably impressed." College punk. "Hey, maybe it's a radio contest. I bet if you say the right words, you win a vacation."

The armature punched four staples through four cardboard flaps. Artie swung a box up onto the pile.

"Art, you made that box upside-down."

The phone stopped ringing.

"Art, if that was the freight manager calling, your ass is plastic grass. Speaking of whom, have a pink slip. Sample order. All that diddley-shit is supposed to be pulled by noon. All for you."

The spring-loaded staple magazine was running low. The air pressure was uneven. A staple jammed up and twisted sideways, wedged all wrong. *Pshkrk.*

"Why me?"

"Years with the firm. You're indispensable. Take the pink slip before my arm falls off."

Artie took the order in his left hand and reached his right arm into the box to unbend the staple from the inside. His index finger snagged on a sharp prong. He couldn't work it loose. He whipped the box to and fro on his arm, tried to shake it loose. Wouldn't shake loose.

"Art, is that your latest attachment? I wish my right arm was so versatile."

Artie grabbed the box under his left elbow and yanked it loose. His right hand gave a sickly whimper through its punctured cuticle. He pulled it out and checked it over. It had self-sealed with no fluid leakage.

"That's real authentic, Art. You know, not every prosthetic gets hangnails. I remember this rubber hand I bought at a novelty shop. . . ."

Artie's plastic third finger was still in fine form hydrodynamically. He held it under the Kid's nose. Vertical.

The Kid laughed and walked to the stencil cutter for a cigarette.

The very first item on the pink slip was a problem. SERIAL # Q-14738 / PRODUCT DESCRIPTION hobbyist models, Glo-Dark Super-Shark Strato-Monitor. Artie had never seen a five-digit item number before, let alone a Q series.

Artie wandered up and down aisles half a city block long, between steel racks three stories high. Scuffling around in his orthopedic nylon shoes, sidestepping pallets loaded with unshipped orders, hopping over jack-handles, Artie explored nooks he'd never even noticed. Inventory tags slid through the focus of his tired eyes. Moonbase Pogocraft. Sunbat Kiteship. Tripontoon Carrier with Conshelf ScubaSled. P-14737. P-14800. Customize Your Own SST. Model T Ford. Stilt-Man. The Human Ear. The Human Lung. Reptiles of the World. Insects of the World . . .

Artie thinking, I'll never find anything in all this crap.

Artie up-angled his eyes, yearning for a clock to say quitting time. Above him, two stories of dusty air and hooded fluorescent tubes. No cranking skylights. He set his elbows on the shelf behind him, hands hanging limp. He bowed his head and stared at his prosthetic, drowsing off, wondering whether it slept when he did.

Artie got to thinking about how he lost his first right hand, the one that came with the rest of him. He thought about the details of the accident. A classic industrial accident.

It was before he worked in shipping—back when he worked in production. Part of his job was mixing colorant powder into barrels of polystyrene granules. His face and arms were always covered with colored dust. Ruby, amber, black, avocado . . . The day of the accident, the injection-molding machines were running amber, and the compression presses were taking ruby. Artie's cheeks were smeared with yellow. His hands looked like sweaty lobster claws.

His main job was feeding the big machines. If their hoppers ran out of plastic, they overheated and broke down. They molded miniature parts, day and night, parts of model kits for kids. Numbered components clustered on stems. Flat twigs of mock machinery. Halves of pistons. Sections of fuselages. Deck A. Wing flap 20. Turret R-1. The presses never stopped crapping them out, heating and recycling, mold and eject, hissing and pounding, water-cooled and pneumatically powered.

Artie was on a stepladder, shoveling granules into the hopper of a compression press. It was steadily turning out a single part for the Mega-Manbot Water Strider set. A very popular model. All the heroes of modern youth seemed to be high-powered machines.

Artie stared into the collection bin of the press, trying to figure out what piece of the Manbot model he was looking at. It couldn't be the cockpit bubble; it wasn't translucent.

Artie figured it out. It was what went inside the cockpit bubble: the pilot. The head and shoulders of a man, mostly covered by helmet, headphones, and goggles. A firm jaw. A resolute mouth.

Hot water trembled inside a rubber hose that hung near Artie's head. It fed under an enamel casing where a temperature gauge was almost in the red. Not his job to fix it. He'd report it to the foreman. He climbed down the stepladder. When the upper side of the mold lifted, he peered in at the lower. One Manbot pilot was mashed on top of another Manbot pilot pancaked over another Manbot pilot that had failed to eject. If the pileup got much bulkier, the mold could be damaged.

He pulled his screwdriver out of his pocket and bent over to dislodge the jam before the next compression cycle. The jam was a stubborn bugger.

Then, instead of his screwdriver at the end of his wrist, he had a compression-molding machine. And a closed mold.

The steady rhythms of factory noise echoed and merged into a buzzing drone in his ears. The hissing of the coolant tube was constant, pure, idiotic. The crack of bones reverberated, a clang of metal bulks not quite touching. With distinct kinesthesia, he felt the skin on his wrist pop and rip, a sliced sausage. Bones crushing themselves to gravel made a crackling in the bursting stink of charred skin and pressure-cooked sinew and the styrene stench of the factory.

He felt molten plastic pump up the veins of his arm. Hot plastic and blood spattered everywhere. The cleanup crew would be mopping and scraping for a week!

Just when he felt his knees give out, some bright foreman saw fit to smash the glass out of a fire-alarm box. An emergency's an emergency, right? The sprinkler system showered him with a fine mist, while he hung by his wrist, until the ejection cycle. They carried him to the loading dock, soaked in grimy broth, for his ride to the hospital.

There he saw a lot of white machines with rubber hoses and tubes and plastic masks and polished metal canisters and white formica counter tops and plastic drinking tumblers and rubber undersheets and rubber bibs on radiologists and see-thru smocks on specialists and a rubber mat on the lobby floor that led to a revolving door, and the next thing he knew, he was stepping through a sliding glass electric-eye door into the plush showroom of the largest prosthetics outlet in the city.

Deep carpets of spun nylon. A wall of grey plexiglas overlooking the parking lot. Recessed fluorescent lights in acoustical ceiling panels. And wood-grain shelves and shelves above and shelves below and more shelves filled with prosthetics, all attractively displayed in styrofoam holders. Here was a patent-pending big toe. Here was an expensive knee, which left the client free to choose the foot of his personal preference. What a selection! Artie thinking, wish I'd brought a date.

All of a sudden, the meditechnical team were all over him with calipers and tape measures.

Wait until you see it, they told him. The Mechand trademark hand is tops in the field. Absolutely. This baby's got every extra in the catalog, they told him. It's more than a hand. It's a job asset. Your earning power is going to soar. And wait until your friends feel your new grip!

Have a look at this photo spread, they told him. The motorized spin-thimble built into the index finger will sink screws or power a wide range of light power tools. The reinforced thumb supports seventy pounds! But most important is the feel. To appreciate that, you've got to try it out at home. No obligation. Only minor implants. A few tests for voltage levels at your motor arcs. A fitting for your shoulder harness. And you're set for life. Guaranteed.

Artie asked for a credit estimate.

Price is no object, they told him. All on the company tab, they assured him. Covered under the group policy.

Artie thinking, I bet I could wangle six fingers out of this deal. Or a secret compartment. Or a decoder ring.

They asked him if he realized how lucky he was to work at a plant with such a generous employee health program. They told him, these babies cost plenty, retail. Plus, you get a month's layoff with full salary to use as a period of adjustment.

Artie thinking, nice idea. I'll learn to jack off lefty.

The first thing he did after installation was to flex his new fingers in and out and listen to the tiny motors whir, forward and reverse. Then he figured out how to crack his knuckles. The report carried a city block.

Artie would get to wondering what happened to the hand the interns removed. Was it floating in a jar for med students to gawk at? Or did they throw it away?

Artie thought about that for a while. Somewhere, in some

zip-locked plastic bag of hospital garbage, in with the pussy swabs and the left-over biscuits . . .

Artie thinking, why do I even think about this?

Q-14738. The inventory tag was dangling from a steel upright across the aisle from Artie. Fine! A start. But there was no pallet of Q-14738 boxes at ground level.

Artie dragged a stepladder to the spot and stepped up for a look at the second shelf. No luck.

Artie fetched an aluminum staircase on coasters that would let him read the stenciling on top of the boxes at the third level. The coasters snagged on some loose excelsior, but he wrestled the thing into position and climbed it. No Q-14738.

He'd need somebody to ride him up to fourth level on the fork lift.

Artie cupped his palms to his mouth and bellowed. "Hey, Kid!" One thing you had to give the New Kid: he could handle a lift truck like it was part of him—steer around any jam, swivel that fork into the tightest spaces, drag an overloaded pallet back out a narrow aisle, full throttle reverse, all the time lowering the merchandise without even looking at it. The Kid could drive.

The truck rumbled around a corner and slammed to a standstill inches behind Artie's back. The heat rash on his neck prickled in a wash of exhaust.

The Kid slung his leg over a canister of propane fuel. "Need a lift?"

"Can we put a pallet up front?"

"*Psh* . . . You scared to fall off? Come on. I want to punch out."

Artie clenched his hands. His right gave a bleat and a whimper, resealing itself.

"Aw, Art, we got the little thing upset! You still want to look for your sample?"

Artie set his left shoe on the right prong of the truck. The prong was no wider than the shoe. He stepped onto the other prong.

"We're off!" the Kid yelled, and the truck lunged down the

aisle, motor knocking. Artie clamped his hands to the rumbling chassis.

"No, I just want to go up!"

"Too late. You got a free ride coming." The Kid shook his hair out behind him. Propane fumes reeked. The truck took two abrupt corners in one whirl of front-axle steering. "Hold on tight. Letting her out on the stretch."

The roller-wheels jumped a smashed carton. Artie could see himself bucked off his perch. He grabbed the safety bars that caged the driver's platform.

"Once around the racks, Art, that's all you're good for. Going up."

With no framework of boards beneath his feet, only the steel fork, Artie was heading for the ceiling. The lift engine whined. The cold cement floor and the Kid's grinning face shot away below him. No hand-holds to brace him, only the shelves rushing past. His shoes vibrated, rising beneath him, then jolted to a dead stop. He was standing at the fourth level.

No Q-14738. Artie hunkered over and rummaged. Nothing. He lifted his eyes.

Overhead, the worn slats of a skewed fiberboard pallet.

Who'd put a pallet on top of the whole rack? Who'd invent a fifth level, just for him? Without looking down, he shouted, "Can you take me any higher?"

A faraway voice: "Can't be done."

He'd have to climb. So he climbed. A firm two-handed grip on the topmost strut of the rack, three stories tall. A heave. A hoist of the leg. He rolled onto his back on the pallet. It didn't teeter. The ceiling was a yard away.

He turned his head. One carton. No label. He reached for it to break it open and look inside.

"Art? You still up there? What would you do if I knocked off work for the day, ha ha ha?"

"What would you do if I dropped a box on your head?"

"I don't have to listen to insults!"

The Kid revved up the truck and rolled away.

What crap, Artie murmuring and reaching to wedge his fingers under the carton flap.

Just then a finger tapped Artie on the neck.

Funny, the things that ran through Artie's head sometimes. Like the time he walked into the downtown prosthetics workshop, late for his periodic manual maintenance check. Before he could even take a number, the meditechnical team had him laid out on a foam rubber couch. Trained professionals jostled around him, a precise blur of smocks, tongue depressors, ammeters, jowls, bifocals, forceps, a test-your-grip machine . . .

How's the old Mechand holding up, they asked him. Bet it doesn't respond the way it used to. *Hm.* Got a deep bruise on the Mount of Jove.

A sticky drawer, Artie explained.

A meditech in a white cap shook her head over Artie's palm and told him there wasn't much future in the hand.

They shook it. It rattled.

Of course, they could overhaul and realign. But would it be worthwhile in the long run, they asked.

Artie explained that he was still making payments on the Radio Feedback Package for the hand.

Do you really want to be stingy about your own hand, they asked. Our suggestion? Replace the old and move up to the latest: the Synthand. A unique achievement in software. The Synthand's movement mechanism is a sinewy net of hydrodynamic mesh, responsive to your wrist through a chemosensitive pad applied over the tiniest of neurolectric cyber-fiber implants.

No printed circuits. No noisy motors. No recharging. Fantastic styling. The sleek line of the thumb. The manicure.

Artie flipped through the brochure. Fashionable! Women prefer . . . Sensual dermal tonus! Executive material tells . . .

There are people these days, they told him, people who beg for an amputation every time they so much as gash their knuckles.

And why? They'd like to be toting a Synthand.

Granted, the period of adjustment is delicate. The instrument is delicate! It has to attune itself to your Na/K balance, your biorhythms, your reflex arcs . . . But it's worth it.

Artie thinking, I feel like I'm getting married.

He only wanted to know one thing: What happens to the Mechand?

Reconditioning. It can be sold used. It'll sure help you finance the Synthand. Somebody's bound to want a strong hand. Look in the classifieds. There's a Wanted To Buy list a yard long of crippl—disabl—prosthetized persons.

It's progress, they told him. Personal progress. What else is there in life but self-improvement?

There was definitely a finger tapping Artie's neck. It seemed to want his attention. So he rolled onto his other elbow to have a look.

At the edge of the pallet, the abandoned Mechand stood on its stump, poised in a nest of frayed straps and rusty buckles, oil smears glinting across flesh-tone tatters in the glare of buzzing fluorescent fixtures.

Artie scrambled back onto his knees and nearly banged his head on a pipe.

Artie thinking, well, well, I didn't expect to meet you here. The last time I saw you, they had you laid out in subsections at the workshop. I guess you're still tuned to my frequency. What a surprise.

The Mechand's gestures were considered and precise. It curled its index finger, beckoning Artie, then pointed straight between his eyes, and revved its drill bit.

Artie edging away, thinking, you don't seem happy. Rough trip crosstown? Anything I can do for you? Anything at all?

Artie dropped the box of Q-14738. It rattled out of sight through a gap between the pallet's slats.

The Mechand shaped itself into a vise and crouched over the

nearest slat. Fiberboard buckled. Splinters curled. The Mechand wrenched up a length of slat and began a slow, steady pounding on the pallet.

Artie trying to think, I appreciate your loyalty, old hand, but honestly, all positions have been filled. Where would I put you? An elbow . . . My left . . . You can't.

He pressed the Synthand to his forehead. It whinnied and trembled, covered in gooseflesh. The Mechand tossed aside the slat and clutched at it. Artie held the hand over his head, where it hissed and sputtered. Three stories below, the slat hit cement.

The Mechand snapped its fingers demandingly with a resounding clang and flying sparks.

Artie getting a firm left-handed grip on the Synthand, thinking, all right, Artie will ride the Mechand on his arm, but only for a while. You'll have to take turns.

He worked the limp Synthand loose, against all its noisy sucking. When the last adhesive snapped, it felt good as picking an old scab.

The Mechand opened its palm to him. Artie heaved the Synthand whistling through the dusty air. The Mechand hopped up and snagged it, a perfect catch, and fell on its back. The two hands lay in a pile, knitting and reknitting their fingers. A whiff of ethyl alcohol mingled with the smell of burnt oil.

Artie thinking, go on, fight it out between you. I never cared for either one of you.

The fingers disengaged. The hands lay on their sides, joined at the wrist. The two-handed wrist stood up on its ten fingers and scuttled to the brink of the pallet.

Artie watched them flip-flop all the way down the side of the rack, holding onto the steel upright with the Mechand, then the Synthand, letting go with the Synthand, then the Mechand. He glimpsed the two of them scurrying down the aisle. They broke stride for a caper, somersaulted a zigzag and rolled on their axis. Artie closed his eyes, feeling dizzy, thinking, I don't blame them, I don't blame them. A lovely couple.

Artie wondered how the two became attracted. A freak com-
plementarity of hormones and guidance telemetry? A certain
scent? What did they have in common? Artie's motor nervous
profile? Or had they sensed each other from afar, even in the
factory, before he came between them?

Artie imagined the heroic journey of the escaped Mechand—
hiding on rooftops, hanging under bridges, clambering across
phone lines. They would do very well without him. They would
thumb a ride to a forest preserve and set up housekeeping in a
cozy dovecote, on top of a post with an embossed plastic label to
tell all the tourists their names.

He didn't blame them. They had no use for him.

He stretched out on the pallet, scratching his back on the slats.
He pulled a smoke from his shirt pocket and a matchbook from
his pants. Striking a light was a challenge, one-handed, but he
managed. He scratched his wrist. It hadn't been uncovered for
months. He rubbed it hard. It felt good.

Artie wondered how he was going to get down.

"THEY MADE US NOT TO BE AND THEY ARE NOT"

Perhaps Kona was a planet where knowledge had
not yet "brought death into the world, and all our woe."
In that case—and you will have to draw your own
conclusions about this—could the Serpent be
represented by a group of squabbling, irritable little
people who only wanted to get back to Earth?

Philippa C. Maddern

Biren was worried about the shuttle's power pack, and was preparing to dismantle it; but that was no reason for the others to
be idle. Erring volunteered to help Biren, and the rest set off on
foot; Alissin and Gerold to collect plant and rock samples respec-
tively, and Jon and Hanna to contact the Konans. Kona was a very
quiet planet. Though they were walking in opposite directions,
Hanna could hear Gerold's voice for a long time, as he proved
conclusively to Alissin that the rule that no explorer should work
alone on a Class B planet was outmoded, impractical, and un-
necessary. Nevertheless, Hanna noticed, he kept beside Alissin
all the time. She thought how glad she was that this was the last
planetfall of the tour. The prospect of not having to put up with
the idiosyncrasies of five other people in close association—not
Gerold's carping, nor Erring's incessant and excessive helpful-
ness, nor even Biren's habitual little grunt—was like daylight at

149

the end of a steep stony tunnel. A very interesting tunnel, thought Hanna, entered of one's own free will, and not nearly so monotonous as life on postwar Terra—but confining, nonetheless. I could be home in six weeks or so, she thought; but knew instantly that the word "home" was mockery from the subconscious. Postwar Terra, with the great rice-producing plains of Asia still wasting year by year from the effects of Enemy bombardment, and the worry over fast-dwindling food sources apparent everywhere in mean-minded husbanding of resources, was a poor cold home to go to. The castle of the victorious, crammed with brand new instruments and ships of war; but with empty larders, and surrounded by salted fields. Words floated into Hanna's mind from a poem written by one of her Linguistic Course friends—"An alien sower came forth to sow our Earth/ With killing seed; it fell upon good ground/And yielded up a minus-thousand-fold . . ."

She became aware of Jon's voice, finishing a question; ". . . isn't it?"

"Sorry? Daydreaming, I'm afraid."

"This is the right direction, isn't it?"

"Should be. If we keep in line with the shuttle and the edge of that bluff, we'll run into what was a large settlement a hundred and fifty years ago."

"Kona years?"

"Yes."

"Hope they're not nomads."

"The reports don't say so," said Hanna wearily, wondering why she continued to fall into the trap of reassuring Jon after two years' close working knowledge of him. A sharp, steady breeze was flowing down from the snow-capped mountains to their right, and the long plain of grass rippled endlessly before it. Ahead of them stretched the bluff, darkly forested; the sky beyond was a clear steely blue. Each colour so exact, thought Hanna —the jointed grass a dark khaki, the pine-green of the trees, the even grey-blue skies. She wanted to consider it further, but Jon was talking again.

"Not a very good report on this one. Even scrappier than the usual prewar type, don't you think?"

Hanna considered (hearing all the time the loud *whish-whish* made by two pairs of feet through the sturdy grass). "Better for me than for you," she said at last. "The language section was the best, but yes, the rest was a bit sketchy."

"Think you'll be able to make yourself understood?"

"Yes," said Hanna patiently (thinking, No birds. I haven't seen any birds. Even on Terra there are some birds left. No wonder it's so quiet here). She added aloud, "I have on all the other planets on this tour."

"What about Achwa?" Jon reminiscently rubbed at the scar on his arm where an Achwan missile had caught him.

"They *understood* us all right. They just didn't *like* us. Prewar survey must have mucked that one up." (And Jon should have been more careful, she thought. It's hard enough to train ethnologists now without them throwing their lives away.)

Jon grunted. "Hope the same thing doesn't happen here while the shuttle's out of action."

No answer. Hanna resolutely fought the impulse to remind Jon that the reports clearly stated the Konans to be "markedly nonaggressive."

"Quiet, isn't it?" he said.

"*Hm.*"

A curious feeling came to Hanna that she and Jon were shrinking under the cold sky, tramping futilely across an unending plain, struggling against the rippling grass as against an immutable current, towards a forest as unattainable as one on a vidscreen.

"It's a long way," said Jon, perhaps feeling something of the same thing.

They trudged on in silence, listening to the steady swish of feet in the grass.

But it was no more than five minutes later that a movement appeared at the edge of the belt of trees, and they knew that the Konans had come to meet them. Both of them, as if by reflex, made little preparatory movements—Jon pulled down the sleeves of his anorak, and Hanna straightened her customary slouch an inch or two. By tacit consent, they slowed down, waiting for the Konans to come up to them. Hanna ran through the stock Konan greeting of a hundred and fifty years ago in her mind. One had to have the mental preparation right—the hairline balance between knowing the phrase exactly, and being prepared to pick up the modifications in the answer. She noted that the Konans apparently still rode Konanhorses. At least the report had prepared them for that.

There were now thirty or forty Konans riding towards them, strung out along the plain in a swift-moving skein. The horses were very tall, and so white that the fleeting shadows on their bodies looked blue. The plain shook softly under their hooves. In a very little time they were near enough for Hanna to see clearly the pale calm face and long hands of the leading rider; and suddenly she felt obscurely resentful that they should so easily and quickly cross the plain that she and Jon had toiled across. Yet at the same time, the beauty of form and movement, the pale changing bow of horsemen over the dark grass pierced into her mind, startling up a flock of shining memories too frail and quick for recognition, but too potent to be ignored.

The foremost riders cried aloud to their horses (they were all riding bareback and bridleless) and stopped no more than three paces from Hanna and Jon. In less than a minute, the other riders, with undisciplined precision, came to rest in a half-circle around the two Terrans. There was silence.

Jon said sardonically, *"After* you."

"We are from Terra, and we bring you greeting," said Hanna. Now that they were all together, she noticed how alike they were, all tall, all classically-featured, all with dark plaits swinging as thick as their wrists. There was no obvious leader to speak to; she addressed the whole group.

And the whole group answered her, with a kind of subdued clamour, not in chorus, but as if each one replied to her individually and simultaneously. Their faces, she saw, were no longer calm; they were twisted in some strong emotion—anger? bewilderment? joy?—no time or use in speculating. Hanna said above the many voices (aware of her mind automatically adapting her words to the epic quality of the language), "If you would converse, let one among you speak, and we will hear."

The group fell silent again. Then hesitantly, after several false starts, one voice sounded. Hanna saw Jon's gaze flicking round to find the speaker, while she concentrated on the words.

"They made us not to be, and they are not," said the voice from one of the group; and when Hanna did not immediately reply, the others chimed in, as if in canon. "They made us not to be . . . they made us not . . . and they are not . . . they made us . . . they made us . . . are not . . . to be . . . are not . . ."

"Who are 'they'?" asked Hanna loudly. But it was no good. The Konans seemed preoccupied with their own words; over and over again, "They made us not to be . . . they made us not . . . they are not . . ."

Jon said, "I'm right, am I? That is what they're saying?" and Hanna nodded. The simple sentence was well within his knowledge. It's just like the voices on tape, she thought uneasily, and wondered what kind of methods the Konans had for passing on language. She said loudly, "Will you hear us?" There was silence for a moment, but the voices started again almost immediately—"They made us not, they made us not, to be, to be, and they are not . . ."

"From where did they come?" asked Hanna desperately, seeking the right phrase to break the lock. "What did they do?" and "To whom do you speak?"

But the Konans seemed almost to have forgotten them. It made no difference what Hanna said to them, or indeed whether she spoke or remained silent. They stayed in their group, chanting, sometimes riding their horses to and fro a few paces. Long after the two Terrans had given up, for the time being, the attempt to communicate, and started the long walk back to the shuttle in the cold evening, the Konan voices floated back over the plain, clear and desolate in the deepening dusk. "They made us not to be, and they are not . . ."

The team discussed the situation that night, talking endlessly, circularly, and almost fruitlessly about it in the cramped control room of the shuttle. Biren had the engineer's annexe littered with power-pack components, but announced with unruffled cheerfulness that there was very little she could do with them, and that she doubted very much whether the shuttle was fit to fly. That knowledge gave the whole discussion a perceptibly uneasy background.

"You mean we're stuck here?" said Gerold in an offended tone.

Biren grunted, and said that all she needed was another power pack, and that she had already called up orbit craft to send another shuttle down with extra ones.

"I *thought*," said Gerold, heavily sarcastic, "that engineers were supposed to check our shuttles before we all happily fly off to unknown planets with them."

"Not my fault," said Biren, unmoved. "If the morons upstairs will stock an A4 shuttle with A3 substitute blocks, I can't do anything but swear at them, and I've done that."

Gerold snorted. Both he and Alissin, Hanna thought, seemed to have been affected, like her, by the peculiarly intractable feel of the planet. They had come back late and tired, Gerold making remarks about "blasted planets where you walk all day and get nowhere," and Alissin saying that she hardly seemed to have done anything in a whole day's work. As if to disprove the point, she was now sitting at the side desk, laying out specimens.

Hanna came out of reverie to hear Jon saying, "It's ridiculous. We've never failed to make contact yet."

She said, "We've made contact. We just don't understand what they're saying."

"You must have got it wrong," said Gerold accusingly.

Hanna let Jon indignantly deny this, and give his opinion that the words were probably some form of ritual.

Gerold said, "Listen to our clever University ethnologist. Give a thing a name and think you understand it," and Jon subsided.

Before the pause became too awkward, Hanna said, "I know I'm not an ethno, but it didn't look like a ritual to me. It was all so—unplanned. Or it looked like that, don't you think, Jon? And why should they have a ritual especially for meeting us?"

"Could be for meeting any strangers."

"Attaboy," muttered Gerold, "my theory right or wrong."

Erring said hastily, "It's only first meeting, after all. You can't be expected to get very far in one meeting."

"Yes, but if only they'd take some notice of us." Jon's voice rose and cracked in frustration.

"Well, they did," said Hanna. "They came to meet us, and responded to a greeting. It's just that we don't understand the notice they take of us."

Jon snapped out, "Oh, *stop* saying we don't understand. We know that, you fool—" and then, in the dreadful pause that followed, "Sorry. But you know what I mean."

Erring said understandingly, "That's okay. That's okay. We know it's hard on you not having a job to go on with."

Biren said, "Do we have to make a really good contact? What's the priority rating of this place?"

Alissin looked up from her plant specimens. "It's quite high. Eight point five, or something like that."

"Have we had any higher than that this trip?"

Everyone tried to repress exasperated sighs. Biren was notoriously vague about anything not directly concerning the working of the ship. Erring said kindly, "Only Vanging, and that was so good the colonists are already going out there."

"How would this one compare with it?"

"We can't tell yet," said Alissin calmly. "The air's very good, and the climate should be all right, but that's about as far as we've got. Oh, and Gerold says the mineral deposits could be all right."

"I did not. I said *some* rock formations like the ones we saw give good results."

Alissin shrugged.

"Don't need to talk to the locals anyway," said Biren, persevering. "It's a big enough planet. Colonists just keep out of the way."

Both Hanna and Jon started to speak, and stopped. "Go on," said Hanna.

"It's too dangerous," said Jon. "They did that three or four times prewar, and none of them really worked. One lot of colonists got massacred about seven years after they arrived, and no one knows why even now, and another lot started a civil war without meaning to, and I forget what happened to the others, but they didn't work out."

"Wouldn't have any trouble with these if all they can do is sit round and talk nonsense."

In the small room, the irritated snorts from Hanna and Jon were perfectly audible. "You know, Biren," said Erring brightly, "I do think Jon and Hanna are right there. After all, this 'making people not to be' could mean killing or dying."

"Well, why didn't they say so?" said Gerold, aggrieved.

"It could be rit—" began Jon, and stopped.

Hanna said slowly, "You know, that's funny. I don't think the language tapes gave the Kona words for 'kill,' or 'die,' or 'dead.' And they're on the standard lists, and the tapes were almost complete."

"And I suppose if you were an ethno, you would conclude from that, the locals are immortal?" said Gerold, sarcastic again. But Hanna did not even hear him. Her lips moved soundlessly, checking off the known vocabulary of the Kona language.

Erring looked pointedly at the clock, and said, "It's getting late. Are we standing watch tonight?"

"Yes, we are," said Gerold. "I wouldn't trust these local bastards as far as I could kick them."

Biren yawned and grunted. "You don't trust anyone that far, so why worry?"

Erring said immediately, "I'll go first watch if you like. Hour and a quarter each? That'd take us till about dawn here, and we can't do much until then."

In silence, the other five climbed into rest suits, and disposed themselves around the floor of the small cabin.

In the middle of the long night, Hanna, sitting watching the red eyes of the alarm system, thought she could hear the chant of Kona voices over the plain. It was too faint to distinguish the words, but inevitably the sentence began in her mind, "They made us not to be, and they are not." She thought again of the rangy white horses and tall riders galloping together effortlessly over the endless plain, and a phrase floated up in her mind— "sea-white, boundlessly beautiful." After a little consideration, she tracked it down as a reference to Peter Beagle's unicorn, in a course she had done on mid-twentieth-century fantasy. She thought of Beagle's unicorns, immortality and beauty and power incarnate, and because of it, almost irrevocably beyond petty mortal transactions. And suddenly the thought came that even a unicorn could be no whiter, no lovelier, no more unreachable, than a Konanhorse. Outside, the chant went on, as thin as the wind. Hanna felt all at once desperately lonely. She thought, I wish we could talk properly. We didn't discuss anything tonight, only scored off each other and refused to face issues. What are we doing, anyway, summing up planets at one a month? We're none of us properly trained or prepared for what we do.

The image of white horses galloping over a dark plain kept breaking into her mind.

The next day Biren elected to go with Alissin and Gerold, and Erring decided to come with Jon and Hanna. Once more they tramped through the dark-green grass, and it was no easier than the first time. The breeze was, if anything, stronger than yesterday's, and colder, more like a river; it quenched even Erring's bright conversation. But this time they could see, even as they set out, the huddle of horses and riders, and the chant came clearly to meet them.

Hanna said, "They must have been at it all night. I heard them during my watch."

"Well, at least we know they don't feel the cold," said Jon. His voice had a resentful edge to it, and his teeth were chattering.

This time the Konans did not come to meet them; but as the three Terrans approached, the group rearranged itself as effortlessly as before into a half-circle facing them. The chant had changed. Hanna could hear that, but in the confusion of voices she could catch only indistinct phrases. She said quickly, seizing the initiative, "We give you greeting. Will you speak with us?"

As before, the Konans had difficulty in allowing one voice to speak alone; but in the end, enough Konans fell silent to make the message understandable. Two or three voices said, "Why did they make us not to be, and why are they not?"

Hanna could hear Jon swearing under his breath; but sudden illumination had come to her. It had taken the Konans all night to reach this question from their previous statement; were they simply very slow conversers, assimilating new ideas only extremely gradually? She said cautiously, "You wish to know why they made you not to be, and why they are not?"

This time, the response was instant. "Yes, we wish to know . . . why did they make us not? . . . we wish to know . . . not to be . . . they are . . . why are they not? . . . we wish to know . . ." She had the reassuring sense of being accepted into their joint comment.

"What did you say?" asked Erring, and she told him briefly the conversation, and her conclusions. "If I'm right, we can manage now," she finished off. "We just have to take things very slowly —say a new modification every couple of hours, though that may be rushing it a bit."

"Every two hours!" Jon was almost shouting. "We can't take that long—it'd take us months—we're supposed to be home next month—we haven't got time—"

Erring patted him on the shoulder and said, "Okay. Okay. Take it easy. We'll work it out."

Hanna said curtly, "Well, we can only go at their pace. If we don't finish in time, it's too bad." Half of her mind was listening intently for any change in the Konan chant; she felt quite incapable of dealing with Jon's problems at the same time. An undercurrent of irritation set up in her mind; against Jon, who was supposed to be interested in aliens, against the dreadful burden of continually adapting to extraterrestrial conditions, against Terran bureaucrats concerned only to push off the munthly quota of colonists from their depleted planet. Deliberately she turned her full concentration to the Konans.

The day dragged wearisomely to a cold end. At dusk the Terrans were very tired; but the Konans seemed perfectly untouched by cold or fatigue, and equally incurious about the state of their visitors. Again, Hanna felt a stab of resentment toward them for their easy mastery of their environment, and wished illogically that one of them would shiver, or drop out and go to sleep, give any indication of something like human endurance. But they continued to sit their tall white horses easily, unhurriedly, apparently untiring.

Still, as she explained to Erring while they tramped back to the shuttle, they had made progress. It appeared that by "they," the Konans meant the prewar survey team. They had made the Konans not to be with—Hanna thought—something like laser guns or flamethrowers. The Konans called it "flying flame." All this had happened "many sun-turns" past, but the Konans seemed unable to say how many.

"But what do they want to know?" asked Erring. "Are they afraid we'll start firing flamethrowers at them too?"

"Oh, I don't think they're frightened of us . . ." Hanna paused, and said at last, uncertainly, "I don't know what they want. They say they don't understand—over and over again, that they don't understand."

"What—they don't understand aggression? That would make sense. The report says they're nonaggressive."

Hanna hesitated again. It was, as far as it went, a good and probably correct answer. "What did you think, Jon?" she asked finally.

Jon said sullenly, "I don't think any of this talk is going to get us anywhere. I think we need the Dixon-Ehrmann approach."

"Which is?"

"The practical nonverbal thing. You live with the people you're studying twenty-four hours a day, and copy their every movement."

Hanna was very tired from long hours of concentration, and very cold. The words snapped out before she could stop them. "Well, (a), if you're going to follow their every movement, you'll have to talk like crazy, and (b), what sort of a horseman do you think you are? Could you ride one of these bloody great brutes for forty hours at a stretch?"

Erring said brightly, "I wonder if Alissin and Gerry have found anything useful today?"

Alissin and Gerold had achieved nothing in their day's work but fatigue and frustration; and Biren had conceived a great dislike of Kona. "Nasty place. Feels too big," she said, cryptically but with decision.

"It can't feel any bigger than it is, and it's about the same size as Terra, so what are you babbling about?" said Gerold.

"Didn't say it was bigger. It just feels bigger."

Hanna said, "Actually, I know what you mean. It feels as if we can't handle it. Every time I look at that blasted plain, I don't think I'm going to be able to get anywhere if I start walking across it. And the people are the same. They've been sitting on those horses for a day and a half now, and they don't even seem to be tired. It's as if the whole thing's on a bigger and stronger scale than we are. As if we were trying to talk to angels or something."

"Back on the old immortality kick, are we?" said Gerold unpleasantly. But Alissin said, ignoring him, "Do you really mean that, Hanna? I mean, have you got any evidence, or are you just saying it?"

A pause; then Hanna said, "Fifty-fifty. It is the way I feel, but there are a few things it would fit in with. This language business

—they don't have a word for 'die,' or 'death,' or not one that I can find. It must be very rare, if there is one. And the language has hardly changed at all since those tapes were made. That's odd. Even in a really highly literate society, it should have changed in a hundred and fifty years. And this thing they keep talking about. It must be the time of the first survey, because they keep saying 'creatures like you,' and they haven't been visited since then. But they use 'we' all the time when they talk about it, and it really means personal involvement in Konan. They've got a different pronoun to mean 'our group in general.' And they just are stronger than we are. They've been on those horses for a day and a half nonstop, and they don't look like wanting to rest. And they move faster, and they seem to have such a lot of time to talk, as if they know there's no hurry at all. Things like that, that I suppose you can explain, but they make a funny impression over-all. Why? Have you—?"

Alissin balanced a slide thoughtfully on one finger. "Oh, just a few odd things, as you say. I can't find any plants with seeds, though it should be autumn-equivalent here. Well, there are lots of ways for plants to reproduce, but I wish I could find traces of some. I mean, if reproduction is at all frequent, there should be traces. And some of the cell structures are odd. I know I haven't got the proper facilities here, but it does make you wonder."

"Yes, doesn't it."

Gerold said, "When we've quite finished the wish-fulfillment, could we possibly get down to possibilities?"

Alissin said tartly, "It's quite possible, and it's not wish-fulfilment. Life extension's been a theoretical possibility since the twentieth century on Terra, and the only reason we haven't got it now is that when it came to the point of doing it commercially, people apparently *weren't* willing to risk it." She added thoughtfully, "They did it by lowering the temperature, too, and this is a coldish planet."

Gerold said, "You're just being unscientific about this, Hanna. Are you suggesting these locals are some kind of spirits—don't eat, don't sleep, don't rest, don't shit—"

Alissin said calmly, "We didn't say anything of the sort. They probably do all those things—though I suppose they might do them at much longer intervals than we expect—but at the moment we simply don't know. I expect Hanna will find out later."

Gerold said loudly, "Well, I'll believe in immortality when I see it." No one answered him, but Hanna heard Alissin mutter, "You could try opening your eyes."

On the third day, Jon refused to go out of the shuttle, on the ground that Hanna was making no progress in talking to the Konans, and would make none until she came round to the Dixon-Ehrmann method. Alissin said she would not go out with Gerold because he talked too much. Erring promptly offered to go with Gerold, and Hanna and Alissin set out together. Hanna found herself almost hating the plains, wondering half-savagely if even an Enemy bombardment could have shrivelled their aloof expanses down to a manageable condition.

Today the Konans had moved a little farther from the shuttle. Hanna moved delicately around to asking them why, and was informed by several voices that this was a settlement. Hanna and Alissin looked round them, but could see nothing but a few humps and hollows, evenly covered with the tough Konan grass. The sequence teased up another memory in Hanna's mind; again, too faint a one for instant reference, but demanding to be shelved for further thought.

In the midst of a long Konan disquisition on the incomprehensibility of the Terran prewar survey, Alissin nudged Hanna's arm. "Do you know what's strange about their faces?" she said.

"No."

"They're all quite symmetrical."

Hanna said irritably, "Of course they are. If they only had one eye, maybe we wouldn't call them humanoids."

"No, I don't mean that. It's what makes them look nonhuman, actually. I mean their faces are perfectly regular. One side's a mirror image of the other."

Hanna looked at the Konans, rapt in saying repeatedly, "Why did they cease to be? It cannot be understood." She saw that Alissin was right. All the faces were as regular as that of a classical statue; it made them look curiously immobile. She thought, Even in little things they are perfect. Not so much as a quirked eyebrow among them. Alissin said, "Biological engineering at some stage, perhaps."

That day, Hanna gathered that some of the prewar team had died trying to follow the Konans up the mountains (which had bewildered and distressed the Konans a good deal), but that some had died in even more distressing—but unspecified—circumstances. Yes, they said repeatedly, they themselves, these people now talking, had seen and spoken with members of the prewar team—"they who looked and talked like you." And at that, some of the Konans began to run their fingers up and down their forearms, in a quick tattoo, and the chant became "Like you, like you, little and short and quick like you." By the end of the day, Hanna's stomach was aching with tension.

She said to Alissin as they tramped back, "You don't remember ever reading about people—I think they're legendary, and I have a feeling it's old British—who outlived their towns, and lived on for centuries as spirits among overgrown heaps of rubble?"

Alissin said, "Not my field, but you wouldn't be thinking of the Danaans, would you? Irish? I had a really old micro of Irish legends when I was a kid."

Hanna nodded slowly. "That would be it. Remind you of anything?"

Alissin indicated the Konans with her chin.

"They were immortal too."

Alissin said flatly, "Only an analogy."

When they got back to the shuttle they found Jon holding forth on the Dixon-Ehrmann method as if it were the key to an eternal paradise.

On the fourth day Hanna raised the problem of a report. As she pointed out, they were halfway through their first week on

Kona, and the preliminary report on an eight point five priority planet would be expected very shortly after that.

Gerold said shortly, "We can't file one. Haven't had any opportunity to move around, so the data's too limited."

"That's silly. We have to put in a report," said Biren.

Alissin said, "I did once hear of a team that didn't. They got all their leave cancelled, and were told to get one out double quick. Then they didn't manage that either."

"What happened to them?" asked Jon, not quite carelessly.

"Oh, they just got told to go back and try again. Well, it was a hell of a planet, and they couldn't communicate with the locals, and there were all sorts of funny things wrong with the balance of the elements. So they flipped on and off it every month for three years before they finished."

There was complete silence in the shuttle. Alissin added apologetically, "It was meant to be a funny story, but it was quite true. I looked up the reports on it."

Everyone looked studiously at the floor. Finally Gerold said, "All right then, we'll put out a report that it's a suitable planet as far as we know."

His words tripped and fell miserably into the general stillness. Hanna and Alissin looked at each other. Both shook their heads, infinitesimally. Gerold said loudly, "All agreed on that?"

Jon said, "Do we all have to write a section as usual?"

"Well, if you think I'm going to use my best forged identiprint just for you—"

"Of course we'll have to put in a caution about the temperature and so on," said Erring hastily.

"And what do you mean by 'and so on'?"

"Well, I do think—"

"Wonderful! What *else* can you do?"

Hanna said, "You may as well stop squabbling. I won't contribute to any report like that one, or have my identiprint on it. Alissin, will you—?"

"No, I won't either."

Gerold hesitated, decided visibly on bluff, and shouted, "Why not? Give me one good reason why not!"

Hanna felt suddenly detached and exhilarated by the need to speak the clear truth. "You've got a lot more than one reason. Look at us—we haven't been here a week, and we're all on razor-edges, and you're willing to send in a false report just to get off the place as quickly as you can. How would you feel if you were a colonist, stuck here for a lifetime? *And* we know the first survey ran into trouble, and we don't yet know how, and we think we may be dealing with immortals, or at least incredibly long-lived and hardy people—"

"You've got no evidence for that—"

"What about the linguistic evidence? What evidence would you accept if you don't accept that?"

"*Any* solid biological stuff—only I notice your tame biologist hasn't produced any yet, trying to make us believe these local bastards are some kind of spirit, don't need any source of energy, anything to eat—"

Alissin started to speak, but Hanna, her detachment submerged in anger, was too intent on answering to let her into the interchange. "We haven't had time to make the necessary communications to carry out biological tests on the Konans and that itself backs up the linguistic evidence for longevity—"

"*That's* a lie—"

"It's damn good evidence at the very least—"

"In *your* mind, perhaps—"

"And yours—"

Suddenly the whole cabinful seemed to be shouting, dividing to take sides for and against Hanna. She shouted above the noise, "*And you can't accept it—*"

Gerold looked round for something to throw, found a pile of Alissin's plastiglas slides, and hurled them straight at Hanna's face. Hanna ducked, and the slides clattered sharply down the wall in the sudden silence.

Hanna said, "Not to be overdramatic, but do you see what I

mean about unusual degrees of tension?"

Gerold said stiffly, "No, I do not."

"Anyway," said Alissin, "there's the food problem. I haven't found any grain or fruit crops here, and that means importing a lot, at least to start off with. And if Terra had enough resources to do that, we wouldn't be racing around looking for ideal planets."

"We can put any reasonable caution in the report. All I object to is this silly talk of immortal locals."

Erring said, "Gerold, do you have some interest in not believing in immortality?" (That's the first time I've ever heard Erring try to be unkind, thought Hanna uneasily.)

Gerold grinned savagely, and said, "Not half the interest you have in thinking I have," and added for good measure, "Little group-therapy specialist."

In the silence, they listened to one another's breathing, and heard, unwillingly, the faint chanting of the Konans, far over the plain.

On the fifth and sixth days, Jon came out with Hanna again, evidently impelled by the need to write up his preliminary report. "After all," he said, "they'll want it pretty soon now, don't you think?"

Hanna did not reply. The elation of telling Gerold unwelcome truths had worn off long ago. She felt depressed, guilty, and uncertain.

"Of course, you won't have to write much. The language report from the first survey was so good."

"I won't write anything. I told you, I'm not putting in a report. At least not if Gerold writes what I think he will."

Jon glanced at her uneasily, and said "Oh, Gerold will be all right. I'll have a talk with him, shall I?"

No answer. Hanna was thinking, Another thing. On any other planet we'd be out of the shuttle and in tents by now. Even on Achwa we were so tired of the shuttle we went outside as soon as we could. But no one's even suggested it here. But of course the tents were army guerrilla ones, from the closing stages of the war, with walls providing one-way vision, and excellent transmission of outside sounds. In brief, very good for observation; but not for giving the secure sense of an environment shut out.

"Shall I?" asked Jon again.

"What? Oh yes, sure." She said, testing, "How about fixing up the tents tonight? Should be all right now."

Jon stared straight in front of him; he muttered quickly, "Too cold," then, more loudly, "Shall I try talking to some of the locals today? It'd be easier on you if they were split into two groups. I mean, we might get on quicker."

"If you think you can manage it," said Hanna, hardly hearing her own reply. For Jon knew as well as she did that the tents were set to keep a steady temperature of twenty-two degrees inside, in outside temperatures ten times lower than anything they had found on Kona.

Jon was saying indignantly, "Of course I can manage it. I may not have had your experience, but I have been working two years, you know."

"I'm sorry." Hanna remembered now that Jon had for many years been the youngest in his child-troop. She wondered how many times, as a little boy, he had had to say "I *can* do it. I *am* big enough."

Whatever his motives, Jon successfully detached a group of Konans from the main body, and worked steadily all the two days, though at the end he had little to report. Hanna was not surprised. She herself had finally concluded that the Konans could not, or would not, tell her any more about the deaths of the first Terran survey, and had turned belatedly to more standard enquiries about Konan life-style. She felt, guiltily, that Gerold had been partly right—they did need to know more about Konan physiology. Yet she herself, engrossed in linguistics, had neglected to make the proper enquiries.

Now, trying to make good the omission, she found again that

there was no quick information to be obtained from the Konans. One morning, for instance, she elicited the statement that "We eat many things, of which the grass is one." But it took her the rest of the day, battling through long discourses on the quality of the grass, and the proper ways of gathering it, to establish that the Konans were actually talking of the plains grass surrounding them, and that they did not eat it every day. And that still left unanswered the questions of how often, and what else, they might eat. She did try, experimentally, to pluck some grass, but though she threw her whole weight against it, not a stalk broke; which only appeared to affirm the perfection of the Konans' digestive systems.

She and Jon returned to the shuttle on the sixth evening to find Gerold busy writing a cautious but smugly favourable report, from which he occasionally read extracts to the rest of the group. Biren, tinkering with the transmitter, announced that the relief shuttle was expected to land sometime after Kona noon the next day. Gerold said, "Good, they can take this report back, and beam it off right away." He and Erring and Jon went into a huddle; they talked—irritatingly—too softly for the others to hear the whole conversation, but too loudly to be ignored. Alissin and Biren worked; Hanna sat and worried. It occurred to her for the first time that in raising the subject of immortality, she might well have produced the uneasiness she had used as evidence for her theory. And what other evidence had she? Conversations with a completely alien people whose language she knew only through short-term study? Her own feelings, helped by a danger-ously ready facility to draw literary comparisons? I could have made a mistake, she thought. We've all been trained so hard to make our decisions quickly, to sum up a planet a month; we'd almost rather make a wrong decision than no decision. What if I've built up this tension for nothing? But all the time, the feel of the unyielding planet pressed through the walls of the shuttle at her. She could not forget the great silent plains, and the solid bar of the mountains behind. She wondered suddenly if some of

the first survey had died from sheer exhaustion, trying to follow
the Konans up the mountains. The plain was bad enough; every
day, one tramped until one was tired, and when one turned
around, the shuttle looked no distance away in the clear air, and
the stretch of grass in front seemed still limitless. What then
would it be like to climb a Konan mountain?

Erring stood up and said, "End of our first week on Kona,
folks! Three weeks today, and we could be off it, and going back
to Terra!" and the sense of longing anticipation went round the
cabin almost as palpably as a breeze.

That night, when Hanna took over the watch, Alissin, who had
preceded her, did not go back to sleep but set up her bench for
work. "Got to prepare some experiments," she said in answer to
Hanna's enquiring look.

"What on?"

"A type of alga. I found it in a puddle out there, and it looks
as if it could be a colony food source, except that it reproduces
damn slowly, even with all the accelerators that I can put on it.
I'm trying a few different environments now." There was a pause,
while she adjusted the settings on an environment hemisphere;
then she said, "Marginal work, really, but I can't do much else
without tissue samples from higher life forms."

Hanna said, with ill-concealed frustration, "We probably won't
be here long enough to get them. Look at the way Gerold's
rushing to get out his preliminary report tomorrow."

Alissin had turned to her algae samples again. She said drily,
"It seems that the only quick way to test out Konan immortality
would be to try to kill some, and see how difficult it is."

It was the day on which Gerold proposed to send out his
report, and Hanna wanted to spend the morning with the Konans, in the faint hope that some knowledge would arrive to
clarify decision. Rather surprisingly, Jon seemed eager to come
too. Alissin also volunteered; but they all knew that this was a

strategic retreat from Gerold's attempts to bully both her and
Hanna into writing reports.

"Very stable weather here," said Alissin as they set off; and it
was true. The breeze was still blowing cold and steady from the
mountains, the sky had never varied from its perfect steel blue,
the unending ripples of grass were the same yesterday, today,
and most likely tomorrow and tomorrow and tomorrow.

Hanna said bitterly, "We hardly know a thing about this place.
We should spend two hundred years just studying it; and we have
to leave it in three weeks because the government wants to shove
colonists out here as fast as they can go."

Jon said "Hurry up, can't you?" He seemed impatient to get
to work.

The Konans had changed no more than the weather. They still
sat their horses apparently unwearying, and the horses themselves were as tall and white and lovely as ever. Every time it is
a shock to see them, thought Hanna. I can't even carry their
image in my mind. Like trying to mount a 3-D projection on a 2-D
screen. It suddenly seemed immensely frustrating that even in
this, the Konans defeated her; she could not even make her ideals
surpass their reality.

Still, she worked away steadily, eliciting small shreds of information from the group, and trying (in case Gerold's preliminary
report did its work too well) to explain the aims of Terran colonization to them. The latter attempt was not successful. The Konans listened, politely, but it made no impression on them.

Once Alissin said, "Jon's group are moving off a bit." Hanna,
deep in the intricacies of Terran colonial policy, hardly heard
her. After some time, Alissin said, "We should get back soon, and
we have to call Jon. He's breaking rule as it is, going so far from
us."

That made Hanna look round; and it was true. Jon's group was
now moving rapidly over the plain towards the shuttle.

"Where is Jon?" said Hanna. "I can't see him."

"He must be there, he was there just before."

"I can't see—"

Then suddenly the tight group broke into a ragged cluster, and the cluster into a line; and both Hanna and Alissin could see clearly a rider in the middle, looking small and out of place, bumping a little to the long stride of his horse. Behind him, another horse bore two Konan riders.

"The fool, the blasted fool! He's gone and tried out his stupid Dixon-Ehrmann method—" Hanna turned to run after them.

"He may be all right. They're only walking."

"Oh, come on!"

Their own group was showing signs of moving in the same direction. Hanna began to run; the horses' walk was a strenuous jog-trot for her and Alissin. Hanna felt her face stiffen with dried sweat.

But Jon rode on, not easily, but at least safely. His companions seemed in high spirits; Hanna could see some of them urging their horses to jump and rear, and sweated again to think that Jon's mount might follow suit. But it continued to walk.

They were halfway to the shuttle by now, and Hanna could see Gerold and Erring and Biren come out to watch the approach. She saw, with alarm, that Gerold carried two pistols. She saw Jon wave to them, with proud affected carelessness, and cursed him more than ever.

All the horses began to trot, and then to canter. Hanna shouted, "Drop *off* you fool, get off while you can!" (knowing all the time that to fall from even a cantering Konanhorse would be very dangerous). But Jon, sliding and bumping perilously, took no notice; and Hanna saw suddenly that he had tied his right wrist to the mane of his horse, evidently to help him keep his grip. She felt her stomach muscles clench with panic.

Erring was shouting now, too: "Jon, are you all right?" Now they were all near enough to the shuttle for Gerold to see Jon's tied hand, and Hanna heard him say, "They've tied him up—the bastards have tied him up!" and he raised one of his pistols. Hanna cried breathlessly, "No, they didn't, Gerry, he did it himself—it's his blasted Dixon-Ehrmann method." But Gerold said, "How do we know that?"

The horses were very near to the shuttle now, and suddenly they began to gallop, past it and in a wide curve around it. They all saw Jon nearly slip, and he screamed. His head whipped back and forth, hitting his hands clenched in his horse's mane; then in a moment the whole mass of horses had gone, streaming past like snowflakes in the wind.

Panic exploded like a bomb among the little group of Terrans. Gerold raised his pistol, and Erring knocked it out of his hand, crying, "You'll hit him, he'll be killed!" Biren and Alissin ran futilely after the horses, and back. Hanna dived for the pistol, and Gerold punched her away. "When they come back again I'm shooting them!" he yelled.

The thunder of hooves approached the shuttle again, and they all ran out to meet it. The Konans were leaning forward, shouting to each other, bringing their horses in a circle round the shuttle. For a moment they could not see Jon; then one horse ran by apparently riderless, but for two hands clasped in his mane, and they saw him dangling like a doll, with his feet rhythmically hitting the ground and bouncing crazily off it again.

A babble of voices. Gerold lifted his pistol and fired, but Jon's horse was past, and the beam tore strips off the next horse and rider. Hanna found herself shouting, "They made us not to be and they are not!" in Konan, again and again. Gerold aimed his pistol once more, and Biren seized the other one; but the race of horses and riders never ceased, and Jon's horse was untouched. Alissin cried, "They don't know they're going to die!" and the tears ran down her face. Some of the horses were slowing now, some running on three legs, and some riders were down. But their pale handsome faces never changed, and none of them cried out, and none fell over. "You can't kill the bloody things," panted Gerold desperately; and at the same time, Hanna heard the roar and whistle of a shuttle landing, and Erring called gladly, "They've come!" and waved wildly. The door of the relief shuttle opened, and a group of Terrans ran out, all armed with pistols, and deployed themselves neatly over the plain. Completely businesslike, they began firing into the mass of Konans, steadily and efficiently saving the stranded shuttle from attack.

Hanna sat down, because her knees folded up. It seemed as if a switch clicked in her brain, so that time went very slowly, and any number of images could parade through her mind simultaneously and without hurry. She saw the Konans galloping to meet them, white horses on a dark plain; and saw too a Konan in front of her stagger forward with half his leg shot off, and lose his other leg to a stray beam, and continue to crawl forward until another shot carved his chest open, all with no expression on his face. She saw gunfire arcing across the plains like flaming swords, a hundred and fifty years ago, and Jon as a little boy saying, "I can! I am big enough!" and the guarded words of the old report: "indigenous humanoids appeared nonaggressive." She heard the Konans saying to her, "It is not to be understood," Alissin commenting, "Try to kill some and see how difficult it is," and heard, too, Gerold cry in anguish, "You can't tell when the bastards are dead, they won't die—" but many of them were dead, caught in crossbeams, and chopped into heaps.

Then the switch clicked back again, and she saw the last of the Konanhorses suddenly double their speed, with no visible effort, so that they raced across the plain faster than the mind could follow, the riders calling to each other in great echoing cries, and were gone behind the bluff like ships gone into hyperspace.

Erring and Alissin were bending over Jon, who lay wounded near what had been his horse.

One of the second shuttle crew came over and said to Gerold, "Too close for comfort. Thought the locals weren't supposed to be dangerous?"

Hanna said, with a hysterical travesty of patience, "No, no, you've got it wrong. No one said they weren't *dangerous,* they said they weren't *aggressive,* and that was right, wasn't it? Erring, wasn't it? Gerold?"

Erring said, taking no notice, "He's alive, anyway. I should think Medcom can deal with him. At least we saved him."

Hanna started to laugh, and Alissin said sharply, "At a cost of how many indigenes, and how much trust? Do you really think his life was worth it?"

Still whooping with laughter, Hanna said, "What did we save him from? For? We haven't got him. He'll die anyway, you know."

SEVEN AMERICAN NIGHTS

Here is Gene Wolfe's most powerful novella
since "The Fifth Head of Cerberus": a phantasmagoria
of life and death, truth and madness in the ruined
continent of North America, seen through the
eyes of a visitor from the civilized East.

Gene Wolfe

ESTEEMED AND LEARNED MADAME:

As I last wrote you, it appears to me likely that your son Nadan (may
Allah preserve him!) has left the old capital and traveled—of his own will
or another's—north into the region about the Bay of Delaware. My
conjecture is now confirmed by the discovery in those regions of the
notebook I enclose. It is not of American manufacture, as you see; and
though it holds only the records of a single week, several suggestive
items therein provide us new reason to hope.

I have photocopied the contents to guide me in my investigations; but
I am alert to the probability that you, Madame, with your superior
knowledge of the young man we seek, may discover implications I have
overlooked. Should that be the case, I urge you to write me at once.

Though I hesitate to mention it in connection with so encouraging a
finding, your most recently due remission has not yet arrived. I assume
that this tardiness results from the procrastination of the mails, which

175

is here truly abominable. I must warn you, however, that I shall be forced to discontinue the search unless funds sufficient for my expenses are forthcoming before the advent of winter.

With inexpressible respect,
HASSAN KERBELAI

Here I am at last! After twelve mortal days aboard the *Princess Fatimah*—twelve days of cold and ennui—twelve days of bad food and throbbing engines—the joy of being on land again is like the delight a condemned man must feel when a letter from the shah snatches him from beneath the very blade of death. America! America! Dull days are no more! They say that everyone who comes here either loves or hates you, America—by Allah I love you now!

Having begun this record at last, I find I do not know where to begin. I had been reading travel diaries before I left home; and so when I saw you, O Book, lying so square and thick in your stall in the bazaar—why should I not have adventures too, and write a book like Osman Aga's? Few come to this sad country at the world's edge after all, and most who do land farther up the coast.

And that gives me the clue I was looking for—how to begin. America began for me as colored water. When I went out on deck yesterday morning, the ocean had changed from green to yellow. I had never heard of such a thing before, neither in my reading, nor in my talks with Uncle Mirza, who was here thirty years ago. I am afraid I behaved like the greatest fool imaginable, running about the ship babbling, and looking over the side every few minutes to make certain the rich mustard color was still there and would not vanish the way things do in dreams when we try to point them out to someone else. The steward told me he knew. Golam Gassem the grain merchant (whom I had tried to avoid meeting for the entire trip until that moment) said, "Yes, yes," and turned away in a fashion that showed he had been avoiding me too, and that it was going to take more of a miracle than yellow water to change his feelings.

One of the few native Americans in first class came out just then: Mister—as the style is here—Tallman, husband of the lovely Madam Tallman, who really deserves such a tall man as myself. (Whether her husband chose that name in self-derision, or in the hope that it would erase others' memory of his infirmity; or whether it was his father's, and is merely one of the countless ironies of fate, I do not know. There was something wrong with his back.) As if I had not made enough spectacle of myself already, I took this Mr. Tallman by the sleeve and told him to look over the side, explaining that the sea had turned yellow. I am afraid Mr. Tallman turned white himself instead, and turned something else too—his back—looking as though he would have struck me if he dared. It was comic enough, I suppose—I heard some of the other passengers chuckling about it afterward—but I don't believe I have seen such hatred in a human face before. Just then the captain came strolling up, and I—considerably deflated but not flattened yet, and thinking that he had not overheard Mr. Tallman and me—mentioned for the final time that day that the water had turned yellow. "I know," the captain said. "It's his country" (here he jerked his head in the direction of the pitiful Mr. Tallman), "bleeding to death."

Here it is evening again, and I see that I stopped writing last night before I had so much as described my first sight of the coast. Well, so be it. At home it is midnight, or nearly, and the life of the cafés is at its height. How I wish that I were there now, with you, Yasmin, not webbed among these red- and purple-clad strangers, who mob their own streets like an invading army, and duck into their houses like rats into their holes. But you, Yasmin, or Mother, or whoever may read this, will want to know of my day —only you are sometimes to think of me as I am now, bent over an old, scarred table in a decayed room with two beds, listening to the hastening feet in the streets outside.

I slept late this morning; I suppose I was more tired from the voyage than I realized. By the time I woke, the whole of the city was alive around me, with vendors crying fish and fruits under my shuttered window, and the great wooden wains the Americans call *trucks* rumbling over the broken concrete on their wide iron wheels, bringing up goods from the ships in the Potomac anchorage. One sees very odd teams here, Yasmin. When I went to get my breakfast (one must go outside to reach the lobby and dining room in these American hotels, which I would think would be very inconvenient in bad weather) I saw one of these *trucks* with two oxen, a horse, and a mule in the traces, which would have made you laugh. The drivers crack their whips all the time.

The first impression one gets of America is that it is not as poor as one has been told. It is only later that it becomes apparent how much has been handed down from the previous century. The streets here are paved, but they are old and broken. There are fine, though decayed, buildings everywhere (this hotel is one— the Inn of Holidays, it is called), more modern in appearance than the ones we see at home, where for so long traditional architecture was enforced by law. We are on Maine Street, and when I had finished my breakfast (it was very good, and very cheap by our standards, though I am told it is impossible to get anything out of season here) I asked the manager where I should go to see the sights of the city. He is a short and phenomenally ugly man, something of a hunchback as so many of them are. "There are no tours," he said. "Not any more."

I told him that I simply wanted to wander about by myself, and perhaps sketch a bit.

"You can do that. North for the buildings, south for the theater, west for the park. Do you plan to go to the park, Mr. Jaffarzadeh?"

"I haven't decided yet."

"You should hire at least two securities if you go to the park —I can recommend an agency."

"I have my pistol."

"You'll need more than that, sir."

Naturally, I decided then and there that I would go to the park, and alone. But I have determined not to spend this, the sole, small coin of adventure this land has provided me so far, before I discover what else it may offer to enrich my existence.

Accordingly, I set off for the north when I left the hotel. I have not, thus far, seen this city, or any American city, by night. What they might be like if these people thronged the streets then, as we do, I cannot imagine. Even by clearest day, there is the impression of carnival, of some mad circus whose performance began a hundred or more years ago and has not ended yet.

At first it seemed that only every fourth or fifth person suffered some trace of the genetic damage that destroyed the old America, but as I grew more accustomed to the streets, and thus less quick to dismiss as Americans and no more the unhappy old woman who wanted me to buy flowers and the boy who dashed shrieking between the wheels of a *truck,* and began instead to look at them as human beings—in other words, just as I would look at some chance-met person on one of our own streets—I saw that there was hardly a soul not marked in some way. These deformities, though they are individually hideous, in combination with the bright, ragged clothing so common here, give the meanest assemblage the character of a pageant. I sauntered along, hardly out of earshot of one group of street musicians before encountering another, and in a few strides passed a man so tall that he was taller seated on a low step than I standing; a bearded dwarf with a withered arm; and a woman whose face had been divided by some devil into halves, one large-eyed and idiotically despairing, the other squinting and sneering.

There can be no question about it—Yasmin must not read this. I have been sitting here for an hour at least, staring at the flame of the candle. Sitting and listening to something that from time to time beats against the steel shutters that close the window of this room. The truth is that I am paralyzed by a fear that entered me—I do not know from whence—yesterday, and has been growing ever since.

Everyone knows that these Americans were once the most skilled creators of consciousness-altering substances the world has ever seen. The same knowledge that permitted them to forge the chemicals that destroyed them, so that they might have bread that never staled, innumerable poisons for vermin, and a host of unnatural materials for every purpose, also contrived synthetic alkaloids that produced endless feverish imaginings.

Surely some, at least, of these skills remain. Or if they do not, then some of the substances themselves, preserved for eighty or a hundred years in hidden cabinets, and no doubt growing more dangerous as the world forgets them. I think that someone on the ship may have administered some such drug to me.

That is out at last! I felt so much better at having written it— it took a great deal of effort—that I took several turns about this room. Now that I have written it down, I do not believe it at all.

Still, last night I dreamed of that bread, of which I first read in the little schoolroom of Uncle Mirza's country house. It was no complex, towering "literary" dream such as I have sometimes had, and embroidered, and boasted of afterward over coffee. Just the vision of a loaf of soft white bread lying on a plate in the center of a small table: bread that retained the fragrance of the oven (surely one of the most delicious in the world) though it was smeared with gray mold. Why would the Americans wish such a thing? Yet all the historians agree that they did, just as they wished their own corpses to appear living forever.

It is only this country, with its colorful, fetid streets, deformed people, and harsh, alien language, that makes me feel as drugged and dreaming as I do. Praise Allah that I can speak Farsi to you, O Book. Will you believe that I have taken out every article of clothing I have, just to read the makers' labels? Will *I* believe it, for that matter, when I read this at home?

The public buildings to the north—once the great center, as I understand it, of political activity—offer a severe contrast to the

streets of the still-occupied areas. In the latter, the old buildings
are in the last stages of decay, or have been repaired by makeshift
and inappropriate means; but they seethe with the life of those
who depend upon such commercial activity as the port yet pro-
vides, and with those who depend on them, and so on. The
monumental buildings, because they were constructed of the
most imperishable materials, appear almost whole, though there
are a few fallen columns and sagging porticos, and in several
places small trees (mostly the sad *carpinus caroliniana*, I believe)
have rooted in the crevices of walls. Still, if it is true, as has been
written, that Time's beard is gray not with the passage of years
but with the dust of ruined cities, it is here that he trails it. These
imposing shells are no more than that. They were built, it would
seem, to be cooled and ventilated by machinery. Many are windowless, their interiors now no more than sunless caves, reeking
of decay; into these I did not venture. Others had had fixed
windows that once were mere walls of glass; and a few of these
remained, so that I was able to sketch their construction. Most,
however, are destroyed. Time's beard has swept away their very
shards.

Though these old buildings (with one or two exceptions) are
deserted, I encountered several beggars. They seemed to be
Americans whose deformities preclude their doing useful work,
and one cannot help but feel sorry for them, though their appearance is often as distasteful as their importunities. They offered to
show me the former residence of their Padshah, and as an excuse
to give them a few coins I accompanied them, making them first
pledge to leave me when I had seen it.

The structure they pointed out to me was situated at the end
of a long avenue lined with impressive buildings; so I suppose
they must have been correct in thinking it once important.
Hardly more than the foundation, some rubble, and one ruined
wing remain now, and it cannot have been originally of an enduring construction. No doubt it was actually a summer palace
or something of that kind. The beggars have now forgotten its

very name, and call it merely "the white house."

When they had guided me to this relic, I pretended that I wanted to make drawings, and they left as they had promised. In five or ten minutes, however, one particularly enterprising fellow returned. He had no lower jaw, so that I had quite a bit of difficulty in understanding him at first; but after we had shouted back and forth a good deal—I telling him to depart and threatening to kill him on the spot, and he protesting—I realized that he was forced to make the sound of *d* for *b*, *n* for *m*, and *t* for *p*; and after that we got along better.

I will not attempt to render his speech phonetically, but he said that since I had been so generous, he wished to show me a great secret—something foreigners like myself did not even realize existed.

"Clean water," I suggested.

"No, no. A great, great secret, Captain. You think all this is dead." He waved a misshapen hand at the desolated structures that surrounded us.

"Indeed I do."   ·

"One still lives. You would like to see it? I will guide. Don't worry about the others—they're afraid of me. I will drive them away."

"If you are leading me into some kind of ambush, I warn you, you will be the first to suffer."

He looked at me very seriously for a moment, and a man seemed to stare from the eyes in that ruined face, so that I felt a twinge of real sympathy. "See there? The big building to the south, on Pennsylvania? Captain, my father's father's father was chief of a department" ("detartnent") "there. I would not betray you."

From what I have read of this country's policies in the days of his father's father's father, that was little enough reassurance, but I followed him.

We went diagonally across several blocks, passing through two ruined buildings. There were human bones in both, and remembering his boast, I asked him if they had belonged to the workers there.

"No, no." He tapped his chest again—a habitual gesture, I suppose—and scooping up a skull from the floor held it beside his own head so that I could see that it exhibited cranial deformities much like his own. "We sleep here, to be shut behind strong walls from the things that come at night. We die here, mostly in wintertime. No one buries us."

"You should bury each other," I said.

He tossed down the skull, which shattered on the terrazzo floor, waking a thousand dismal echoes. "No shovel, and few are strong. But come with me."

At first sight the building to which he led me looked more decayed than many of the ruins. One of its spires had fallen, and the bricks lay in the street. Yet when I looked again, I saw that there must be something in what he said. The broken windows had been closed with ironwork at least as well made as the shutters that protect my room here; and the door, though old and weathered, was tightly shut, and looked strong.

"This is the museum," my guide told me. "The only part left, almost, of the Silent City that still lives in the old way. Would you like to see inside?"

I told him that I doubted that we would be able to enter.

"Wonderful machines." He pulled at my sleeve. "You *see* in, Captain. Come."

We followed the building's walls around several corners, and at last entered a sort of alcove at the rear. Here there was a grill set in the weed-grown ground, and the beggar gestured toward it proudly. I made him stand some distance off, then knelt as he had indicated to look through the grill.

There was a window of unshattered glass beyond the grill. It was very soiled now, but I could see through into the basement of the building, and there, just as the beggar had said, stood an orderly array of complex mechanisms.

I stared for some time, trying to gain some notion of their

purpose; and at length an old American appeared among them, peering at one and then another, and whisking the shining bars and gears with a rag.

The beggar had crept closer as I watched. He pointed at the old man, and said, "Still come from north and south to study here. Someday we are great again." Then I thought of my own lovely country, whose eclipse—though without genetic damage—lasted twenty-three hundred years. And I gave him money, and told him that, yes, I was certain America would be great again someday, and left him, and returned here.

I have opened the shutters so that I can look across the city to the obelisk and catch the light of the dying sun. Its fields and valleys of fire do not seem more alien to me, or more threatening, than this strange, despondent land. Yet I know that we are all one —the beggar, the old man moving among the machines of a dead age, those machines themselves, the sun, and I. A century ago, when this was a thriving city, the philosophers used to speculate on the reason that each neutron and proton and electron exhibited the same mass as all the others of its kind. Now we know that there is only one particle of each variety, moving backward and forward in time, an electron when it travels as we do, a positron when its temporal displacement is retrograde, the same few particles appearing billions of billions of times to make up a single object, and the same few particles forming all the objects, so that we are all the sketches, as it were, of the same set of pastels.

I have gone out to eat. There is a good restaurant not far from the hotel, better even than the dining room here. When I came back the manager told me that there is to be a play tonight at the theater, and assured me that because it is so close to his hotel (in truth, he is very proud of this theater, and no doubt its proximity to his hotel is the only circumstance that permits the hotel to remain open) I will be in no danger if I go without an escort. To tell the truth, I am a little ashamed that I did not hire a boat today to take me across the channel to the park; so now I will attend the play, and dare the night streets.

Here I am again, returned to this too-large, too-bare, uncarpeted room, which is already beginning to seem a second home, with no adventures to retail from the dangerous benighted streets. The truth is that the theater is hardly more than a hundred paces to the south. I kept my hand on the butt of my pistol and walked along with a great many other people (mostly Americans) who were also going to the theater, and felt something of a fool.

The building is as old as those in the Silent City, I should think; but it has been kept in some repair. There was more of a feeling of gaiety (though to me it was largely an alien gaiety) among the audience than we have at home, and less of the atmosphere of what I may call the sacredness of Art. By that I knew that the drama really is sacred here, as the colorful clothes of the populace make clear in any case. An exaggerated and solemn respect always indicates a loss of faith.

Having recently come from my dinner, I ignored the stands in the lobby at which the Americans—who seem to eat constantly when they can afford it—were selecting various cold meats and pastries, and took my place in the theater proper. I was hardly in my seat before a pipe-puffing old gentleman, an American, desired me to move in order that he might reach his own. I stood up gladly, of course, and greeted him as "Grandfather," as our own politeness (if not theirs) demands. But while he was settling himself and I was still standing beside him, I caught a glimpse of his face from the exact angle at which I had seen it this afternoon, and recognized him as the old man I had watched through the grill.

Here was a difficult situation. I wanted very much to draw him into conversation, but I could not well confess that I had been spying on him. I puzzled over the question until the lights were extinguished and the play began.

It was Vidal's *Visit to a Small Planet*, one of the classics of the old American theater, a play I have often read about but never (until now) seen performed. I would have liked it much better if it had been done with the costumes and settings of its proper period; unhappily, the director had chosen to "modernize" the entire affair, just as we sometimes present *Rustam Beg* as if Rustam had been a hero of the war just past. General Powers was a contemporary American soldier with the mannerisms of a cowardly bandit, Spelding a publisher of libelous broadsheets, and so on. The only characters that gave me much pleasure were the limping spaceman, Kreton, and the ingenue, Ellen Spelding, played as and by a radiantly beautiful American blonde.

All through the first act my mind had been returning (particularly during Spelding's speeches) to the problem of the old man beside me. By the time the curtain fell, I had decided that the best way to start a conversation might be to offer to fetch him a kebab —or whatever he might want—from the lobby, since his threadbare appearance suggested that he might be ready enough to be treated, and the weakness of his legs would provide an admirable excuse. I tried the gambit as soon as the flambeaux were relit, and it worked as well as I could have wished. When I returned with a paper tray of sandwiches and bitter drinks, he remarked to me quite spontaneously that he had noticed me flexing my right hand during the performance.

"Yes," I said, "I had been writing a good deal before I came here."

That set him off, and he began to discourse, frequently with a great deal more detail than I could comprehend, on the topic of writing machines. At last I halted the flow with some question that must have revealed that I knew less of the subject than he had supposed. "Have you ever," he asked me, "carved a letter in a potato, and moistened it with a stamp pad, and used it to imprint paper?"

"As a child, yes. We use a turnip, but no doubt the principle is the same."

"Exactly; and the principle is that of extended abstraction. I ask you—on the lowest level, what is communication?"

"Talking, I suppose."

His shrill laugh rose above the hubbub of the audience. "Not at all! Smell" (here he gripped my arm), "smell is the essence of communication. Look at that word *essence* itself. When you smell another human being, you take chemicals from his body into your own, analyze them, and from the analysis you accurately deduce his emotional state. You do it so constantly and so automatically that you are largely unconscious of it, and say simply, 'He seemed frightened,' or 'He was angry.' You see?"

I nodded, interested in spite of myself.

"When you speak, you are telling another how you would smell if you smelled as you should and if he could smell you properly from where he stands. It is almost certain that speech was not developed until the glaciations that terminated the Pliocene stimulated mankind to develop fire, and the frequent inhalation of wood smoke had dulled the olfactory organs."

"I see."

"No, you hear—unless you are by chance reading my lips, which in this din would be a useful accomplishment." He took an enormous bite of his sandwich, spilling pink meat that had surely come from no natural animal. "When you write, you are telling the other how you would speak if he could hear you, and when you print with your turnip, you are telling him how you would write. You will notice that we have already reached the third level of abstraction."

I nodded again.

"It used to be believed that only a limited number K of levels of abstraction were possible before the original matter disappeared altogether—some very interesting mathematical work was done about seventy years ago in an attempt to derive a generalized expression for K for various systems. Now we know that the number can be infinite if the array represents an open curve, and that closed curves are also possible."

"I don't understand."

"You are young and handsome—very fine looking, with your wide shoulders and black mustache; let us suppose a young woman loves you. If you and I and she were crouched now on the limb of a tree, you would scent her desire. Today, perhaps she tells you of that desire. But it is also possible, is it not, that she may write you of her desire?"

Remembering Yasmin's letters, I assented.

"But suppose those letters are perfumed—a musky, sweet perfume. You understand? A closed curve—the perfume is not the odor of her body, but an artificial simulation of it. It may not be what she feels, but it is what she tells you she feels. Your real love is for a whale, a male deer, and a bed of roses." He was about to say more, but the curtain went up for the second act.

I found that act both more enjoyable, and more painful, than the first. The opening scene, in which Kreton (soon joined by Ellen) reads the mind of the family cat, was exceptionally effective. The concealed orchestra furnished music to indicate cat thoughts; I wish I knew the identity of the composer, but my playbill does not provide the information. The bedroom wall became a shadow screen, where we saw silhouettes of cats catching birds, and then, when Ellen tickled the real cat's belly, making love. As I have said, Kreton and Ellen were the play's best characters. The juxtaposition of Ellen's willowy beauty and high-spirited naiveté, and Kreton's clear desire for her illuminated perfectly the Paphian difficulties that would confront a powerful telepath, were such persons to exist.

On the other hand, Kreton's summoning of the presidents, which closes the act, was as objectionable as it could possibly have been made. The foreign ruler conjured up by error was played as a Turk, and as broadly as possible. I confess to feeling some prejudice against that bloodthirsty race myself, but what was done was indefensible. When the president of the World Council appeared, he was portrayed as an American.

By the end of that scene I was in no very good mood. I think that I have not yet shaken off the fatigues of the crossing; and they, combined with a fairly strenuous day spent prowling around the ruins of the Silent City, had left me now in that state in which the smallest irritation takes on the dimensions of a mortal insult. The old curator beside me discerned my irascibility, but mistook the reason for it, and began to apologize for the state of the American stage, saying that all the performers of talent emigrated as soon as they gained recognition, and returned only when they had failed on the eastern shore of the Atlantic.

"No, no," I said. "Kreton and the girl are very fine, and the rest of the cast is at least adequate."

He seemed not to have heard me. "They pick them up wherever they can—they choose them for their faces. When they have appeared in three plays, they call themselves actors. At the Smithsonian—I am employed there, perhaps I've already mentioned it —we have tapes of real theater: Laurence Olivier, Orson Welles, Katharine Cornell. Spelding is a barber, or at least he was. He used to put his chair under the old Kennedy statue and shave the passersby. Ellen is a trollop, and Powers a drayman. That lame fellow Kreton used to snare sailors for a singing house on Portland Street."

His disparagement of his own national culture embarrassed me, though it put me in a better mood. (I have noticed that the two often go together—perhaps I am secretly humiliated to find that people of no great importance can affect my interior state with a few words or some mean service.) I took my leave of him and went to the confectioner's stand in the lobby. The Americans have a very pretty custom of duplicating the speckled eggs of wild birds in marzipan, and I bought a box of these—not only because I wanted to try them myself, but because I felt certain they would prove a treat for the old man, who must seldom have enough money to afford luxuries of that kind. I was quite correct—he ate them eagerly. But when I sampled one, I found its odor (as though I were eating artificial violets) so unpleasant that I did not take another.

"We were speaking of writing," the old man said. "The closed curve and the open curve. I did not have time to make the point that both could be achieved mechanically; but the monograph I am now developing turns upon that very question, and it happens that I have examples with me. First the closed curve. In the days when our president was among the world's ten most powerful men—the reality of the Paul Laurent you see on the stage there —each president received hundreds of requests every day for his signature. To have granted them would have taken hours of his time. To have refused them would have raised a brigade of enemies."

"What did they do?"

"They called upon the resources of science. That science devised the machine that wrote this."

From within his clean, worn coat he drew a folded sheet of paper. I opened it and saw that it was covered with the text of what appeared to be a public address, written in a childish scrawl. Mentally attempting to review the list of the American presidents I had seen in some digest of world history long ago, I asked whose hand it was.

"The machine's. Whose hand is being imitated here is one of the things I am attempting to discover."

In the dim light of the theater it was almost impossible to make out the faded script, but I caught the word *Sardinia*. "Surely, by correlating the contents to historical events it should be possible to date it quite accurately."

The old man shook his head. "The text itself was composed by another machine to achieve some national psychological effect. It is not probable that it bears any real relationship to the issues of its day. But now look here." He drew out a second sheet, and unfolded it for me. So far as I could see, it was completely blank. I was still staring at it when the curtain went up.

As Kreton moved his toy aircraft across the stage, the old man took a final egg and turned away to watch the play. There was still half a carton left, and I, thinking that he might want more later, and afraid that they might be spilled from my lap and lost underfoot, closed the box and slipped it into the side pocket of my jacket.

The special effects for the landing of the second spaceship were well done; but there was something else in the third act that gave me as much pleasure as the cat scene in the second. The final curtain hinges on the device our poets call *the Peri's asphodel,* a trick so shopworn now that it is acceptable only if it can be presented in some new light. The one used here was to have John—Ellen's lover—find Kreton's handkerchief and, remarking that it seemed perfumed, bury his nose in it. For an instant, the shadow wall used at the beginning of the second act was illuminated again to graphically (or I should say, pornographically) present Ellen's desire, conveying to the audience that John had, for that moment, shared the telepathic abilities of Kreton, whom all of them had now entirely forgotten.

The device was extremely effective, and left me feeling that I had by no means wasted my evening. I joined the general applause as the cast appeared to take their bows; then, as I was turning to leave, I noticed that the old man appeared very ill. I asked if he were all right, and he confessed ruefully that he had eaten too much, and thanked me again for my kindness—which must at that time have taken a great deal of resolution.

I helped him out of the theater, and when I saw that he had no transportation but his feet, told him I would take him home. He thanked me again, and informed me that he had a room at the museum.

Thus the half-block walk from the theater to my hotel was transformed into a journey of three or four kilometers, taken by moonlight, much of it through rubble-strewn avenues of the deserted parts of the city.

During the day I had hardly glanced at the stark skeleton of the old highway. Tonight, when we walked beneath its ruined overpasses, they seemed inexpressibly ancient and sinister. It occurred to me then that there may be a time-flaw, such as astronomers report from space, somewhere in the Atlantic. How is it that this western shore is more antiquated in the remains of a civilization not yet a century dead than we are in the shadow of

Darius? May it not be that every ship that plows that sea moves through ten thousand years?

For the past hour—I find I cannot sleep—I have been debating whether to make this entry. But what good is a travel journal, if one does not enter everything? I will revise it on the trip home, and present a cleansed copy for my mother and Yasmin to read.

It appears that the scholars at the museum have no income but that derived from the sale of treasures gleaned from the past; and I bought a vial of what is supposed to be the greatest creation of the old hallucinatory chemists from the woman who helped me get the old man into bed. It is—it was—about half the height of my smallest finger. Very probably it was alcohol and nothing more, though I paid a substantial price.

I was sorry I had bought it before I left, and still more sorry when I arrived here; but at the time it seemed that this would be my only opportunity, and I could think of nothing but to seize the adventure. After I have swallowed the drug I will be able to speak with authority about these things for the remainder of my life.

Here is what I have done. I have soaked the porous sugar of one of the eggs with the fluid. The moisture will soon dry up. The drug—if there is a drug—will remain. Then I will rattle the eggs together in an empty drawer, and each day, beginning tomorrow night, I will eat one egg.

I am writing today before I go down to breakfast, partly because I suspect that the hotel does not serve so early. Today I intend to visit the park on the other side of the channel. If it is as dangerous as they say, it is very likely I will not return to make an entry tonight. If I do return—well, I will plan for that when I am here again.

After I had blown out my candle last night I could not sleep, though I was tired to the bone. Perhaps it was only the excitement of the long walk back from the museum; but I could not free my mind from the image of Ellen. My wandering thoughts associated her with the eggs, and I imagined myself Kreton, sitting up in bed with the cat on my lap. In my daydream (I was not asleep) Ellen brought me my breakfast on a tray, and the breakfast consisted of the six candy eggs.

When my mind had exhausted itself with this kind of imagery, I decided to have the manager procure a girl for me so that I could rid myself of the accumulated tensions of the voyage. After about an hour during which I sat up reading, he arrived with three; and when he had given me a glimpse of them through the half-open door, he slipped inside and shut it behind him, leaving them standing in the corridor. I told him I had only asked for one.

"I know, Mr. Jaffarzadeh, I know. But I thought you might like to have a choice."

None of them—from the glimpse I had had—resembled Ellen; but I thanked him for his thoughtfulness and suggested that he bring them in.

"I wanted to tell you first, sir, that you must allow me to set the price with them—I can get them for much less than you, sir, because they know they cannot deceive me, and they must depend on me to bring them to my guests in the future." He named a sum that was in fact quite trivial.

"That will be fine," I said. "Bring them in."

He bowed and smiled, making his pinched and miserly face as pleasant as possible and reminding me very much of a picture I had once seen of an imp summoned before the court of Suleiman. "But first, sir, I wished to inform you that if you would like all three—together—you may have them for the price of two. And should you desire only two of the three, you may have them for one and one half the price of one. All are very lovely, and I thought you might want to consider it."

"Very well, I have considered it. Show them in."

"I will light another candle," he said, bustling about the room. "There is no charge, sir, for candles at the rate you're paying. I can put the girls on your bill as well. They'll be down as room service—you understand, I'm sure."

When the second candle was burning and he had positioned it to his liking on the nightstand between the two beds, he opened the door and waved in the girls, saying, "I'll go now. Take what you like and send out the others." (I feel certain this was a stratagem—he felt I would have difficulty in getting any to leave, and so would have to pay for all three.)

Yasmin must never see this—that is decided. It is not just that this entire incident would disturb her greatly, but because of what happened next. I was sitting on the bed nearest the door, hoping to decide quickly which of the three most resembled the girl who had played Ellen. The first was too short, with a wan, pinched face. The second was tall and blond, but plump. The third, who seemed to stumble as she entered, exactly resembled Yasmin.

For a few seconds I actually believed it was she. Science has so accustomed us to devising and accepting theories to account for the facts we observe, however fantastic, that our minds must begin their manufacture before we are aware of it. Yasmin had grown lonely for me. She had booked passage a few days after my own departure, or perhaps had flown, daring the notorious American landing facilities. Arriving here, she had made inquiries at the consulate, and was approaching my door as the manager lit his candle, and not knowing what was taking place had entered with prostitutes he had engaged.

It was all moonshine, of course. I jumped to my feet and held up the candle, and saw that the third girl, though she had Yasmin's large, dark eyes and rounded little chin, was not she. For all her night-black hair and delicate features, she was indisputably an American; and as she came toward me (encouraged, no doubt, because she had attracted my attention) I saw that like Kreton in the play she had a club foot.

As you see, I returned alive from the park after all. Tonight before I retire I will eat an egg; but first I will briefly set down my experiences.

The park lies on the opposite side of the Washington Channel,

between the city and the river. It can be reached by land only at
the north end. Not choosing to walk so far and return, I hired a
little boat with a tattered red sail to carry me to the southern tip,
which is called Hains Point. Here there was a fountain, I am told,
in the old times; but nothing remains of it now.

We had clear, sunny spring weather, and made our way over
exhilarating swells of wave with nothing of the deadly wallowing
that oppressed me so much aboard the *Princess Fatimah*. I sat in
the bow and watched the rolling greenery of the park on one side
of the channel and the ruins of the old fort on the other, while
an elderly man handled the tiller, and his thin, sun-browned
granddaughter, aged about eleven, worked the sail.

When we rounded the point, the old man told me that for very
little more he would take me across to Arlington to see the
remains of what is supposed to be the largest building of the
country's antiquity. I refused, determined to save that experience
for another time, and we landed where a part of the ancient
concrete coping remained intact.

The tracks of old roads run up either shore; but I decided to
avoid them, and made my way up the center, keeping to the
highest ground in so far as I could. Once, no doubt, the whole
area was devoted to pleasure. Very little remains, however, of the
pavilions and statuary that must have dotted the ground. There
are little, worn-away hills that may once have been rockeries but
are now covered with soil, and many stagnant pools. In a score
of places I saw the burrows of the famous giant American rats,
though I never saw the animals themselves. To judge from the
holes, their size has not been exaggerated—there were several I
could have entered with ease.

The wild dogs, against which I had been warned by both the
hotel manager and the old boatman, began to follow me after I
had walked about a kilometer north. They are short-haired, and
typically blotched with black and brown flecked with white. I
would say their average weight was about twenty-five kilos. With
their erect ears and alert, intelligent faces they did not seem

particularly dangerous; but I soon noticed that whichever way I turned, the ones in back of me edged nearer. I sat on a stone with my back to a pool and made several quick sketches of them, then decided to try my pistol. They did not seem to know what it was, so I was able to center the red aiming laser very nicely on one big fellow's chest before I pressed the stud for a high energy pulse.

For a long time afterward, I heard the melancholy howling of these dogs behind me. Perhaps they were mourning their fallen leader. Twice I came across rusting machines that may have been used to take invalids through the gardens in such fair weather as I myself experienced today. Uncle Mirza says I am a good colorist, but I despair of ever matching the green-haunted blacks with which the declining sun painted the park.

I met no one until I had almost reached the piers of the abandoned railway bridge. Then four or five Americans who pretended to beg surrounded me. The dogs, who as I understand it live mostly upon the refuse cast up by the river, were more honest in their intentions and cleaner in their persons. If these people had been like the pitiful creatures I had met in the Silent City, I would have thrown them a few coins; but they were more or less able-bodied men and women who could have worked, and chose instead to rob. I told them that I had been forced to kill a fellow countryman of theirs (not mentioning that he was a dog) who had assaulted me; and asked where I could report the matter to the police. At that they backed off, and permitted me to walk around the northern end of the channel in peace, though not without a thousand savage looks. I returned here without further incident, tired and very well satisfied with my day.

I have eaten one of the eggs! I confess I found it difficult to take the first taste; but marshaling my resolution was like pushing at a wall of glass—all at once the resistance snapped, and I picked the thing up and swallowed it in a few bites. It was piercingly sweet, but there was no other flavor. Now we will see. This is more frightening than the park by far.

Nothing seemed to be happening, so I went out to dinner. It was twilight, and the carnival spirit of the streets was more marked than ever—colored lights above all the shops, and music from the rooftops where the wealthier natives have private gardens. I have been eating mostly at the hotel, but was told of a "good" American-style restaurant not too far south on Maine Street.

It was just as described—people sitting on padded benches in alcoves. The table tops are of a substance like fine-grained, greasy, artificial stone. They looked very old. I had the Number One Dinner—buff-colored fish soup with the pasty American bread on the side, followed by a sandwich of ground meat and raw vegetables doused with a tomato sauce and served on a soft, oily roll. To tell the truth, I did not much enjoy the meal; but it seems a sort of duty to sample more of the American food than I have thus far.

I am very tempted to end the account of my day here, and in fact I laid down this pen when I had written *thus far,* and made myself ready for bed. Still, what good is a dishonest record? I will let no one see this—just keep it to read over after I get home.

Returning to the hotel from the restaurant, I passed the theater. The thought of seeing Ellen again was irresistible; I bought a ticket and went inside. It was not until I was in my seat that I realized that the bill had changed.

The new play was *Mary Rose.* I saw it done by an English company several years ago, with great authenticity; and it struck me that (like Mary herself) it had far outlived its time. The American production was as inauthentic as the other had been correct. For that reason, it retained—or I should have said it had acquired —a good deal of interest.

Americans are superstitious about the interior of their country, not its coasts, so Mary Rose's island had been shifted to one of the huge central lakes. The highlander, Cameron, had accordingly become a Canadian, played by General Powers' former aide. The Speldings had become the Morelands, and the Morelands had become Americans. Kreton was Harry, the knife-throwing wounded soldier; and my Ellen had become Mary Rose.

The role suited her so well that I imagined the play had been selected as a vehicle for her. Her height emphasized the character's unnatural immaturity, and her slenderness, and the vulnerability of her pale complexion, would have told us, I think, if the play had not, that she had been victimized unaware. More important than any of these things was a wild and innocent affinity for the supernatural, which she projected to perfection. It was that quality alone (as I now understood) that had made us believe on the preceding night that Kreton's spaceship might land in the Speldings' rose garden—he would have been drawn to Ellen, though he had never seen her. Now it made Mary Rose's disappearances and reappearances plausible and even likely; it was as likely that unseen spirits lusted for Mary Rose as that Lieutenant Blake (previously John Randolf) loved her.

Indeed it was more likely. And I had no sooner realized that, than the whole mystery of *Mary Rose*—which had seemed at once inexplicable and banal when I had seen it well played in Teheran —lay clear before me. We of the audience were the envious and greedy spirits. If the Morelands could not see that one wall of their comfortable drawing room was but a sea of dark faces, if Cameron had never noticed that we were the backdrop of his island, the fault was theirs. By rights then, Mary Rose should have been drawn to us when she vanished. At the end of the second act I began to look for her, and in the beginning of the third I found her, standing silent and unobserved behind the last row of seats. I was only four rows from the stage, but I slipped out of my place as unobtrusively as I could, and crept up the aisle toward her.

I was too late. Before I had gone halfway, it was nearly time for her entrance at the end of the scene. I watched the rest of the play from the back of the theater, but she never returned.

Same night. I am having a good deal of trouble sleeping, though while I was on the ship I slept nine hours a night, and was off as soon as my head touched the pillow.

The truth is that while I lay in bed tonight I recalled the old curator's remark that the actresses were all prostitutes. If it is true and not simply an expression of hatred for younger people whose bodies are still attractive, then I have been a fool to moan over the thought of Mary Rose and Ellen when I might have had the girl herself.

Her name is Ardis Dahl—I just looked it up in the playbill. I am going to the manager's office to consult the city directory there.

Writing before breakfast. Found the manager's office locked last night. It was after two. I put my shoulder against the door and got it open easily enough. (There was no metal socket for the bolt such as we have at home—just a hole mortised in the frame.) The directory listed several Dahls in the city, but since it was nearly eight years out of date it did not inspire a great deal of confidence. I reflected, however, that in a backwater like this people were not likely to move about so much as we do at home, and that if it were not still of some utility, the manager would not be likely to retain it; so I selected the one that appeared from its address to be nearest the theater, and set out.

The streets were completely deserted. I remember thinking that I was now doing what I had previously been so afraid to do, having been frightened of the city by reading. How ridiculous to suppose that robbers would be afoot now, when no one else was. What would they do, stand for hours at the empty corners?

The moon was full and high in the southern sky, showering the street with the lambent white fluid of its light. If it had not been for the sharp, unclean odor so characteristic of American residential areas, I might have thought myself walking through an illustration from some old book of wonder tales, or an actor in a children's pantomime, so bewitched by the scenery that he has forgotten the audience.

(In writing that—which to tell the truth I did not think of at the time, but only now, as I sat here at my table—I realized that that is in fact what must happen to the American girl I have been in the habit of calling Ellen but must now learn to call Ardis. She could never perform as she does if it were not that in some part of her mind her stage became her reality.)

The shadows about my feet were a century old, tracing faithfully the courses they had determined long before New Tabriz came to jewel the lunar face with its sapphire. Webbed with thoughts of her—my Ellen, my Mary Rose, my Ardis!—and with the magic of that pale light that commands all the tides, I was elevated to a degree I cannot well describe.

Then I was seized by the thought that everything I felt might be no more than the effect of the drug.

At once, like someone who falls from a tower and clutches at the very wisps of air, I tried to return myself to reality. I bit the interiors of my cheeks until the blood filled my mouth, and struck the unfeeling wall of the nearest building with my fist. In a moment the pain sobered me. For a quarter hour or more I stood at the curbside, spitting into the gutter and trying to clean and bandage my knuckles with strips torn from my handkerchief. A thousand times I thought what a sight I would be if I did in fact succeed in seeing Ellen, and I comforted myself with the thought that if she were indeed a prostitute it would not matter to her— I could offer her a few additional rials and all would be well.

Yet that thought was not really much comfort. Even when a woman sells her body, a man flatters himself that she would not do so quite so readily were he not who he is. At the very moment I drooled blood into the street, I was congratulating myself on the strong, square face so many have admired; and wondering how I should apologize if in kissing her I smeared her mouth with red.

Perhaps it was some faint sound that brought me to myself;

perhaps it was only the consciousness of being watched. I drew my pistol and turned this way and that, but saw nothing.

Yet the feeling endured. I began to walk again; and if there was any sense of unreality remaining, it was no longer the unearthly exultation I had felt earlier. After a few steps I stopped and listened. A dry sound of rattling and scraping had followed me. It too stopped now.

I was nearing the address I had taken from the directory. I confess my mind was filled with fancies in which I was rescued by Ellen herself, who in the end should be more frightened than I, but who would risk her lovely person to save mine. Yet I knew these *were* but fancies, and the thing pursuing me was not, though it crossed my mind more than once that it might be some *druj* made to seem visible and palpable to me.

Another block, and I had reached the address. It was a house no different from those on either side—built of the rubble of buildings that were older still, three-storied, heavy-doored, and almost without windows. There was a bookshop on the ground floor (to judge by an old sign) with living quarters above it. I crossed the street to see it better, and stood, wrapped again in my dreams, staring at the single thread of yellow light that showed between the shutters of a gable window.

As I watched that light, the feeling of being watched myself grew upon me. Time passed, slipping through the waist of the universe's great hourglass like the eroded soil of this continent slipping down her rivers to the seas. At last my fear and desire —desire for Ellen, fear of whatever it was that glared at me with invisible eyes—drove me to the door of the house. I hammered the wood with the butt of my pistol, though I knew how unlikely it was that any American would answer a knock at such a time of night, and when I had knocked several times, I heard slow steps from within.

The door creaked open until it was caught by a chain. I saw a gray-haired man, fully dressed, holding an old-fashioned, long-barreled gun. Behind him a woman lifted a stub of smoking candle to let him see; and though she was clearly much older than Ellen, and was marked, moreover, by the deformities so prevalent here, there was a certain nobility in her features and a certain beauty as well, so that I was reminded of the fallen statue that is said to have stood on an island farther north, and which I have seen pictured.

I told the man that I was a traveler—true enough!—and that I had just arrived by boat from Arlington and had no place to stay, and so had walked into the city until I had noticed the light of his window. I would pay, I said, a silver rial if they would only give me a bed for the night and breakfast in the morning, and I showed them the coin. My plan was to become a guest in the house so that I might discover whether Ellen was indeed one of the inhabitants; if she were, it would have been an easy matter to prolong my stay.

The woman tried to whisper in her husband's ear, but save for a look of nervous irritation he ignored her. "I don't dare let a stranger in." From his voice I might have been a lion, and his gun a trainer's chair. "Not with no one here but my wife and myself."

"I see," I told him. "I quite understand your position."

"You might try the house on the corner," he said, shutting the door, "but don't tell them Dahl sent you." I heard the heavy bar dropped into place at the final word.

I turned away—and then by the mercy of Allah who is indeed compassionate happened to glance back one last time at the thread of yellow between the shutters of that high window. A flicker of scarlet higher still caught my attention, perhaps only because the light of the setting moon now bathed the rooftop from a new angle. I think the creature I glimpsed there had been waiting to leap upon me from behind, but when our eyes met it launched itself toward me. I had barely time to lift my pistol before it struck me and slammed me to the broken pavement of the street.

For a brief period I think I lost consciousness. If my shot had not killed the thing as it fell, I would not be sitting here writing this journal this morning. After half a minute or so I came to myself enough to thrust its weight away, stand up, and rub my bruises. No one had come to my aid; but neither had anyone rushed from the surrounding houses to kill and rob me. I was as alone with the creature that lay dead at my feet as I had been when I only stood watching the window in the house from which it had sprung.

After I found my pistol and assured myself that it was still in working order, I dragged the thing to a spot of moonlight. When I glimpsed it on the roof, it had seemed a feral dog, like the one I had shot in the park. When it lay dead before me, I had thought it a human being. In the moonlight I saw it was neither, or perhaps both. There was a blunt muzzle; and the height of the skull above the eyes, which anthropologists say is the surest badge of humanity and speech, had been stunted until it was not greater than I have seen in a macaque. Yet the arms and shoulders and pelvis—even a few filthy rags of clothing—all bespoke mankind. It was a female, with small, flattened breasts still apparent on either side of the burn channel.

At least ten years ago I read about such things in Osman Aga's *Mystery Beyond the Sun's Setting;* but it was very different to stand shivering on a deserted street corner of the old capital and examine the thing in the flesh. By Osman Aga's account (which no one, I think, but a few old women has ever believed) these creatures were in truth human beings—or at least the descendants of human beings. In the last century, when the famine gripped their country and the irreversible damage done to the chromosomal structures of the people had already become apparent, some few turned to the eating of human flesh. No doubt the corpses of the famine supplied their food at first; and no doubt those who ate of them congratulated themselves that by so doing they had escaped the effects of the enzymes that were then still used to bring slaughter animals to maturity in a matter of months. What they failed to realize was that the bodies of the human beings they ate had accumulated far more of these unnatural substances than were ever found in the flesh of the short-lived cattle. From them, according to *Mystery Beyond the Sun's Setting*, rose such creatures as the thing I had killed.

But Osman Aga has never been believed. So far as I know, he is a mere popular writer, with a reputation for glorifying Caspian resorts in recompense for free lodging, and for indulging in absurd expeditions to breed more books and publicize the ones he has already written—crossing the desert on a camel and the Alps on an elephant—and no one else has ever, to my knowledge, reported such things from this continent. The ruined cities filled with rats and rabid bats, and the terrible whirling dust storms of the interior, have been enough for other travel writers. Now I am sorry I did not contrive a way to cut off the thing's head; I feel sure its skull would have been of interest to science.

As soon as I had written the preceding paragraph, I realized that there might still be a chance to do what I had failed to do last night. I went to the kitchen, and for a small bribe was able to secure a large, sharp knife, which I concealed beneath my jacket.

It was still early as I ran down the street, and for a few minutes I had high hopes that the thing's body might still be lying where I had left it; but my efforts were all for nothing. It was gone, and there was no sign of its presence—no blood, no scar from my beam on the house. I poked into alleys and waste cans. Nothing. At last I came back to the hotel for breakfast, and I have now (it is mid-morning) returned to my room to make my plans for the day.

Very well. I failed to meet Ellen last night—I shall not fail today. I am going to buy another ticket for the play, and tonight I will not take my seat, but wait behind the last row where I saw her standing. If she comes to watch at the end of the second act as she did last night, I will be there to compliment her on her performance and present her with some gift. If she does not come, I will make my way backstage—from what I have seen of these Americans, a quarter rial should get me anywhere, but I am willing to loosen a few teeth if I must.

What absurd creatures we are! I have just reread what I wrote this morning, and I might as well have been writing of the philosophic speculations of the Congress of Birds or the affairs of the demons in Domdaniel, or any other subject on which neither I nor anyone else knows or can know a thing. O Book, you have heard what I supposed would occur, now let me tell you what actually took place.

I set out as I had planned to procure a gift for Ellen. On the advice of the hotel manager, I followed Maine Street north until I reached the wide avenue that passes close by the obelisk. Around the base of this still imposing monument is held a perpetual fair in which the merchants use the stone blocks fallen from the upper part of the structure as tables. What remains of the shaft is still, I should say, upwards of one hundred meters high; but it is said to have formerly stood three or four times that height. Much of the fallen material has been carted away to build private homes.

There seems to be no logic to the prices in this country, save for the general rule that foodstuffs are cheap and imported machinery—cameras and the like—costly. Textiles are expensive, which no doubt explains why so many of the people wear ragged clothes that they mend and dye in an effort to make them look new. Certain kinds of jewelry are quite reasonable; others sell for much higher prices than they would in Teheran. Rings of silver or white gold set, usually, with a single modest diamond, may be had in great numbers for such low prices that I was tempted into buying a few to take home as an investment. Yet I saw bracelets that would have sold at home for no more than half a rial, for which the seller asked ten times that much. There were many interesting antiques, all of which are alleged to have been dug from the ruined cities of the interior at the cost of someone's life. When I had talked to five or six vendors of such items, I was able to believe that I knew how the country was depopulated.

After a good deal of this pleasant, wordy shopping, during which I spent very little, I selected a bracelet made of old coins —many of them silver—as my gift to Ellen. I reasoned that women always like jewelry, and that such a showy piece might be of service to an actress in playing some part or other, and that the coins must have a good deal of intrinsic value. Whether she will like it or not—if she ever receives it—I do not know; it is still in the pocket of my jacket.

When the shadow of the obelisk had grown long, I returned here to the hotel and had a good dinner of lamb and rice, and retired to groom myself for the evening. The five remaining candy eggs stood staring at me from the top of my dresser. I remembered my resolve, and took one. Quite suddenly I was struck by the conviction that the demon I believed I had killed the night before had been no more than a phantom engendered by the action of the drug.

What if I had been firing my pistol at mere empty air? That seemed a terrible thought—indeed it seems so to me still. A worse one is that the drug really may have rendered visible—as some say those ancient preparations were intended to—a real but spiritual being. If such things in fact walk what we take to be unoccupied rooms and rooftops, and the empty streets of night, it would explain many sudden deaths and diseases, and perhaps the sudden changes for the worse we sometimes see in others and others in us, and even the birth of evil men. This morning I called the thing a *druj;* it may be true.

Yet if the drug had been in the egg I ate last night, then the egg I held was harmless. Concentrating on that thought, I forced myself to eat it all, then stretched myself upon the bed to wait.

Very briefly I slept and dreamed. Ellen was bending over me, caressing me with a soft, long-fingered hand. It was only for an instant, but sufficient to make me hope that dreams are prophecies.

If the drug was in the egg I consumed, that dream was its only result. I got up and washed, and changed my clothes, sprinkling my fresh shirt liberally with our Pamir rosewater, which I have observed the Americans hold in high regard. Making certain my ticket and pistol were both in place, I left for the theater.

The play was still *Mary Rose*. I intentionally entered late (after Harry and Mrs. Otery had been talking for several minutes), then lingered at the back of the last row as though I were too polite to disturb the audience by taking my seat. Mrs. Otery made her exit; Harry pulled his knife from the wood of the packing case and threw it again, and when the mists of the past had marched across the stage, Harry was gone, and Moreland and the parson were chatting to the tune of Mrs. Moreland's knitting needles. Mary Rose would be on stage soon. My hope that she would come out to watch the opening scene had come to nothing; I would have to wait until she vanished at the end of Act II before I could expect to see her.

I was looking for a vacant seat when I became conscious of someone standing near me. In the dim light I could tell little except that he was rather slender, and a few centimeters shorter than I.

Finding no seat, I moved back a step or two. The newcomer touched my arm and asked in a whisper if I could light his cigarette. I had already seen that it was customary to smoke in the theaters here, and I had fallen into the habit of carrying matches to light the candles in my room. The flare of the flame showed the narrow eyes and high cheekbones of Harry—or as I preferred to think of him, Kreton. Taken somewhat aback, I murmured some inane remark about the excellence of his performance.

"Did you like it? It is the least of all parts—I pull the curtain to open the show, then pull it again to tell everyone it's time to go home."

Several people in the audience were looking angrily at us, so we retreated to a point at the head of the aisle that was at least legally in the lobby, where I told him I had seen him in *Visit to a Small Planet* as well.

"Now *there* is a play. The character—as I am sure you saw—is good and bad at once. He is benign, he is mischievous, he is hellish."

"You carried it off wonderfully well, I thought."

"Thank you. This turkey here—do you know how many roles it has?"

"Well, there's yourself, Mrs. Otery, Mr. Amy—"

"No, no." He touched my arm to stop me. "I mean *roles,* parts that require real acting. There's one—the girl. She gets to skip about the stage as an eighteen-year-old whose brain atrophied at ten; and at least half what she does is wasted on the audience because they don't realize what's wrong with her until Act I is almost over."

"She's wonderful," I said. "I mean Mlle. Dahl."

Kreton nodded and drew on his cigarette. "She is a very competent ingenue, though it would be better if she weren't quite so tall."

"Do you think there's any chance that she might come out here —as you did?"

"Ah," he said, and looked me up and down.

For a moment I could have sworn that the telepathic ability he was credited with in *Visit to a Small Planet* was no fiction; nevertheless, I repeated my question: "Is it probable or not?"

"There's no reason to get angry—no, it's not likely. Is that enough payment for your match?"

"She vanishes at the end of the second act, and doesn't come on stage again until near the close of the third."

Kreton smiled. "You've read the play?"

"I was here last night. She must be off for nearly forty minutes, including the intermission."

"That's right. But she won't be here. It's true she goes out front sometimes—as I did myself tonight—but I happen to know she has company backstage."

"Might I ask who?"

"You might. It's even possible I might answer. You're Moslem, I suppose—do you drink?"

"I'm not a *strict* Moslem; but no, I don't. I'll buy you a drink gladly though, if you want one, and have coffee with you while you drink it."

We left by a side door and elbowed our way through the crowd in the street. A flight of narrow and dirty steps descending from the sidewalk led us to a cellar tavern that had all the atmosphere of a private club. There was a bar with a picture (now much dimmed by dirt and smoke) of the cast of a play I did not recognize behind it, three tables, and a few alcoves. Kreton and I slipped into one of these and ordered from a barman with a misshapen head. I suppose I must have stared at him, because Kreton said, "I sprained my ankle stepping out of a saucer, and now I am a convalescent soldier. Should we make up something for him too? Can't we just say the potter is angry sometimes?"

"The potter?" I asked.

" 'None answered this; but after Silence spake/A Vessel of a more ungainly Make:/They sneer at me for leaning all awry;/What! Did the Hand then of the Potter shake?' "

I shook my head. "I've never heard that; but you're right, he looks as though his head had been shaped in clay, then knocked in on one side while it was still wet."

"This is a republic of hideousness as you have no doubt already seen. Our national symbol is supposed to be an extinct eagle; it is in fact the nightmare."

"I find it a very beautiful country," I said. "Though I confess that many of your people are unsightly. Still there are the ruins, and you have such skies as we never see at home."

"Our chimneys have been filled with wind for a long time."

"That may be for the best. Blue skies are better than most of the things made in factories."

"And not all our people are unsightly," Kreton murmured.

"Oh no. Mlle. Dahl—"

"I had myself in mind."

I saw that he was baiting me, but I said, "No, you aren't hideous —in fact, I would call you handsome in an exotic way. Unfortunately, my tastes run more toward Mlle. Dahl."

"Call her Ardis—she won't mind."

The barman brought Kreton a glass of green liqueur, and me a cup of the weak, bitter American coffee.

"You were going to tell me who she is entertaining."

"Behind the scenes." Kreton smiled. "I just thought of that— I've used the phrase a thousand times, as I suppose everyone has. This time it happens to be literally correct, and its birth is suddenly made plain, like Oedipus's. No, I don't think I promised I would tell you that—though I suppose I said I might. Aren't there other things you would really rather know? The secret hidden beneath Mount Rushmore, or how you might meet her yourself?"

"I will give you twenty rials to introduce me to her, with some assurance that something will come of the introduction. No one need ever find out."

Kreton laughed. "Believe me, I would be more likely to boast of my profit than keep it secret—though I would probably have to divide my fee with the lady to fulfil the guarantee."

"You'll do it then?"

He shook his head, still laughing. "I only pretend to be corrupt; it goes with this face. Come backstage after the show tonight, and I'll see that you meet Ardis. You're very wealthy, I presume, and if you're not, we'll say you are anyway. What are you doing here?"

"Studying your art and architecture."

"Great reputation in your own country, no doubt?"

"I am a pupil of Akhon Mirza Ahmak; he has a great reputation, surely. He even came here, thirty years ago, to examine the miniatures in your National Gallery of Art."

"Pupil of Akhon Mirza Ahmak, pupil of Akhon Mirza Ahmak," Kreton muttered to himself. "That is very good—I must remember it. But now"—he glanced at the old clock behind the bar— "it's time we got back. I'll have to freshen my makeup before I go on in the last act. Would you prefer to wait in the theater, or just come around to the stage door when the play's over? I'll give you a card that will get you in."

"I'll wait in the theater," I said, feeling that would offer less chance for mishap; also because I wanted to see Ellen play the ghost again.

"Come along then—I have a key for that side door."

I rose to go with him, and he threw an arm about my shoulder that I felt it would be impolite to thrust away. I could feel his hand, as cold as a dead man's, through my clothing, and was reminded unpleasantly of the twisted hands of the beggar in the Silent City.

We were going up the narrow stairs when I felt a gentle touch inside my jacket. My first thought was that he had seen the outline of my pistol, and meant to take it and shoot me. I gripped his wrist and shouted something—I do not remember what. Bound together and struggling, we staggered up the steps and into the street.

In a few seconds we were the center of a mob—some taking his side, some mine, most only urging us to fight, or asking each other what the disturbance was. My pocket sketchpad, which he must have thought held money, fell to the ground between us. Just then the American police arrived—not by air as the police would have come at home, but astride shaggy, hulking horses, and swinging whips. The crowd scattered at the first crackling arc from the lashes, and in a few seconds they had beaten Kreton to the ground. Even at the time I could not help thinking what a terrible thing it must be to be one of these people, whose police are so quick to prefer any prosperous-looking foreigner to one of their own citizens.

They asked me what had happened (my questioner even dismounted to show his respect for me), and I explained that Kreton had tried to rob me, but that I did not want him punished. The truth was that seeing him sprawled unconscious with a burn across his face had put an end to any resentment I might have felt toward him; out of pity, I would gladly have given him the few rials I carried. They told me that if he had attempted to rob me he must be charged, and that if I would not accuse him they would do so themselves.

I then said that Kreton was a friend; and that on reflection I felt

certain that what he had attempted had been intended as a prank.
(In maintaining this I was considerably handicapped by not
knowing his real name, which I had read on the playbill but
forgotten, so that I was forced to refer to him as "this poor
man.")

At last the policeman said, "We can't leave him in the street,
so we'll have to bring him in. How will it look if there's no
complaint?"

Then I understood that they were afraid of what their superiors
might say if it became known that they had beaten him unconscious when no charge was made against him; and when I became
aware that if I would not press charges, the charges they would
bring themselves would be far more serious—assault or attempted murder—I agreed to do what they wished, and signed
a form alleging the theft of my sketchbook.

When they had gone at last, carrying the unfortunate Kreton
across a saddlebow, I tried to reenter the theater. The side door
through which we had left was locked, and though I would gladly
have paid the price of another ticket, the box office was closed.
Seeing that there was nothing further to be done, I returned
here, telling myself that my introduction to Ellen, if it ever came,
would have to wait for another day.

Very truly it is written that we walk by paths that are always
turning. In recording these several pages I have managed to
restrain my enthusiasm, though when I described my waiting at
the back of the theater for Ardis, and again when I recounted how
Kreton had promised to introduce me to her, I was forced for
minutes at a time to lay down my pen and walk about the room
singing and whistling, and—to reveal everything—jumping over
the beds! But now I can conceal no longer. I have seen her! I have
touched her hand; I am to see her again tomorrow; and there is
every hope that she will become my mistress!

I had undressed and laid myself on the bed (thinking to bring
this journal up to date in the morning) and had even fallen into
the first doze of sleep, when there was a knock at the door. I

slipped into my robe and pressed the release.

It was the only time in my life that for even an instant I thought I might be dreaming—actually asleep—when in truth I was up and awake.

How feeble it is to write that she is more beautiful in person than she appears on the stage. It is true, and yet it is a supreme irrelevance. I have seen more beautiful women—indeed Yasmin is, I suppose, by the formal standards of art, more lovely. It is not Ardis' beauty that draws me to her—the hair like gold, the translucent skin that then still showed traces of the bluish makeup she had worn as a ghost, the flashing eyes like the clear, clean skies of America. It is something deeper than that; something that would remain if all that were somehow taken away. No doubt she has habits that would disgust me in someone else, and the vanity that is said to be so common in her profession, and yet I would do anything to possess her.

Enough of this. What is it but empty boasting, now that I am on the point of winning her?

She stood in my doorway. I have been trying to think how I can express what I felt then. It was as though some tall flower, a lily perhaps, had left the garden and come to tap at my door, a thing that had never happened before in all the history of the world, and would never happen again.

"You are Nadan Jaffarzadeh?"

I admitted that I was, and shamefacedly, twenty seconds too late, moved out of her way.

She entered, but instead of taking the chair I indicated, turned to face me; her blue eyes seemed as large as the colored eggs on the dresser, and they were filled with a melting hope. "You are the man, then, that Bobby O'Keene tried to rob tonight."

I nodded.

"I know you—I mean, I know your face. This is insane. You came to *Visit* on the last night and brought your father, and then to *Mary Rose* on the first night, and sat in the third or fourth row. I thought you were an American, and when the police told me your name I imagined some greasy fat man with gestures. Why on earth would Bobby want to steal from *you?*"

"Perhaps he needed the money."

She threw back her head and laughed. I had heard her laugh in *Mary Rose* when Simon was asking her father for her hand; but that had held a note of childishness that (however well suited to the part) detracted from its beauty. This laugh was the merriment of houris sliding down a rainbow. "I'm sure he did. He always needs money. You're sure, though, that he meant to rob you? You couldn't have . . ."

She saw my expression and let the question trail away. The truth is that I was disappointed that I could not oblige her, and at last I said, "If you want me to be mistaken, Ardis, then I was mistaken. He only bumped against me on the steps, perhaps, and tried to catch my sketchbook when it fell."

She smiled, and her face was the sun smiling upon roses. "You would say that for me? And you know my name?"

"From the program. I came to the theater to see you—and that was not my father, who it grieves me to say is long dead, but only an old man, an American, whom I had met that day."

"You brought him sandwiches at the first intermission—I was watching you through the peephole in the curtain. You must be a very thoughtful person."

"Do you watch everyone in the audience so carefully?"

She blushed at that, and for a moment could not meet my eyes.

"But you will forgive Bobby, and tell the police that you want them to let him go? You must love the theater, Mr. Jef—Jaff—"

"You've forgotten my name already. It is Jaffarzadeh, a very commonplace name in my country."

"I hadn't forgotten it—only how to pronounce it. You see, when I came here I had learned it without knowing who you were, and so I had no trouble with it. Now you're a real person to me and I can't say it as an actress should." She seemed to notice the chair behind her for the first time, and sat down.

I sat opposite her. "I'm afraid I know very little about the theater."

"We are trying to keep it alive here, Mr. Jaffar, and—"

"Jaffarzadeh. Call me Nadan—then you won't have so many syllables to trip over."

She took my hand in hers, and I knew quite well that the gesture was as studied as a salaam and that she felt she was playing me like a fish; but I was beside myself with delight. To be played by *her!* To have *her* eager to cultivate my affection! And the fish will pull her in yet—wait and see!

"I will," she said, "Nadan. And though you may know little of the theater, you feel as I do—as we do—or you would not come. It has been such a long struggle; all the history of the stage is a struggle, the gasping of a beautiful child born at the point of death. The moralists, censorship and oppression, technology, and now poverty have all tried to destroy her. Only we, the actors and audiences, have kept her alive. We have been doing well here in Washington, Nadan."

"Very well indeed," I said. "Both the productions I have seen have been excellent."

"But only for the past two seasons. When I joined the company it had nearly fallen apart. We revived it—Bobby and Paul and I. We could do it because we cared, and because we were able to find a few naturally talented people who can take direction. Bobby is the best of us—he can walk away with any part that calls for a touch of the sinister . . ."

She seemed to run out of breath. I said, "I don't think there will be any trouble about getting him free."

"Thank God. We're getting the theater on its feet again now. We're attracting new people, and we've built up a following— people who come to see every production. There's even some money ahead at last. But *Mary Rose* is supposed to run another two weeks, and after that we're doing *Faust,* with Bobby as Mephistopheles. We've simply no one who can take his place, no one who can come close to him."

"I'm sure the police will release him if I ask them to."

"They *must*. We have to have him tomorrow night. Bill—someone you don't know—tried to go on for him in the third act tonight. It was just ghastly. In Iran you're very polite; that's what I've heard."

"We enjoy thinking so."

"We're not. We never were; and as . . ."

Her voice trailed away, but a wave of one slender arm evoked everything—the cracked plaster walls became as air, and the decayed city, the ruined continent, entered the room with us. "I understand," I said.

"They—we—were betrayed. In our souls we have never been sure by whom. When we feel cheated we are ready to kill; and maybe we feel cheated all the time."

She slumped in her chair, and I realized, as I should have long before, how exhausted she was. She had given a performance that had ended in disaster, then had been forced to plead with the police for my name and address, and at last had come here from the station house, very probably on foot. I asked when I could obtain O'Keene's release.

"We can go tomorrow morning, if you'll do it."

"You wish to come too?"

She nodded, smoothed her skirt, and stood. "I'll have to know. I'll come for you about nine, if that's all right."

"If you'll wait outside for me to dress, I'll take you home."

"That's not necessary."

"It will only take a moment," I said.

The blue eyes held something pleading again. "You're going to come in with me—that's what you're thinking, I know. You have two beds here—bigger, cleaner beds than the one I have in my little apartment; if I were to ask you to push them together, would you still take me home afterward?"

It was as though I were dreaming indeed—a dream in which everything I wanted—the cosmos purified—delivered itself to me. I said, "You won't have to leave at all—you can spend the night with me. Then we can breakfast together before we go to release your friend."

She laughed again, lifting that exquisite head. "There are a hundred things at home I need. Do you think I'd have breakfast with you without my cosmetics, and in these dirty clothes?"

"Then I will take you home—yes, though you lived in Kazvin. Or on Mount Kaf."

She smiled. "Get dressed, then. I'll wait outside, and I'll show you my apartment; perhaps you won't want to come back here afterward."

She went out, her wooden-soled American shoes clicking on the bare floor, and I threw on trousers, shirt, and jacket, and jammed my feet into my boots. When I opened the door, she was gone. I rushed to the barred window at the end of the corridor, and was in time to see her disappear down a side street. A last swirl of her skirt in a gust of night wind, and she had vanished into the velvet dark.

For a long time I stood there looking out over the ruinous buildings. I was not angry—I do not think I could be angry with her. I was, though here it is hard to tell the truth, in some way glad. Not because I feared the embrace of love—I have no doubt of my ability to suffice any woman who can be sated by man—but because an easy exchange of my cooperation for her person would have failed to satisfy my need for romance, for adventure of a certain type, in which danger and love are twined like coupling serpents. Ardis, my Ellen, will provide that, surely, as neither Yasmin nor the pitiful wanton who was her double could. I sense that the world is opening for me only now; that I am being born; that that corridor was the birth canal, and that Ardis in leaving me was drawing me out toward her.

When I returned to my own door, I noticed a bit of paper on the floor before it. I transcribe it exactly here, though I cannot transmit its scent of lilacs.

You are a most attractive man and I want very much to stretch the truth and tell you you can have me freely when Bobby is free but I won't sell myself etc. Really I *will* sell myself for Bobby but I have other fish to fry tonight. I'll see you in the morning and if you can get Bobby out or even try hard you'll have (real) love from the vanishing

Mary Rose

Morning. Woke early and ate here at the hotel as usual, finishing about eight. Writing this journal will give me something to do while I wait for Ardis. Had an American breakfast today, the first time I have risked one. Flakes of pastry dough toasted crisp and drenched with cream, and with it strudel and the usual American coffee. Most natives have spiced pork in one form or another, which I cannot bring myself to try; but several of the people around me were having egg dishes and oven-warmed bread, which I will sample tomorrow.

I had a very unpleasant dream last night; I have been trying to put it out of my mind ever since I woke. It was dark, and I was under an open sky with Ardis, walking over ground much rougher than anything I saw in the park on the farther side of the channel. One of the hideous creatures I shot night before last was pursuing us—or rather, lurking about us, for it appeared first to the left of us, then to the right, silhouetted against the night sky. Each time we saw it, Ardis grasped my arm and urged me to shoot, but the little indicator light on my pistol was glowing red to show that there was not enough charge left for a shot. All very silly, of course, but I am going to buy a fresh powerpack as soon as I have the opportunity.

It is late afternoon—after six—but we have not had dinner yet. I am just out of the tub, and sit here naked, with today's candy egg laid (pinker even than I) beside this book on my table. Ardis and I had a sorry, weary time of it, and I have come back here to make myself presentable. At seven we will meet for dinner; the curtain goes up at eight, so it can't be a long one, but I am going backstage to watch the play from the wings, where I will be able to talk to her when she isn't performing.

I just took a bite of the egg—no unusual taste, nothing but an unpleasant sweetness. The more I reflect on it, the more inclined I am to believe that the drug was in the first I ate. No doubt the monster I saw had been lurking in my brain since I read *Mysteries,* and the drug freed it. True, there were bloodstains on my clothes (the Peri's asphodel!) but they could as easily have come from my cheek, which is still sore. I have had my experience, and all I have left is my candy. I am almost tempted to throw out the rest. Another bite.

Still twenty minutes before I must dress and go for Ardis—she showed me where she lives, only a few doors from the theater. To work then.

Ardis was a trifle late this morning, but came as she had promised. I asked where we were to go to free Kreton, and when she told me—a still-living building at the eastern end of the Silent City—I hired one of the rickety American caleches to drive us there. Like most of them, it was drawn by a starved horse; but we made good time.

The American police are organized on a peculiar system. The national secret police (officially, the Federated Enquiry Divisions) are in a tutorial position to all the others, having power to review their decisions, promote, demote, and discipline, and as the ultimate reward, enroll personnel from the other organizations. In addition they maintain a uniformed force of their own. Thus when an American has been arrested by uniformed police, his friends can seldom learn whether he has been taken by the local police, by the F.E.D. uniformed national force, or by members of the F.E.D. secret police posing as either of the foregoing.

Since I had known nothing of these distinctions previously, I had no way of guessing which of the three had O'Keene; but the local police to whom Ardis had spoken the night before had given her to understand that he had been taken by them. She explained all this to me as we rattled along, then added that we were now going to the F.E.D. Building to secure his release. I must have looked as confused as I felt at this, because she added, "Part of it is a station for the Washington Police Department—they rent the space from the F.E.D."

My own impression (when we arrived) was that they did no such thing—that the entire apparatus was no more real than one of the scenes in Ardis's theater, and that all the men and women to whom we spoke were in fact agents of the secret police, wielding ten times the authority they pretended to possess, and going through a solemn ritual of deception. As Ardis and I moved from office to office, explaining our simple errand, I came to think that she felt as I did, and that she had refrained from expressing these feelings to me in the cab not only because of the danger, the fear that I might betray her or the driver be a spy, but because she was ashamed of her nation, and eager to make it appear to me, a foreigner, that her government was less devious and meretricious than is actually the case.

If this is so—and in that windowless warren of stone I was certain it was—then the very explanation she proffered in the cab (which I have given in its proper place) differentiating clearly between local police, uniformed F.E.D. police, and secret police, was no more than a children's fable, concealing an actuality less forthright and more convoluted.

Our questioners were courteous to me, much less so to Ardis, and (so it seemed to me) obsessed by the idea that something more lay behind the simple incident we described over and over again—so much so in fact that I came to believe it myself. I have neither time nor patience enough to describe all these interviews, but I will attempt to give a sample of one.

We went into a small, windowless office crowded between two others that appeared empty. A middle-aged American woman was seated behind a metal desk. She appeared normal and reasonably attractive until she spoke; then her scarred gums showed that she had once had two or three times the proper number of teeth—forty or fifty, I suppose, in each jaw—and that the dental surgeon who had extracted the supernumerary ones had not always, perhaps, selected those he suffered to remain as wisely as he might. She asked, "How is it outside? The weather? You see, I don't know, sitting in here all day."

Ardis said, "Very nice."

"Do you like it, *Hajji?* Have you had a pleasant stay in our great country?"

"I don't think it has rained since I've been here."

She seemed to take the remark as a covert accusation. "You came too late for the rains, I'm afraid. This is a very fertile area, however. Some of our oldest coins show heads of wheat. Have you seen them?" She pushed a small copper coin across the desk, and I pretended to examine it. There are one or two like it in the bracelet I bought for Ardis, and which I still have not presented to her. "I must apologize on behalf of the District for what happened to you," the woman continued. "We are making every effort to control crime. You have not been victimized before this?"

I shook my head, half suffocated in that airless office, and said I had not been.

"And now you are here." She shuffled the papers she held, then pretended to read from one of them. "You are here to secure the release of the thief who assaulted you. A very commendable act of magnanimity. May I ask why you brought this young woman with you? She does not seem to be mentioned in any of these reports."

I explained that Ardis was a coworker of O'Keene's, and that she had interceded for him.

"Then it is you, Ms. Dahl, who are really interested in securing this prisoner's release. Are you related to him?"

And so on.

At the conclusion of each interview we were told either that the matter was completely out of the hands of the person to whom we had just spent half an hour or an hour talking, that it was necessary to obtain a clearance from someone else, or that an additional deposition had to be made. About two o'clock we were sent to the other side of the river—into what my guidebooks insist is an entirely different jurisdiction—to visit a penal facility. There we were forced to look for Kreton among five hundred or so miserable prisoners, all of whom stank and had lice. Not finding him, we returned to the F.E.D. Building past the half-overturned and yet still brooding figure called the Seated Man, and the ruins and beggars of the Silent City, for another round of interrogations. By five, when we were told to leave, we were both exhausted, though Ardis seemed surprisingly hopeful. When I left her at the door of her building a few minutes ago, I asked her what they would do tonight without Kreton.

"Without Harry, you mean." She smiled. "The best we can, I suppose, if we must. At least Paul will have someone ready to stand in for him tonight."

We shall see how well it goes.

I have picked up this pen and replaced it on the table ten times at least. It seems very likely that I should destroy this journal instead of continuing with it, were I wise; but I have discovered a hiding place for it which I think will be secure.

When I came back from Ardis's apartment tonight there were only two candy eggs remaining. I am certain—absolutely certain —that three were left when I went to meet Ardis. I am almost equally sure that after I had finished making the entry in this book, I put it, as I always do, at the left side of the drawer. It was on the right side.

It is possible that all this is merely the doing of the maid who cleans the room. She might easily have supposed that a single candy egg would not be missed, and have shifted this book while cleaning the drawer, or peeped inside out of curiosity.

I will assume the worst, however. An agent sent to investigate my room might be equipped to photograph these pages—but he might not, and it is not likely that he himself would have a reading knowledge of Farsi. Now I have gone through the book and eliminated all the passages relating to my reason for visiting this leprous country. Before I leave this room tomorrow I will arrange indicators—hairs and other objects whose positions I shall carefully record—that will tell me if the room has been searched again.

Now I may as well set down the events of the evening, which were truly extraordinary enough.

I met Ardis as we had planned, and she directed me to a small restaurant not far from her apartment. We had no sooner seated ourselves than two heavy-looking men entered. At no time could I see plainly the face of either, but it appeared to me that one was the American I had met aboard the *Princess Fatimah* and that the other was the grain dealer I had so assiduously avoided there, Golam Gassem. It is impossible, I think, for my divine Ardis ever to look less than beautiful; but she came as near to it then as the laws of nature permit—the blood drained from her face, her mouth opened slightly, and for a moment she appeared to be a lovely corpse. I began to ask what the trouble was, but before I could utter a word she touched my lips to silence me, and then, having somewhat regained her composure, said, "They have not seen us. I am leaving now. Follow me as though we were finished eating." She stood, feigned to pat her lips with a napkin (so that the lower half of her face was hidden) and walked out into the street.

I followed her, and found her laughing not three doors away from the entrance to the restaurant. The change in her could not have been more startling if she had been released from an enchantment. "It is so funny," she said. "Though it wasn't then. Come on, we'd better go; you can feed me after the show."

I asked her what those men were to her.

"Friends," she said, still laughing.

"If they are friends, why were you so anxious that they not see you? Were you afraid they would make us late?" I knew that such a trivial explanation could not be true, but I wanted to leave her a means of evading the question if she did not want to confide in me.

She shook her head. "No, no. I didn't want either to think I did not trust him. I'll tell you more later, if you want to involve yourself in our little charade."

"With all my heart."

She smiled at that—that sun-drenched smile for which I would gladly have entered a lion pit. In a few more steps we were at the rear entrance to the theater, and there was no time to say more. She opened the door, and I heard Kreton arguing with a woman I later learned was the wardrobe mistress. "You are free," I said, and he turned to look at me.

"Yes. Thanks to you, I think. And I do thank you."

Ardis gazed on him as though he were a child saved from drowning. "Poor Bobby. Was it very bad?"

"It was frightening, that's all. I was afraid I'd never get out. Do you know Terry is gone?"

She shook her head, and said, "What do you mean?" but I was certain—and here I am not exaggerating or coloring the facts, though I confess I have occasionally done so elsewhere in this chronicle—that she had known it before he spoke.

"He simply isn't here. Paul is running around like a lunatic. I hear you missed me last night."

"God, yes," Ardis said, and darted off too swiftly for me to follow.

Kreton took my arm. I expected him to apologize for having tried to rob me, but he said, "You've met her, I see."

"She persuaded me to drop the charges against you."

"Whatever it was you offered me—twenty rials? I'm morally entitled to it, but I won't claim it. Come and see me when you're ready for something more wholesome—and meanwhile, how do you like her?"

"That is something for me to tell her," I said, "not you."

Ardis returned as I spoke, bringing with her a balding black man with a mustache. "Paul, this is Nadan. His English is very good—not so British as most of them. He'll do, don't you think?"

"He'll have to—you're sure he'll do it?"

"He'll love it," Ardis said positively, and disappeared again.

It seemed that "Terry" was the actor who played Mary Rose's husband and lover, Simon; and I—who had never acted in so much as a school play—was to be pressed into the part. It was about half an hour before curtain time, so I had all of fifty minutes to learn my lines before my entrance at the end of the first act.

Paul, the director, warned me that if my name were used, the audience would be hostile; and since the character (in the version of the play they were presenting) was supposed to be an American, they would see errors where none existed. A moment later, while I was still in frantic rehearsal, I heard him saying, "The part of Simon Blake will be taken by Ned Jefferson."

The act of stepping onto the stage for the first time was really the worst part of the entire affair. Fortunately I had the advantage of playing a nervous young man come to ask for the hand of his sweetheart, so that my shaky laughter and stammer became "acting."

My second scene—with Mary Rose and Cameron on the magic island—ought by rights to have been much more difficult than the first. I had had only the intermission in which to study my lines, and the scene called for pessimistic apprehension rather than mere anxiety. But all the speeches were short, and Paul had been able by that time to get them lettered on large sheets of paper, which he and the stage manager held up in the wings. Several times I was forced to extemporize, but though I forgot the playwright's words, I never lost my sense of the *trend* of the play, and was always able to contrive something to which Ardis and Cameron could adapt their replies.

In comparison to the first and second acts, my brief appearance in the third was a holiday; yet I have seldom been so exhausted as I was tonight when the stage darkened for Ardis's final confrontation with Kreton, and Cameron and I, and the middle-aged people who had played the Morelands were able to creep away.

We had to remain in costume until we had taken our bows, and it was nearly midnight before Ardis and I got something to eat at the same small, dirty bar outside which Kreton had tried to rob me. Over the steaming plates she asked me if I had enjoyed acting, and I had to nod.

"I thought you would. Under all that solidity you're a very dramatic person, I think."

I admitted it was true, and tried to explain why I feel that what I call *the romance of life* is the only thing worth seeking. She did not understand me, and so I passed it off as the result of having been brought up on the *Shah Namah,* of which I found she had never heard.

We went to her apartment. I was determined to take her by force if necessary—not because I would have enjoyed brutalizing her, but because I felt she would inevitably think my love far less than it was if I permitted her to put me off a second time. She showed me about her quarters (two small rooms in great disorder), then, after we had lifted into place the heavy bar that is the sigil of every American dwelling, put her arms about me. Her breath was fragrant with the arrack I had bought for her a few minutes before. I feel sure now that for the rest of my life that scent will recall this evening to me.

When we parted, I began to unloose the laces that closed her blouse, and she at once pinched out the candle. I pleaded that she was thus depriving me of half the joy I might have had of her love; but she would not permit me to relight it, and our caresses and the embraces of our couplings were exchanged in perfect darkness. I was in ecstasy. To have seen her, I would have blinded myself; yet nothing could have increased my delight.

When we separated for the last time, both spent utterly, and she left to wash, I sought for matches. First in the drawer of the unsteady little table beside the bed, then among the disorder of my own clothes, which I had dropped to the floor and we had kicked about. I found some eventually, but could not find the candle—Ardis, I think, had hidden it. I struck a match; but she had covered herself with a robe. I said, "Am I never to see you?"

"You will see me tomorrow. You're going to take me boating, and we'll picnic by the water, under the cherry trees. Tomorrow night the theater will be closed for Easter, and you can take me to a party. But now you are going home, and I am going to go to sleep." When I was dressed and standing in her doorway, I asked her if she loved me; but she stopped my mouth with a kiss.

I have already written about the rest—returning to find two eggs instead of three, and this book moved. I will not write of that again. But I have just—between this paragraph and the last—read over what I wrote earlier tonight, and it seems to me that one sentence should have had more weight than I gave it: when I said that in my role as Simon I never lost the *trend* of the play.

What the fabled secret buried by the old Americans beneath their carved mountain may be I do not know; but I believe that if it is some key to the world of human life, it must be some form of that. Every great man, I am sure, consciously or not, in those terms or others, has grasped that secret—save that in the play that is our life we can grapple that trend and draw it to left or right if we have the will.

So I am doing now. If the taking of the egg was not significant, yet I will make it so—indeed I already have, when I infused one egg with the drug. If the scheme in which Ardis is entangled—with Golam Gassem and Mr. Tallman if it be they—is not some affair of statecraft and dark treasure, yet I will make it so before the end. If our love is not a great love, destined to live forever in the hearts of the young and the mouths of the poets, it will be so before the end.

Once again I am here; and in all truth I am beginning to wonder if I do not write this journal only to read it. No man was ever happier than I am now—so happy, indeed, that I was sorely tempted not to taste either of the two eggs that remain. What if the drug, in place of hallucination, self-knowledge, and euphoria, brings permanent and despairing madness? Yet I have eaten it nonetheless, swallowing the whole sweet lump in a few bites. I would rather risk whatever may come than think myself a coward. With equanimity I await the effects.

The fact is that I am too happy for all the Faustian determination I penned last night. (How odd that *Faust* will be the company's next production. Kreton will be Mephistopheles of course
—Ardis said as much, and it would be certain in any case. Ardis
herself will be Margaret. But who will play the Doctor?) Yet now,
when all the teeth-gritting, table-pounding determination is
gone, I know that I will carry out the essentials of the *plan* more
surely than ever—with the ease, in fact, of an accomplished vio-
linist sawing out some simple tune while his mind roves elsewhere. I have been looking at the ruins of the Jeff (as they call it),
and it has turned my mind again to the fate of the old Americans.
How often they, who chose their leaders for superficial appear-
ances of strength, wisdom, and resolution, must have elected
them only because they were as fatigued as I was last night.

I had meant to buy a hamper of delicacies, and call for Ardis
about one, but she came for me at eleven with a little basket
already packed. We walked north along the bank of the channel
until we reached the ruins of the old tomb to which I have already
referred, and the nearly circular artificial lake the Americans call
the Basin. It is rimmed with flowering trees—old and gnarled,
but very beautiful in their robes of white blossom. For some little
American coin we were given command of a bright blue boat with
a sail twice or three times the size of my handkerchief, in which
to dare the halcyon waters of the lake.

When we were well away from the people on shore, Ardis asked
me, rather suddenly, if I intended to spend all my time in America
here in Washington.

I told her that my original plan had been to stay here no more
than a week, then make my way up the coast to Philadelphia and
the other ancient cities before I returned home; but that now that
I had met her I would stay here forever if she wished it.

"Haven't you ever wanted to see the interior? This strip of
beach we live on is kept half alive by the ocean and the trade that
crosses it; but a hundred miles inland lies the wreck of our entire
civilization, waiting to be plundered."

"Then why doesn't someone plunder it?" I asked.

"They do. A year never passes without someone bringing some great prize out—but it is so large . . ." I could see her looking beyond the lake and the fragrant trees. "So large that whole cities are lost in it. There was an arch of gold at the entrance to St. Louis—no one knows what became of it. Denver, the Mile High City, was nested in silver mines; no one can find them now."

"Many of the old maps must still be in existence."

Ardis nodded slowly, and I sensed that she wanted to say more than she had. For a few seconds there was no sound but the water lapping against the side of the boat.

"I remember having seen some in the museum in Teheran— not only our maps, but some of your own from a hundred years ago."

"The courses of the rivers have changed," she said. "And when they have not, no one can be sure of it."

"Many buildings must still be standing, as they are here, in the Silent City."

"That was built of stone—more solidly than anything else in the country. But yes, some, many, are still there."

"Then it would be possible to fly in, land somewhere, and pillage them."

"There are many dangers, and so much rubble to look through that anyone might search for a lifetime and only scratch the surface."

I saw that talking of all this only made her unhappy, and tried to change the subject. "Didn't you say that I could escort you to a party tonight? What will that be like?"

"Nadan, I have to trust someone. You've never met my father, but he lives close to the hotel where you are staying, and has a shop where he sells old books and maps." (So I had visited the right house—almost—after all!) "When he was younger, he wanted to go into the interior. He made three or four trips, but never got farther than the Appalachian foothills. Eventually he married my mother and didn't feel any longer that he could take the risks . . ."

"I understand."

"The things he had sought to guide him to the wealth of the past became his stock in trade. Even today, people who live farther inland bring him old papers; he buys them and resells them. Some of those people are only a step better than the ones who dig up the cemeteries for the wedding rings of the dead women."

I recalled the rings I had bought in the shadow of the broken obelisk, and shuddered, though I do not believe Ardis observed it.

"I said that some of them were hardly better than the grave robbers. The truth is that some are worse—there are people in the interior who are no longer people. Our bodies are poisoned —you know that, don't you? All of us Americans. They have adapted—that's what Father says—but they are no longer human. He made his peace with them long ago, and he trades with them still."

"You don't have to tell me this."

"Yes I do—I must. Would you go into the interior, if I went with you? The government will try to stop us if they learn of it, and to confiscate anything we find."

I assured her with every oath I could remember that with her beside me I would cross the continent on foot if need be.

"I told you about my father. I said that he sells the maps and records they bring him. What I did not tell you is that he reads them first. He has never given up, you see, in his heart."

"He has made a discovery?" I asked.

"He's made many—hundreds. Bobby and I have used them. You remember those men in the restaurant? Bobby went to each of them with a map and some of the old letters. He's persuaded them to help finance an expedition into the interior, and made each of them believe that we'll help him cheat the other—that keeps them from combining to cheat us, you see."

"And you want me to go with you?" I was beside myself with joy.

"We weren't going to go at all—Bobby was going to take the money, and go to Baghdad or Marrakesh, and take me with him.

But, Nadan," here she leaned forward, I remember, and took my hands in hers, "there really is a secret. There are many, but one better—more likely to be true, more likely to yield truly immense wealth than all the others. I know you would share fairly with me. We'll divide everything, and I'll go back to Teheran with you."

I know that I have never been more happy in my life than I was then, in that silly boat. We sat together in the stern, nearly sinking it, under the combined shade of the tiny sail and Ardis's big straw hat, and kissed and stroked one another until we would have been pilloried a dozen times in Iran.

At last, when I could bear no more unconsummated love, we ate the sandwiches Ardis had brought, and drank some warmish, fruit-flavored beverage, and returned to shore.

When I took her home a few minutes ago, I very strongly urged her to let me come upstairs with her; I was on fire for her, sick to impale her upon my own flesh and pour myself into her as some mad god before the coming of the Prophet might have poured his golden blood into the sea. She would not permit it— I think because she feared that her apartment could not be darkened enough to suit her modesty. I am determined that I will yet see her.

I have bathed and shaved to be ready for the party, and as there is still time I will insert here a description of the procession we passed on the way back from the lake. As you see, I have not yet completely abandoned the thought of a book of travels.

A very old man—I suppose a priest—carried a cross on a long pole, using it as a staff, and almost as a crutch. A much younger one, fat and sweating, walked backward before him swinging a smoking censer. Two robed boys carrying large candles preceded them, and they were followed by more robed children, singing, who fought with nudges and pinches when they felt the fat man was not watching them.

Like everyone else, I have seen this kind of thing done much better in Rome; but I was more affected by what I saw here. When the old priest was born, the greatness of America must have been a thing of such recent memory that few can have realized it had passed forever; and the entire procession—from the flickering candles in clear sunshine, to the dead leader lifted up, to his inattentive, bickering followers behind—seemed to me to incarnate the philosophy and the dilemma of these people. So I felt, at least, until I saw that they watched it as uncomprehendingly as they might if they themselves were only travelers abroad, and I realized that its ritualized plea for life renewed was more foreign to them than to me.

It is very late—three, my watch says.

I resolved again not to write in this book. To burn it or tear it to pieces, or to give it to some beggar; but now I am writing once again because I cannot sleep. The room reeks of my vomit, though I have thrown open the shutters and let in the night.

How could I have loved that? (And yet a few moments ago, when I tried to sleep, visions of Ellen pursued me back to wakefulness.)

The party was a masque, and Ardis had obtained a costume for me—a fantastic gilded armor from the wardrobe of the theater. She wore the robes of an Egyptian princess, and a domino. At midnight we lifted our masks and kissed, and in my heart I swore that tonight the mask of darkness would be lifted too.

When we left, I carried with me the bottle we had brought, still nearly half full; and before she pinched out the candle I persuaded her to pour out a final drink for us to share when the first frenzy of our desire was past. She—it—did as I asked, and set it on the little table near the bed. A long time afterward, when we lay gasping side by side, I found my pistol with one groping hand and fired the beam into the wide-bellied glass. Instantly it filled with blue fire from the burning alcohol. Ardis screamed, and sprang up.

I ask myself now how I could have loved; but then, how could I in one week have come so near to loving this corpse-country? Its eagle is dead—Ardis is the proper symbol of its rule.

One hope, one very small hope remains. It is possible that what I saw tonight was only an illusion, induced by the egg. I know now that the thing I killed before Ardis's father's house was real, and between this paragraph and the last I have eaten the last egg. If hallucinations now begin, I will know that what I saw by the light of the blazing arrack was in truth a thing with which I have lain, and in one way or another will see to it that I never return to corrupt the clean wombs of the women of our enduring race. I might seek to claim the miniatures of our heritage after all, and allow the guards to kill me—but what if I were to succeed? I am not fit to touch them. Perhaps the best end for me would be to travel alone into this maggot-riddled continent; in that way I will die at fit hands.

Later. Kreton is walking in the hall outside my door, and the tread of his twisted black shoe jars the building like an earthquake. I heard the word *police* as though it were thunder. My dead Ardis, very small and bright, has stepped out of the candle-flame, and there is a hairy face coming through the window.

The old woman closed the notebook. The younger woman, who had been reading over her shoulder, moved to the other side of the small table and seated herself on a cushion, her feet politely positioned so that the soles could not be seen. "He is alive then," she said.

The older woman remained silent, her gray head bowed over the notebook, which she held in both hands.

"He is certainly imprisoned, or ill; otherwise he would have been in touch with us." The younger woman paused, smoothing the fabric of her *chador* with her right hand, while the left toyed with the gem simulator she wore on a thin chain. "It is possible that he has already tried, but his letters have miscarried."

"You think this is his writing?" the older woman asked, opening the notebook at random. When the younger did not answer she added, "Perhaps. Perhaps."

Arcs & Secants

"Moongate," KATE WILHELM'S nineteenth story for *Orbit*, came out of the author's intense interest in the Oregon desert. The curious heaps of stones described in the story actually occur in Oregon; nobody knows who put them there or why.

A long time ago we wrote to an ex-Clarion student, "The story is fuzzier than it ought to be because the language is fuzzy. You ought to go through this carefully, line by line, & make sure every word is what you really mean. The story is powerful, & I think you ought to be able to sell it, but not if the editor's eyes keep crossing while he reads it."

Another ex-Clarion student wrote at about the same time: "A few words about how the yarrow stalks have fallen. My apartment has been broken into and ripped off twice: the first time, they got away with a typewriter; the second, about $300 worth of camera equipment. I had a '64 Mercury. Somebody ripped the chrome swan hood ornament from it. The car broke down and I left it stalled in the parking lot of a nearby apartment complex. It was worth about fifty dollars to a junk dealer. The manager had it towed away; I kept putting off getting it back because I couldn't afford the charges and had no place to store it. I finally got a registered letter from the wrecking company saying they would auction off the car if I didn't come down and pay off the towing and garage costs, an amount a little better than $300. . . . I recently took a short sojourn through the English department of LSU [Louisiana State University], mainly because I thought I

234

could come out ahead with financial aid. I now owe the state $700. . . . I sometimes have the feeling I have been convicted, of a crime I have no memory of committing, and sentenced to life as a character in a Fellini movie."

PAMELA SARGENT ("The Novella Race"), who lives in Binghamton, New York, has never won a Nebula or Hugo or attended a writers' conference.

CARTER SCHOLZ ("The Eve of the Last Apollo," *Orbit 18*) sent us an invitation to join an art pyramid: "Please send one piece of art (poem, graphic, hunch, etc.) to the first person on this list. Eliminate their name, and add your own at the bottom. Duplicate the top part of this invitation and send it to five people who will never let the on-going documentation of our civilization falter."

R. A. LAFFERTY ("Bright Coins in Never-Ending Stream") wrote to his agent, in response to our criticism of an earlier version of this story: ". . . What is wrong with worms? Just keep saying, 'They taste like shrimp, they taste like shrimp.' "

TERRY CARR, editor of *Universe* and an old friend, sent us a riddle on a postcard, then the answer on another postcard. Then he sent us another riddle: "How do you keep a turkey in suspense?" and never sent the answer. After about two weeks we realized that *was* the answer.

TERRENCE L. BROWN ("The Synergy Sculpture") is a new writer who lives in Hood River, Oregon, a town of about 4,000 souls where we grew up; we and Mr. Brown are the only members of the world's most exclusive writers' organization, SFWHRO.

We wrote to a promising young writer during the worst month of a bad winter, "I think this is pretty convincing, but it sure is dismal. You are forgetting the implied contract between the writer & reader—'you pay your money, and I'll show you something keen.' A suicidal old guy in a hospital is not keen."

JOHN ANTHONY CROSS ("The Birds Are Free") told us some stories about ducks and geese which are too indelicate to print here.

We find ourselves writing to more and more young writers, "You really ought to do something about your spelling." Some of our best writers are shaky spellers, and Samuel R. Delany is a basket case in that regard, but bad spelling does not guarantee good writing. Every writer who can't spell should marry someone who can.

STEVE CHAPMAN ("A Right-Handed Wrist") spent some time in a plastics fabricating plant like the one described in his story. Sometimes this kind of thing works and sometimes not; Mark Twain, for instance, never got any fiction out of his printshop experience.

During the bad month referred to above, we wrote to a friend: "I have a cracked great toe (a jar of chicken stock fell out of the freezer on it) and am hobbling. Kate's pinched nerve is getting better slowly. One of our dumb cats behaved oddly one evening and it cost us $42 to find out that nothing was wrong with him. So it goes, but at least *it is raining.*"

PHILIPPA C. MADDERN (" 'They Made Us Not to Be and They Are Not' ") is one of the star pupils of a writers' workshop Ursula K. Le Guin conducted in Australia a few years ago. She has sold several stories to magazines and anthologies, and it is our opinion that she will be heard from a lot.

We had a letter from HARRY HARRISON; the contents were not memorable, but the address was: Pilot View, Bullock Harbour, Dalkey, County Dublin, Ireland.

GENE WOLFE ("Seven American Nights") grew up in Texas, spent some time in the Army, became an engineer, and worked for a large corporation, all without becoming brainwashed by Texas, the Army, engineering, or large corporations. His first science fiction story appeared in *Orbit 2*, eleven years ago; since then he has contributed sixteen more to these pages.

Stories intended for publication should be accompanied by stamped, self-addressed envelopes, and should be sent to Damon Knight, 1645 Horn Lane, Eugene, Oregon 97404.

Index to Volumes 11–20

[*All references are to volumes.*]

Authors

The Skinny People of Leptophlebo Street, 16
Le Guin, Ursula K.
Direction of the Road, 12
The Stars Below, 14

McClintock, Michael W.
Under Jupiter, 19
McEvoy, Seth
Which in the Wood Decays, 17
Macfarlane, W.
Gardening Notes from All Over, 13
McIntyre, Vonda N.
The Genius Freaks, 12
Spectra, 11
Maddern, Philippa C.
"They Made Us Not to Be and They Are Not," 20
Martin, George R. R.
Meathouse Man, 18
Millar, Jeff
Toto, I Have a Feeling We're Not in Kansas Anymore, 17
Miller, Jesse
Phoenix House, 16
Moore, Raylyn
Fun Palace, 17
A Modular Story, 18

O'Donnell, Kevin, Jr.
Night Shift, 19
Orr, William F.
Euclid Alone, 16
The Mouth Is for Eating, 13

Piserchia, Doris
A Brilliant Curiosity, 16
Half the Kingdom, 12
Idio, 13

242

Titles